Running Home

Barbara Ellen Brink

Visit Barbara Ellen Brink at www.barbaraellenbrink.com

Cover design by Katharine A. Brink

Author photo by Barbara E Brink

Edited by Nancy Hudson

This novel is a work of fiction. Names, characters, businesses, places, events and incidents are either the products of the author's imagination or used in a fictitious manner. Any resemblance to actual persons, living or dead, or actual events is purely coincidental.

ISBN-10:1469914085
ISBN-13:978-1469914084

Other novels by this author

The Second Chances Series:
Alias Raven Black
Trial By Fire

Split Sense

The Fredrickson Winery Series:
Entangled
Crushed
Savor

The Double Barrel Mysteries:
Roadkill
Much Ado About Murder
Midsummer Madness

The Amish Bloodsuckers Trilogy:
Chosen
Shunned
Reckoning

Running Home

Prologue

California

Ivy ached bone deep. Up half the night with two sick children, she was ready to drop onto the couch and curl into a ball of oblivion. She clicked the television on and turned the volume low. The early morning news would undoubtedly put her to sleep, but it was a link to the outside world. Sometimes she felt as though she were living on an island apart from everyone else on earth. Her own little Alcatraz. The telephone rang just as she settled onto the sofa with a blanket tucked up to her chin. She sighed and reached out for the phone on the end table.

"Hello?"

"It's me. Sorry I missed our night out. I had to work late and didn't want to wake you, so I just camped out here at the office."

Ivy closed her eyes. She didn't know her husband anymore. He was missing more than he was around and his lies had grown bolder with the telling. She pictured him now sitting behind his modern glass and chrome desk, staring out the window of his fancy high-rise office, blonde hair hanging over his forehead like a young Robert Redford. He would look anything but sorry. With a cappuccino in hand and the newspaper spread out to the financial section, he would barely remember what he had called about. She was tempted to hang up. After last night she didn't have the energy for an argument.

"Ivy?" Todd said when she didn't respond immediately.

Her eyes fluttered open. "I'm here. Forgive me if I don't yell and scream. I'm too tired. I was up all night myself. Except–in my case–with the kids. They have the flu."

His silence lasted several seconds as though searching for the right touch of sympathy to infuse his next words. Ivy wished Todd would just admit he didn't want the responsibility of a family. That he never had. It would be easier than pretending everything was normal. She could see the truth in his eyes when he thought she wasn't looking; like millstones around his neck, his family was keeping him from the life he yearned for. As an important executive he could hardly be expected to stay home and nurse sick children.

"Are they feeling better this morning?" he asked.

"They're finally sleeping. Are you planning on stopping by the house sometime today to wish your son happy birthday?" Ivy asked, knowing full well he'd forgotten.

"Of course, babe," he said and actually had the gall to sound offended. "I'll be home for dinner. I got a great gift for him." He paused, and she could hear the crinkling of newspaper pages. "Want me to stop and pick up a cake, or will anyone feel like eating?"

There was a smile in his voice, but Ivy was no longer captivated by his false charm. The past eight years had insured that. Now, with her energy sapped and her emotions fluctuating between depression and anger, his charm didn't even break through the surface of her weariness. She was just so tired; tired of feeling like a single parent, tired of the lies, tired of being alone.

"I'm sure Caleb would appreciate the thought even if he doesn't feel like eating tonight." She purposely swallowed down her anger for the children's sake. They loved their father and needed what little attention he could spare them. Once upon a time she'd craved his attention too, but times change. The inattentive moments he shared with her now, filled with phone calls and work on his laptop, couldn't fill the dark void of her heart. Lying in bed alone at night she'd try to remember what loving her husband felt like. After so long without, she wasn't sure if she ever had. Now there was only emptiness.

"I'll be home by seven at the latest," he promised.

She replaced the phone in its cradle and settled back, a small groan escaping her lips. The weather report was coming up on the news and she turned the volume up.

"Rain, rain, and more rain is in our forecast for the next three days. But don't let it dampen your spirits, folks. Next week I predict we will have a return of our glorious sunshine. Stay tuned for more after these messages." The weatherman's plaster of Paris smile held firm until a commercial for dog food came on in his place.

Ivy clicked the remote and the screen went black. Rain, rain, and more rain. Sometimes she felt as though she were drowning.

✝✝✝

Todd pushed a lock of blonde hair back from his forehead and folded the paper. The early morning sun filled his office with a warm light, forcing shadows into the corners and under the furniture. He got up from his desk and stood at the window, hands in the pockets of his charcoal slacks. Storm clouds formed in the distance, a dark line on the horizon. He rubbed the stubble on his jaw as he stared out at the cityscape. He loved this view and doubted he could ever tire of it. But this time he was pushed into a corner he couldn't get out of. Like the shadows under the furniture.

Lights flashed below as two police cruisers went speeding through traffic on their way to an emergency. At this height the sound never reached his ears. He once felt insulated from the rest of the world up here, like a king in a castle. Now the time had come to abdicate the throne before he was impeached.

He released a heavy sigh. There were only two options left to him. He could try to create a false trail that would lead to someone else in the company and take the heat off him, which wouldn't work for long. Or he could run.

Reluctantly, he turned away from the window. The surface of his desk was cluttered with papers and files. He didn't know why he bothered to go through the ritual of work when he would probably be gone in a few days. Monroe Industries would get along without him just as surely as they had before he came. Jack Monroe would make certain of that. He picked up the trashcan and sent the entire contents of the desk's glass top into the garbage with one sweep of his arm. He'd had enough corporate politics to last a lifetime. By this time next week, he'd be lounging on a beach somewhere sipping pina coladas.

He glanced at the credenza behind him where the obligatory framed photos of his family lined the top. Caleb and Riley's smiling faces peered back at him, their eyes full of innocence and faith. They trusted him like no one else. His kids. His blood. The two souls in this town he regretted disappointing. He'd take them with him if he could, but he couldn't. He was a miserable father; even he knew that. Ivy needed them more than he did, and they needed her. Kids were fragile creatures. They expected things, things that he couldn't buy them.

He opened the left-hand drawer of his desk and took out a small jewel CD case, snapped it open and stared at the tiny disc inside. There was no turning back. He'd made a bargain with the devil and now it was time to pay up. He clicked the case shut and slipped it into the breast pocket of his suit coat, shrugged into the coat and headed for the door.

Sheila, his newest secretary, looked up from her keyboard and smiled as he pulled the door shut and approached her desk. "Good morning, Mr. Winter. I have that letter ready for you to sign. And Mr. Monroe called last evening right after you left for the night. He asked that you return his call this morning as soon as you got in. I didn't realize you were already in your office, sir," she apologized as though she should have been able to see through the locked door.

Todd gave her a careless wave of his hand. "If he calls again tell him I'm in a conference or something. I have to go shopping." He pushed the elevator button.

"Shopping?"

"It's my son's birthday. A boy doesn't turn seven every day, you know." The doors on the elevator opened and he stepped inside. "By the way," he called out as he pushed the button for the street level, "you better cancel any appointments I have. I'm not coming back."

He walked out onto the sidewalk a few moments later. The building towered above him, hundreds of office windows watching his departure. Instead of getting his Mercedes from the underground garage he decided to walk a while. Maybe the exercise would clear his head. He was still tired and lethargic after last night. He couldn't survive on three hours of sleep for long. He wasn't old by any means, but he wasn't twenty anymore either. One of these days his vices were bound to catch up with him.

He felt the hairs on the back of his neck rise as though someone were watching him. He turned and panned the street, his eyes narrowed intently. Just the usual suspects. People hurried along, minding their own business. No one seemed the least bit interested in another suit leaving an office building. He snorted a derisive laugh and turned up the sidewalk. It was definitely time to get out of town. He was getting paranoid.

†††

"Where's daddy? I thought he was gonna be here for my birthday." Caleb stood at her elbow, disappointment slowly stealing the eagerness from his face. He'd taken a shower earlier and his blonde curls were slicked down over his forehead in a bumpy wave.

Ivy wished she had never told the kids their father promised to be home. He seldom kept promises, at least not recently. He'd raise their hopes and then dash them to the ground.

Rain fell off and on during the afternoon, just as the forecaster predicted, but as evening approached, the sky cleared and now the sun's departing rays faded into shades of amber on the horizon.

"He must be running late, honey. Why don't we go ahead and have dinner. I'm sure he'll be home soon." She put an arm around his thin shoulders and gave him a hug. "Come on. You'll feel better with a little soup in your tummy."

"I see Daddy's car coming!" Riley stood at the front window peeking between the drapes, only her little pajama clad bottom sticking out into the room.

Ivy returned Caleb's excited grin with a grin of her own, but her lips felt stiff and unnatural. She wished she were happy that Todd finally showed up. She was merely relieved. She couldn't bear her son's disappointment one more time. Her gut wrenched with pain whenever Caleb begged for Todd's attention. Like a love-starved puppy he always wanted more.

Caleb's eyes lit with anticipation. "Can I go outside and see what he brought me?"

6

She nodded and watched him go. His bare feet slapped the entrance tiles as he sprinted to the front door and pulled it open. Riley quickly followed, and Ivy slowly trailed behind.

When she stepped out on the front porch, Todd was lifting a shiny red bicycle from the trunk of his car. Caleb jumped excitedly beside him.

"Look, Mommy. Daddy bought me a two-wheeler! It doesn't even have training wheels," he yelled, beaming with pride.

"I see that." Ivy met Todd's gaze and felt a chill run through her. Something was different. His lips curved but the smile didn't reach his eyes.

"Hey, babe," Todd looked up at her from the bottom of the steps. He ran a hand through his hair, pushing it back from his forehead. "Sorry I'm late."

"Had to work after hours again tonight?" Ivy couldn't help but ask. She sounded bitter and vengeful, and she hated herself for it.

He nodded. "Something like that." He ruffled Caleb's hair and grinned. "How about getting your shoes on and I'll teach you to ride this big boy tonight?"

"Yeah!" Caleb flew up the steps and back into the house before Ivy could stop him.

She frowned. "Todd, it's getting dark and almost their bedtime. It's not time to start something like this."

He held her gaze. "There won't be any better time than now. It's not going to hurt him to stay up a little later and play with his dad." His voice brooked no argument.

"Can I stay up late too, Daddy?" asked Riley, her eyes wide and eager. She glanced back at Ivy as though expecting an argument.

Ivy turned and fled into the house. When had she become the big bad wolf; the one that made sure everyone ate their vegetables and brushed their teeth and went to bed on time? Riley's expression said it all. Todd was the fun parent and she was the crabby one. She didn't like what she

7

was becoming, but what could she do? Short of leaving her husband, nothing would change. Life was complicated and unfair, but she had the kids to think about.

Caleb passed her on his way back outside, a happy grin stretching his face. He'd pulled on socks and tennis shoes and carried his bicycle helmet by the strap.

"Mommy, aren't you going to watch me ride my bike?" he asked, excitement nearly coming out his pores.

Ivy took the helmet from his hand and set it over his blonde curls. "I'll be out later. I've got to put things away in the kitchen, honey," she said as she fastened the strap below his chin. "Have fun."

He ran out to his waiting father. She closed the door carefully behind him, then leaned her head against the wood panel and let tears fill her eyes. She didn't know why she cried. Probably just tired from being up all night with the kids. She didn't cry often or vent her feelings at every turn. She only cried when there was no other option, when she'd damned up so much pain that there wasn't anywhere else for the flood to go but out, crashing over the walls she'd built to keep it in. Hot tears coursed down her cheeks for long seconds before she straightened, wiped her face on the sleeve of her shirt, and headed for the kitchen.

†††

Brenna sat in the black car parked at the curb, obviously impatient to be gone. "Come on, Todd. We're going to miss our flight," she called through the open window.

Todd flashed her a grin before locking the front door of the house. "Don't worry, babe. I wouldn't miss it for the world."

He started down the brick walkway; his leather overnight bag slung over one shoulder. One last time he turned to look back at the rambling stucco house he had gone out on a financial limb to own. He thought if he had the perfect house he would be satisfied, but he wasn't. The women he got involved with over the years, and even the important position he acquired at Monroe Industries had fallen short of his expectations. He felt deflated, like a kid a week after Christmas and everything he opened was already broken.

No one could say he didn't love his kids, and Ivy, in his way, but that wasn't enough. They could never fulfill all his needs and he certainly had never been able to fulfill theirs. He had a deep-seated belief they would be better off without him. To desert them and run probably qualified as the most unselfish thing he'd ever done.

As he approached the car he watched the woman waiting for him. She was young, beautiful, and sexy, but realistically she wouldn't be enough either.

A rush of adrenaline pumped through his veins as he thought about his plans. He'd taken care of the little matter of finding a suitable hiding place for the disc until he could safely leave the country and start a new life. Tomorrow he would no longer be Todd Winter, husband and father, but a man without ties to anyone or anything, even a country. He wished things could be different. He didn't like leaving his kids behind and possibly never seeing them again, but they would be safer in the long run. After all, he hadn't left them with nothing. And Ivy, the perfect wife and mother, would no doubt see to their every need.

Brenna showed her displeasure and impatience with an audible sigh as he finally slid into the bucket seat beside her. "Can we go now?" she asked. "Besides not wanting to meet up with your wife and kids, it would be good to be gone before Monroe Industries realizes you've flown the coop with their company secrets."

"Don't worry so much. Ivy took the kids to the dentist this morning and before anyone realizes what's missing we'll be lying on a beach soaking up the rays."

He'd said his personal goodbyes last night. Ivy hadn't been very communicative after he kept the kids up past their bedtimes, but it gave him a chance to spend quality time with Caleb and Riley. He hoped they wouldn't hate him after his disappearance.

Brenna let out the clutch as she shifted into first and took off with a squeal of tires. She sent him a slanting glance as he barely got the door slammed shut in time.

"I just have one more stop to make at the bank." He placed his hand on her thigh and squeezed, a crooked grin on his handsome face.

Her dark brows drew together but she didn't say anything, just shifted into second and rounded the corner so abruptly he banged his head against the door. He laughed and pulled the seatbelt across his chest, pushing the buckle securely in place. He was in for the ride of his life.

{1}

Nebraska

Music blared from the direction of the den where the kids sat glued to the huge flat screen watching cartoons, their mouths slack and their eyes wide. You'd think neither of them had ever seen a television before. Ivy peeked around the corner watching them. "Are you two all right in here?" she asked.

They continued to stare unblinkingly ahead, but Caleb's head bobbed ever so slightly. It was enough to assure her they were still alive, if only barely.

"All right. If you need anything, just call me. I'll be in the kitchen with Aunt Holly."

She paused in the doorway watching them, the two most precious souls in the world to her. She hoped running home had been the right thing to do. The kids couldn't understand leaving everything they knew in California to move to a place they didn't remember. But like Scarlet O'Hara when her world was falling apart, Ivy felt the pull of home. The foggy apparitions of a life filled with love and stability led her on. Whether the ghostly childhood memories were real or imagined she couldn't clearly remember, having been skewed by time and distance.

Shortly after Todd flew to Chicago on business two weeks ago, everything came crashing in. She'd been bombarded with calls from his office asking if she knew where he was or if she'd heard from him. She wasn't good at guessing games and demanded to know what was going on...

Her voice rose as a million questions filled her mind. "I don't understand. Why are you asking me where he is? You sent him to Chicago!"

The president of Monroe Industries, whom she'd only met at the company gala the year before, came on the line, cutting off Todd's secretary with clipped words. "Jack Monroe here. I'm sorry to inform you Mrs. Winter that your husband left town in a storm cloud of suspicion. Seven hundred thousand dollars has been diverted from an investment account and no one knows where the money is. We did not authorize your husband's trip and are as completely in the dark as you seem to be." His tone held a touch of doubt as to her culpability.

Ivy tightened her grip on the phone, not answering the pointed barb. Her mind spun in confusion at his words.

"If you do hear from him, I strongly urge you to let us know immediately. There are some very serious unanswered questions that must be resolved for security reasons."

Ivy knew there was something they weren't saying, something worse than stolen money, but she didn't ask. She couldn't ask. The situation was bad enough without drowning in the horrid details of her husband's sins.

Then the FBI got involved. They questioned her endlessly about Todd's job, his contacts, even their private life. They sent men to the house to search Todd's home office and personal effects. They put a tap on her phone, assuming he would eventually call to check up on the kids, if not her.

They informed her that a surveillance camera at the airport had picked up Todd traveling with an unidentified woman. One of the agents handed her a photograph. "Have you ever seen this woman before?"

Ivy studied the picture. The young woman fit the two requirements Todd expected of anyone he ran around with: female and not his wife. She handed the picture back and shook her head. "No. She doesn't look familiar."

When Todd finally called, Ivy knew the tap on the line would record their conversation, but she didn't care. "What in the world are you doing, Todd? Have you gone completely crazy? Mr. Monroe said you stole a lot of money from the company. Why would you do something like that?"

He gave a short bark of a laugh. "He said that? Good old Jack, can't own up to the trouble he's in."

"Todd, please–what is going on? The FBI are involved, and they seem to think I know something. You've got to come home and straighten this out. Where are you?"

"Acapulco." He paused, and Ivy could hear music in the background. It sounded like he was at a club or something. "Ivy, I'm not coming back. It's not working for me. Home, family, the job." His voice was soft and placating. "We never should have married so young. We made a lot of mistakes. I didn't date around enough. Didn't know what I really wanted."

"So, all those affairs *after* we married didn't count as dating around? Does the new blonde know what you want? Or is she going to find out eventually it isn't her either?" she asked, her voice shaking with anger.

"Look–I can't do this anymore. You and the kids want something from me I can't give, and I want something you can't give. Let's call it a draw."

"What couldn't I give you, Todd? I tried everything I know." A knot formed in her throat and she tried to swallow. She didn't want to fall victim to Todd's callous behavior anymore.

He chuckled, seemingly oblivious to her pain. "Excitement, baby. Excitement."

The FBI finally gave up and cleared out. As far as she knew no information had been discovered at the house to lead them to Todd and he never called again.

She didn't waste any time, but put the house up for sale, hired a moving company to pack and ship the rest of their belongings, minus Todd's which she donated to Goodwill, and took the kids on a jet back home to Nebraska.

Her sister's invitation to stay with her and her husband until Ivy could find a place to rent had been a godsend. She felt as if her entire world had fallen in. She might be free of Todd at last, a bittersweet sensation to say the least, but as a single parent she now needed to find a job to support the three of them and secure a place to live.

"Are you sure you don't mind watching the kids while I go out to look at apartments?" she asked Holly once more.

Holly rolled her eyes toward the ceiling and planted her hands on her hips. "I'm perfectly capable of watching two small children for a few hours. I'm not a complete idiot you know." She pointed a knowing finger in Ivy's direction. "If you're not ready to go apartment hunting, don't rush it. You can stay here for as long as you need to. Bill and I don't mind. Just take it easy for a while and relax. You've been under enough stress lately with all that's been going on. No one expects you to figure everything out in a couple of days."

Ivy nodded. "I know, but I need to be doing something. And we can't keep living here indefinitely, no matter how sweet you've been about it. For one thing," she added, "I'm sure Bill would like to have his big screen TV back. Those two have taken possession of it and that's nine-tenths of the law, as they say."

"Don't worry; it wouldn't hurt Bill any to be weaned from the remote control for awhile. Might even do our marriage some good. I can't remember the last time he opted to take me to bed early rather than finish watching some stupid game he already knew the outcome of."

"I thought watching games was sort of in his job description. He is a sports columnist after all," she teased.

"He doesn't have to like it so much or stay out late every night attending games."

Bitterness tinged Holly's words and Ivy knew she was hurting inside. Her sister's marriage was not as perfect as Ivy had imagined it to be from the safe distance of California. If she'd known they were struggling, she never would have added her problems to the mix by moving in, even for a few days. "Maybe he's just avoiding us. I'm sure our being underfoot around here is cramping his style. Once we get a place of our own you two can work things out."

Holly handed her the key to the car, her eyes glistening with unshed tears, but she managed a smile.

"I'm on my way then." Ivy picked up her purse and reached in for her little compact mirror. She quickly reapplied a touch of lipstick, snapped the mirror shut and looked down at her black slacks and yellow tank top. They would have to do. Besides, she was apartment-hunting not going on a blind date.

"The real-estate agent said he'd meet me at the first place in-," she glanced at her watch and groaned, "exactly twelve minutes. Pray I hit all green lights, Hol." She opened the door to the garage.

"Don't hurry back. I'll feed the kids and tuck them in," Holly called before the door swung shut behind her.

Holly's little red Honda had a lot of pep, and Ivy darted in and out of rush-hour traffic like a pro. With thirty seconds to spare she parked in front of a three-story brick apartment building and turned off the ignition. She glanced around for the man she was supposed to meet but didn't see him waiting so she hopped out of the car, locked the door, and made her way to the front entrance.

The building was secure, in a loose definition of the term. She watched an elderly woman hold the door for a young Hispanic man as she waited out front. Mid-westerners obviously weren't as worried about crime as Californians.

"Are you Ms. Thompson?"

With the move back to Omaha she had decided to change from her married name to her maiden name and was slightly surprised at how easy it was to make the transformation. She turned, smiling. The man with the deep, mellow, voice was well over six feet tall. He wasn't handsome in the modern sense of the word, a Hollywood pretty boy, but with a slightly crooked nose that looked as though it had been broken at one time, a solid, square chin, and a wide engaging mouth, he was definitely attractive.

"Ms. Thompson?" he asked again.

"Sorry," she said, extending her hand. "Yes, I'm Ivy Thompson."

He shook her hand and fished in his coat pocket for a business card. She dutifully read the name beneath a picture that resembled a passport photo. The man was not photogenic. He was frowning in the photo as though someone had insulted his mother.

"I'm Samson," he said. Small lines gathered at the corners of his brown eyes as he squinted against the late afternoon sun. "I know you talked to Tony Harper on the phone, but he was unable to make it and asked me to take you around, if that's all right." He absently ran a hand through thick, brown hair and she had to suppress a giggle at the thought that her favorite Bible story character had come to life in a pinstripe suit and shiny, black, leather shoes.

"No problem."

"Then let's get started, shall we?" He unlocked the front door and led the way down the hall to the elevator.

When he pushed open the door of the third-floor apartment and stood back to give her room to enter, she felt her first jangle of nerves. The simple process of renting a place to live now seemed like a life-changing step. Whatever she finally settled on would be where she and the children would begin their new lives apart from Todd. She drew a deep breath and walked into the small two-bedroom apartment.

Off to her left was a small kitchenette. There were the basic appliances, stove, refrigerator, and built-in microwave. The white walls and beige carpeting throughout felt sterile, lacking originality. She hoped they allowed renters to at least paint the walls a different color. She paused in the door of the tiny bathroom and remembered the fancy marble tile, double-headed shower, and sunken tub in the master bathroom in their home back in California. The snug space was a far cry from what she was used to, but in a way that was comforting. Todd had always presented her with *things*, to try and compensate for his lack of time, love and care. Life would be simpler here certainly, and she hoped, happier.

"I understand you have two children. Perhaps you'd rather look at something larger." Mr. Sinclair had given her space as she wandered through the rooms, but now he stepped forward and handed her a printout of another place in a fancy high-rise on the other side of town. Ivy quickly glanced through flowery descriptions of a spacious, three-bedroom condo with two and a half baths, before she read the price in small print in the bottom corner.

"I don't think so." She reluctantly handed the flyer back. Money would be tight from now on and she had to be careful that she didn't get them into a bind.

"Can I show you something?" He turned and led her back down the short hall to the front room. The west wall had a large sliding glass door covered from top to bottom with heavy brown drapes. He pulled the curtain back and slid the door open in one smooth motion.

"Come on out," he said as he stepped onto the wooden deck.

She followed him, her eyes widening at the view. The setting sun was molten orange, appearing to melt into the pond that lay spread out before her. A bicycle path wound around, disappearing into a wooded area below the pond. In the final glow of the setting sun a family of ducks sat bobbing on the waters' surface, intermittently quacking softly as they shook out their feathers and one by one tucked their heads beneath their wings. She could still hear the hum of traffic in the distance, but the peacefulness of this setting was a balm to her soul.

"You have perfect timing, Mr. Sinclair." She fixed him with a piercing look. "I know you could have heard on the news when the sun was going to set, but how did you get those ducks to sit so nicely at just the right moment?"

He grinned, and his teeth gleamed white against his tan. "That's a realtor's secret, Ms. Thompson." He turned and went back inside before she could respond.

Ivy stood for a moment enjoying the view before following him in. Mr. Sinclair leaned against the wall, folder in hand, waiting patiently. He'd taken off his suit coat and draped it over one arm. His shirt stretched taunt across a broad chest and one stray lock of brown hair fell over his forehead giving him a very appealing bad boy look. She imagined he wouldn't have any trouble attracting *Delilah's.*

"Do you want to check out the next one on the list? You can follow in your car or ride along with me. Which would work for you?" he asked.

"Why waste time? I'll take this one. You knew I would, didn't you?" Her teasing tone elicited a smile from him.

He pulled away from the wall. "For your price range this is the best deal in town. Small but clean, and as you've seen, the deck has a pretty nice view. There's also a park a couple of blocks from here that the kids might enjoy. I think you'll be glad you signed." He shrugged back into his coat and held the door open.

She stepped out into the hallway, her nervousness from before gone, and she felt calm in her decision. "Thank you. I appreciate you filling in for Mr. Harper. I hope you didn't have to change your plans for me."

"No problem. Just doing my job."

When the doors of the elevator opened on the first floor again, he stood back and let her off first, then he hurried to open the entrance door as well. She hadn't been the target of so much gallantry for a long time. The attention gave her a curiously feminine feeling. She glanced at him as they walked outside, and she realized there was something about the man that made her feel glad she was a woman.

"I'll make sure you have the papers to sign first thing in the morning. Can I meet you for coffee?"

She must have appeared a bit shocked because he laughed. "If you'd rather meet at the office, we can. I just prefer a more relaxed atmosphere when I do business. There's a coffee shop near here. I've become quite addicted to their almond mocha. Afterwards I could present you with the keys to your new castle and go through everything with you."

"Do you always take so much time with a client who is just renting? I assume most agents prefer a sale."

"Hey in this economy we take whatever we can get." He grinned. "Besides, I try to treat all my clients equally, with respect and helpfulness."

Ivy tried to look serious. "Would you really treat some gray-haired old lady with a sagging chest and knee-high panty hose falling down around her ankles, the same? Would you ask *her* out for coffee?"

He hesitated, apparently sensing a test. "I don't know if I'd ask her out for coffee, but I'd pick one up for her."

She adjusted the strap of her purse over her shoulder. The man was not a smooth operator like Todd or he would have had a line out faster than she could bat an eye. Not that her husband was the ideal example to strive for. Todd was a thief, a liar, and not to be trusted. She just wondered if a man really existed in this world who did things out of the kindness of his heart? She would like to think so. She'd lost faith in mankind as well as in God the last few years. Maybe she should give him a chance. She would find out soon enough if his good guy persona was just a ploy.

"Tell me where and when and I'll meet you there."

He pulled out a pen and started to write the address down.

She remembered that Holly had to work at the shop in the morning. Her sister was already sweet enough to let her use her car, but she didn't think she would want to take Caleb and Riley to work with her. "Oh, sorry. I don't have anywhere to leave the kids tomorrow morning. Could we meet in the evening?"

He didn't even flinch but held out the slip of paper on which he'd written the name and address of the coffee shop. "Don't sweat it. They'll love the place. Maggie has great donuts and bagels as well as coffee. Is eight o'clock too early? We can get a bite to eat, and then they can come along and see their new home." He held the door of the Honda open while she slid in.

"If you're sure."

"See you in the morning." He gave her a friendly wave and walked to a dark blue Pontiac parked along the street.

Ivy leaned back against the leather seat of the Honda and stared through the front windshield into the darkening night. Streetlights came on one by one, and she had a clear view of the comings and goings of her soon to be new neighbors. Samson Sinclair's eyes flashed in her mind, so clear they seemed to be totally lacking in guile. Could she possibly have met a man without a secret agenda?

{2}

Ivy parked the little red Honda out front of the Mocha Shack and turned to smile into the back seat at her kids already clambering to get out of their seatbelts.

"All right, you two. I don't want Mr. Sinclair getting hot coffee spilled in his lap. So, try to behave yourselves. After breakfast, we'll go see our new home and you can decide where all your toys are going to go."

"Why can't we go back to our old house? I liked it there." Caleb frowned up at her as he released his belt and automatically began helping his little sister.

"You already know why, honey. I told you that Daddy wasn't coming back, and we have to start a new life. This is where I grew up. I want us to start our new life here. Give it a try. I know you miss the house and your friends, but you'll make new friends, and I think you'll like the place I rented. There is a pond in the back and bike paths where we can ride to the park. It'll be great, you'll see."

Riley grinned. "I like it, Mommy."

"How can you like it, Riley? You haven't even seen the apartment yet." Caleb shook his head with all the disgust a big brother can muster and opened the door of the car.

"I still like it," she said. She slid across the seat and out Caleb's open door.

Ivy locked the car and entered the small shop. The smells that greeted them were a heavenly combination of fresh-brewed coffee, sticky buns, cinnamon rolls and other goodies that made the kids' eyes light up when they viewed them in the glass cases.

"Mommy, I want that one." Riley pointed at a chocolate frosted donut covered with multi-colored sprinkles.

"You just lick off all the frosting and leave the donut," her brother said.

"Do not!"

"Do too!"

"That's enough. Have you already forgotten you're supposed to be on your best behavior? I don't care which donut you pick but no more arguing. Understand?"

"They wouldn't be a very convincing brother and sister if they never argued."

Samson Sinclair stood behind them. He grinned, and she felt color wash up into her cheeks. She didn't know why he had that effect on her. She couldn't remember blushing since she was in high school.

"Good morning, Mr. Sinclair." Trying not to look flustered, she made the introductions. "These are my children, Caleb and Riley. Kids, say hello to Mr. Sinclair."

Caleb did a terrific imitation of Todd's business voice. "How do you do, Mr. Sinclair?"

"How do you do, Caleb. Nice to meet you – both," he added with a wink in Riley's direction. Riley grabbed Ivy's hand and peeked out at him from around her mother's legs.

"Did you pick a donut yet? They all look pretty yummy," he said, viewing the selection with a practiced eye.

Before the kids could answer, a woman appeared from the kitchen with another tray of fresh rolls. She trudged along heavily, her sagging upper arms swinging alongside the tray she carried like pendulums in full action. Ivy noticed the apron she wore covered a blue double-knit polyester pantsuit that *had* to be against some fire code and pulled halfway over her beehive hairdo was a black hairnet that looked more like a Jewish cap on her gray head than protection against falling split-ends. With as much spray as she obviously used to get her hair to stay that way, there wasn't much chance of any escaping.

"Well, well, well, if it isn't Samson Sinclair back again for the third time this week. If you don't start watching what you eat, young man, you're going look like Hank and me." The woman slid the tray under the glass where they could get a better look at the fresh assortment. "I see you brought company with you today. Good morning! Like to have a taste test?" She held out two sugarcoated donut holes on toothpicks, which the kids eagerly took and poked into their mouths.

"What do you say?" Ivy prompted. The kids mumbled a suitable response with mouths full and Samson laughed.

"I think they like your cooking, Maggie."

"I'll be sure and let Hank know. He's really the genius chef around here. I'm just the help," she whispered conspiratorially behind a pudgy hand.

They soon had their sweets loaded on a tray with milks and coffees. The group sat down in one of the booths against the window where they had a view of early morning traffic.

"Sounds like you come here often," Ivy said, to fill the void.

"I do. It's close to where I live, and Maggie and Hank are old friends."

He passed the kids their plates and cups and did something Ivy hadn't seen done in many years. He bowed his head silently over his food. She waited in shocked silence. What sort of man stopped to pray these days?

He looked up. "I think you have my coffee."

"Huh?"

"My coffee?" He raised his eyebrows at her blank expression. "This one is plain. I had the almond mocha."

"Oh – I'm sorry." She quickly passed him the one in her hand and took her own a little clumsily, sloshing hot liquid over the side and onto her hand. "Ouch!"

"Let me see." Before she could protest, he reached across, took her hand in his, and dabbed at the reddened skin with a paper napkin. "Doesn't look like you'll get a blister."

Their eyes met across the small booth and she realized she was holding her breath. He smiled and sat back, gently releasing her hand to pick up a donut. She sipped her coffee and watched him talk and joke with the children. There was something different about him. He didn't seem hurried or as though he was putting on an act, but warm and caring and truly interested in what the kids had to say. Even Caleb seemed to like him, and she could tell he had been planning to put up a mean resistance. He didn't want any man getting near his mother at this point and she couldn't blame him. Not that she was looking for a man. Definitely *not* looking.

The last time she'd been looking, she'd been in high school. She fell in love with Todd Winter her senior year. At twenty-two, he was the older man who would take her away from her mundane life. Much to her parent's horror and through her own naivety, they were married the day after she graduated. She soon found out why he was in such a hurry to tie the knot. She wanted to believe he couldn't live another day without her, but it was her savings account he couldn't live without. With over five thousand dollars saved from working after school and summers since she was fourteen, she was obviously an attractive catch for a man who had run out of funding and needed support through his last year of college while he spent all his free time *studying* pretty coeds.

She took a gulp of hot coffee to nix the memories and turned to stare out the window. It was hard to believe that eight years ago she was a naïve nineteen-year-old. But she was still young. Todd may have stolen those years of her life, but he had given her Caleb and Riley; she wouldn't trade them for anything, not even a chance to start fresh. She glanced back at Samson Sinclair. Although, starting off with the right man would have been advantageous.

Ivy watched the interaction between this man and her children and couldn't help wishing Todd had been someone her kids could play with and look up to, that she could respect and love. Too bad do-overs weren't possible in real life. She cleared her throat and set her cup down.

"You look as though you want to get down to business. Sorry I've been stalling. I'm enjoying your kids. I have a couple of nieces and nephews, but they live in Chicago, and I don't get to see them as much as I'd like to. One of these days I need to find the right girl, so I can settle down and have some of my own."

She couldn't believe a man this perfect and unattached sat before her now. God certainly liked to pull dirty tricks. She could have used this opportunity about eight years ago. But she doubted she would have had the sense back then to pick a decent guy over Todd.

She shook her head. "No, that's fine. I just don't want to keep you any longer than necessary. I'm sure you have more important things to do."

"Not really. You're my priority right now." He reached over and carefully wiped a blob of frosting from Riley's cheek.

Ivy tensed, and her voice came out sounding stiff and formal. "I appreciate that, Mr. Sinclair."

He glanced up. A frown laced his brows. "Why don't you call me Samson? Everyone does."

Before she could answer, Maggie's voice boomed across the room. "Samson, you two want anymore coffee?"

"See?" Samson grinned and called back, "No thanks, Maggie. We're fine."

Ivy laughed and relaxed for the first time since meeting Samson Sinclair. "I'm sorry I'm so uptight. I really do appreciate all you're doing. Please call me Ivy."

"Ivy. That's a nice name. Like a strong green vine that's reaching for something."

"Clinging, more like, for a stable place to hang on. At least lately. We need to put down roots. We've been living with my sister and her husband for the last few days. It will be nice to have a place of our own again."

"Where did you live before?"

"California." She didn't embellish, and he didn't ask. He sipped his coffee and watched her.

"Mommy, can we go see what the new donuts look like that Maggie brought out?" Caleb asked, his eyes wide with eagerness.

Riley's shrill, little voice chimed in. "Yeah, can we?"

"Riley, bring it down a decibel or two, okay? Yes, but stay where I can see you."

They ran off to stand with their noses pressed against the glass case while Maggie arranged fresh donuts and chatted with them.

"How old is Caleb?"

"He's seven. Riley's four."

"I don't know if you'd be interested, but I teach a Sunday school class for small boys at church. I'd love to have him come. Of course, there are classes for all ages including adults, so you'd certainly be welcome too."

At thirteen years old, Ivy loved church and always went along with a friend that lived down the block. Her parents didn't belong to a church and except for Christmas, never bothered to attend one. Why they felt it necessary that one day of the year, she never did understand. If you ignored God the rest of the year, would He want you to come to His house for His birthday? She hadn't thought so at the time and still didn't. Not that she sought out God anymore anyway. Not since the last time she went to church.

"I don't think so." She stared down at her hands. They began to shake at the thought. "We've been doing just fine without God so far," she said, a tinge of bitterness in her voice.

"I'm sorry you feel that way, Ivy. I don't mean to pressure you; I thought it would be fun for the kids. They could meet new friends in a safe environment and -"

"Safe? How can you be sure it would be safe?"

"Well, I'd be there to watch out for them. I've attended services there nearly my entire life. There are good people there. Maggie and Hank are members. In fact, Hank taught my Sunday school class when I was a boy."

She ran her finger nervously around the rim of her empty cup, refusing to meet his eye.

"What's wrong, Ivy? Maybe I shouldn't ask, but is there some reason you're mad at God?"

She looked up at his question. Had she been angry with God all this time? No. She simply quit believing because he didn't live up to her expectations. She glanced away from Samson's probing gaze. "I'm not angry with God. You have to believe in God to be angry at him, don't you?"

Samson leaned forward, his voice low and confident. "You believe in God, Ivy. You've just forgotten how to trust."

"Are you a therapist as well as a real estate agent?" she asked, the bite back in her words. "I don't remember asking for your opinion on my belief system."

He had the good sense to appear chagrined. He started to apologize but Caleb and Riley interrupted. They ran back from the counter, two more sugared donut holes in their greedy little hands. Ivy felt immense relief wash over her.

"Hey - slow down, you two. You've had enough sugar for today. Let's sign those papers and go see our new home." She looked across at Samson who still wore his religious *I care about you* look.

"Whatever you say. You're the boss." He drew the contract from his jacket pocket and Ivy signed all the appropriate places.

"There you go," he said as he handed her a copy. "The place is all yours. I'll take you through the building and show you the laundry room, the pool and workout room, and how to get into everything with your access key."

Ivy stood and slung her purse over her shoulder. "That's quite all right, Mr. Sinclair, but we can find everything on our own. Give me the key, and we'll be on our way." She held out her hand and after only a slight hesitation, he took the key from his pocket and handed it to her.

"Thanks for breakfast and – everything. Say goodbye to Mr. Sinclair, kids."

"But I thought his name was Samson now." Riley looked up at Ivy with a puzzled expression. "Can't he come too?"

Samson smiled and bent down to eye level with Riley. "Sorry, I have to go to the office and get my paper work done. But it has been very nice to meet all of you, and I hope we meet again soon."

The kids waved as Ivy backed them toward the door and made her escape. She actually drew a sigh of relief when they were in the car and headed for the apartment. They'd probably never meet Mr. Sinclair again, and that was certainly for the best. His probing unnerved her. The audacity of the man to tell her that she had forgotten how to trust! Where did he get off analyzing someone he just met? That technique probably didn't get him a lot of second dates.

Maybe she had forgotten how to trust, but that was old news. At the fragile age of thirteen her trust in God had violently been ripped away. And since living with Todd, *trust* had been replaced in her dictionary with *look before you leap.* But Samson Sinclair didn't know about Todd. He wasn't talking about her distrust of men. Her mouth drew into a thin line. Why should she trust in a God who had never

28

been there when she needed Him most? She had been taking care of herself and the kids for quite some time now, without any help from anyone – especially God.

{3}

Samson watched them go and then slid back into his seat at the booth. He dropped his head into his hands and groaned. To say that their second meeting hadn't gone well was to put it mildly.

"What's the matter, Samson? That young woman and her kids giving you a hard time?" Maggie stood at his elbow with a fresh pot of coffee in her hand and a teasing smile on her face. "Mind if I sit a spell? I don't have any customers right now, and you look as though you could use some cheering up." At his nod she squeezed slowly into the booth, her stomach pressed tightly against the edge of the table.

"How are you, Maggie? I didn't have a chance to talk to you earlier with business to take care of and all," Samson said, hoping to head off her earlier line of questioning.

Maggie took a plastic fork from her apron pocket and stuck it through her hairnet to scratch at her scalp. She used the pointed prongs in several more areas until she finally satisfied her itch and leaned back with a sigh.

"Ah, that feels better. I hate wearing these things, but I think it makes people feel better when they see me in them. It gives the illusion that we're sanitary people." She laughed, but the action appeared to push her stomach painfully against the edge of the table, so she stopped.

"So, what's the story with the woman and children? Or is this secret FBI business you can't talk about?"

"The situation is complicated. Ivy doesn't know I'm working for the bureau. I hate to put you in this position, but if she and the kids come back in here again, will you please not mention anything about me? Just avoid the topic."

"Samson Sinclair, are you lying to that nice, young woman to get information for the FBI?" Maggie's voice rose and carried to the far corner of the shop where two women sat eating bagels. They both turned to take in the soap opera playing out at the booth by the window.

Samson touched Maggie's hand. "Could you talk quieter, please? The whole world will soon know my entire life, and I'd prefer they didn't." He inclined his head toward the audience in the back.

"I'm sorry, but you didn't answer my question. Are you tricking that woman?" Maggie asked, sounding anything but sorry. Her gray eyes pierced him to his soul.

"I'm supposed to be investigating her. She moved here from California. She thinks I'm her realtor. I rented her an apartment in my building." He met her gaze and saw disappointment there. He glanced out the window, his jaw tightening with irritation. "It's my job. I can't just tell my superiors to go fly a kite."

"Is she supposed to be a terrorist or something?"

He shook his head. "Her husband is the criminal. They're using her to get to him, hoping he'll turn up or call or something and they can get a fix on him."

Worry filled Maggie's eyes, and she reached across and took Samson's hand in her own. "I saw the way you looked at that woman. You're attracted to her and nothing good can come of that. She's a married woman with two children. You better think long and hard before getting too close.

Remember what happened to another Samson who went into the Philistines' camp."

He wished he'd been named anything but Samson. He was so sick of trying to live up to his name one minute and live it down the next. "I know what you're saying, and I appreciate your concern, but there's no need to worry. This is business – not personal. I have to keep an eye on her. That's all." He ran a hand through his hair and leaned back in his seat trying to appear nonchalant.

"Are you going to sit there and tell me you're *not* attracted to her?"

As hard as he tried, Samson couldn't think of an answer that would satisfy Maggie. He knew she was right. He *was* walking into the enemy's camp. Ivy may not be a Philistine, but by her own admission she chose not to believe. At the least, she had some very big spiritual questions to resolve. And she was married. He wasn't free to pursue her even if her husband *was* a jerk who stole from the company he worked for and ran off with another woman. Watching the passing cars through the Café window, he knew that becoming romantically involved with a married woman was not something he could do.

He shook his head. "Whether or not I'm attracted to Ivy Winter has no bearing on my job. I've been ordered to watch her, and I will. If it makes you feel any better, I'll be careful."

"It won't be easy now that you live in the same building."

"Not just the same building," he admitted reluctantly. "She's in the apartment next door. And I don't think she'll be too pleased when she finds out. I asked if the kids would like to go to Sunday school with me, and she made a beeline for the door. I think she needs someone to talk to, someone she can trust. I'm not a good candidate. If she finds out I'm spying on her for the FBI, she'll certainly never trust *me* again." He wrapped his hands around the warm cup Maggie had refilled and stared down into the black liquid as though he'd find the answer there. "I don't want to be a stumbling block to her. I just don't know what to do."

"Well, strike up the band and play the Halleluiah Chorus! I believe this is the first time I've ever heard you admit you don't know what to do. You've always been confident and known what you wanted, Samson. But what about God? What about waiting on him? Sometimes you have to walk by faith. You don't know his purpose yet in bringing you into this family's life, but he does. Instead of solving everything yourself maybe you should let God do what he does best."

She glanced up when the doorbell chimed. Customers filed in, and she hurriedly squeezed out from behind the table and hauled herself to her feet.

"I've got to go now, but you think about what I said, you hear?" She patted his hand, retrieved the pot of coffee, and went to wait on her customers.

He smiled after her, unsure whether to be annoyed or thankful that she cared. Maggie was always quick to share words of wisdom even when he didn't want to hear them. But she was right this time. He did tend to act before he had a clear plan. Waiting was not one of his strong points. If he wanted to do his job and be a light to Ivy at the same time, he needed to look to God for guidance, because on his own he was sure to mess up.

††††

Ivy and the kids returned to the house a little after noon. Holly was working at the store, and the kids went into the den to take advantage of the big screen television while they still had the chance. She sat down with a soda to relax, and her thoughts went back to the morning just past.

They had gone through the apartment building to familiarize themselves with everything. The kids wanted to see the duck pond up close, so they walked out the back door of the building and down to the water's edge. A few ducks floated lazily along, quacking to one another as though in conversation. Caleb and Riley watched them for a few minutes, and then turned their attention to the bike path winding away into a wooded area.

"Could we ride our bikes through there, Mommy?" Caleb asked, pointing toward the trees.

"When the truck brings all our stuff, we'll look for the bikes right away. Mr. Sinclair said that path leads to a park. We can ride to the park on Saturdays and maybe have a picnic." Ivy lifted her daughter into her arms and swung her around. Riley squealed with delight until Ivy plopped her back on the ground and sat on the grass beside her.

"What do you think, you two? Do you like the place?" she asked the children. She still worried whether or not she had done the right thing by moving them here. The alternative, of course, would be to stay in California and possibly have people snub them and make cruel remarks behind their backs when the news came out about Todd. She didn't want the children to know what their father had done until they were old enough to understand. They already had to deal with the fact that he'd left them.

"I like it," Riley answered, leaning against Ivy.

Ivy put an arm around her and hugged her close. "You already said *you* liked it before you saw it. What about you, Caleb?

Caleb stood beside them, his hands in the pockets of his Levi's, squinting against the brightness of the sun. He looked so much like Todd in that stance Ivy had to swallow a lump that formed in her throat. The love she felt for Todd died long ago, but she could still remember the good times. Sometimes she felt like a complete failure. Marriage meant forever, till death do us part. Even the fairy tales said, "and they lived happily ever after." The words they'd spoken at their own wedding had been a promise of exactly that, and she'd tried so hard to live up to them even when Todd cheated and lied. But now he'd finally left them for good, and she didn't feel the bond of that promise any longer.

"I think it's okay," Caleb said. He looked up at the building behind them and waved. "Hey, there's Mr. Sinclair. Is he on our balcony?" he asked.

Ivy swiveled around to take a look. Samson stood on the balcony next door to theirs. He must be showing another apartment. He waved and then turned and went back in through the sliding glass door. Wanting to avoid another meeting with the Good Samaritan, she'd taken the kids and walked around the outside of the building to their car.

The telephone rang, bringing her back to the present, and she got up to answer it. "Hello." There was silence on the other end of the line. "Hello?" she said again, a little louder. She started to hang up.

"Mrs. Todd Winter?" a voice asked, too soft to distinguish whether it was male or female.

"Yes."

"We want the computer disc your husband left with you." There was something sinister in the voice. Could this be another FBI agent calling? She'd had about enough of their bullying.

"Excuse me? Who is this? I don't know what you're talking about, but I plan to lodge a complaint if you don't stop harassing me. I've already told you people I don't know anything about Todd's business."

"Stop playing games, Mrs. Winter. The disc. We want it. Don't disappoint us or something bad could happen to your family."

"How dare you–," she began, but a soft click told her the anonymous caller had hung up. She set the phone down and stepped back from it as though it were a coiled serpent. What was that about? Disc? What disc?

The FBI searched their home and took Todd's computer. They never mentioned a disc. If he'd deleted anything from his hard drive she was sure they had ways to retrieve it. If Todd had burned discs with company information, she didn't know where he would have hidden them. The FBI took whatever they wanted, and she'd packed up the rest of Todd's papers from the file cabinet and desk and sent them back to Monroe Industries. She shouldn't be blamed if something came up missing.

The phone rang again, and she froze. She let the thing ring five times before she got up the nerve to answer it. Her hand shook as she picked up the receiver and held it to her ear.

"Hello?"

"Holly!" Ivy slumped into the kitchen chair with relief. "Thank God it's you."

"Of course, it's me. Who else would it be?"

"I don't know." Ivy closed her eyes. She couldn't get the ominous sound of that voice and the threats out of her mind.

"Okay…anyway, I was calling to ask if you could pick me up in an hour. Business is really slow today, so I think I'll come home early and let Lisa close up."

"Sure. We'll be there."

"How did the kids like the apartment?"

"They seemed okay with it. The truck is supposed to arrive tomorrow morning, and we can start moving in. Once they have their own furniture and toys in their rooms it will make the place seem more like home." She rubbed the back of her neck, feeling stress in every muscle. "It's good for the kids to be around family for a change. We didn't know a soul out in California when we moved there. It's nice to be back," she said.

"I'm glad you're back too, Ivy. I missed you. I better go. Lisa needs to use the phone – something about a Chinese vase. I'll see you in an hour, okay?"

"Sure."

Ivy hung up the phone and let her head drop into her hands. So far getting away from the problem did not seem to be working. She drew a deep breath and slowly released it, feeling some of her earlier tension evaporate. It was probably just a prank call and nothing to get worked up about. Some kook got hold of information he shouldn't have and used it to feel powerful. He probably found out about her husband's crimes and decided to get in on the game. That must be the explanation. What else could it be?

She put her nervousness to work making bologna sandwiches for the kid's lunch, and while they ate, she tried to plan what furniture she would use in their new place. They had too many pieces to fit into a small, two-bedroom apartment. Caleb and Riley would have to use bunk beds and share a room for now, but she was keeping the king-sized bed for herself. It was perfect in the early mornings when the kids came running to snuggle with her while they watched cartoons and she got in a few more winks. She would keep a television for her room and sell the others. The entertainment center, with the top of the line stereo system Todd had insisted upon, would fit in the corner of the small living room, and the overstuffed loveseat and matching recliners, would complete the room beautifully. The rest would have to be stored or sold. They would have a simple home, not the decorative masterpiece their California stucco had been, but a home where the kids could play in any room without worrying they might mess something up. She looked over the layout plan she had sketched and smiled. She was beginning to think that small was better; one bathroom to scrub was definitely better than four.

Riley finished her sandwich and milk and stood beside Ivy, trying to see over her shoulder at the sketch. "What'cha doing, Mommy? Colorin'?"

Ivy lifted her on her lap and showed her the drawing of their new apartment. She pointed out the different rooms and where they would put their things.

Riley turned her head to look up at her mother's face. "What about the fish? You didn't leave room for their big glass house," she said, a frown creasing her smooth forehead.

Ivy had completely forgotten the fish. Todd had brought a huge aquarium home one day, set up with exotic fish that cost him more per pound than lobster, and you couldn't even eat them. The children wanted a puppy, but Todd said a dog caused too much trouble and made messes and he hated messes. So, he tried to pacify them with expensive fish they couldn't hold, touch, or even feed because they might give them too much and kill them. Caleb never cared about them, but Riley stood in front of the glass with her little face pressed to it and made fish kisses at them, talking in a language only the fish understood.

"I'm sorry, Riley. We couldn't bring them. They couldn't travel on the truck with the furniture, so I had to sell them back to the pet store." Seeing the look of gloom that filled her daughter's face, she hugged her tight.

"Don't worry, we'll get more fish. But we won't be able to have such a large home for them. We'll have to get babies and a small aquarium that will fit in your room, all right?"

"Okay, but I get to name them, right?"

"You can name them anything you like, Sweetie." She smiled as Riley climbed down from her lap.

"I get new fishes, Caleb," she announced to her brother who still sat on a barstool at the kitchen counter eating the rest of a bag of barbecue potato chips.

He snorted. "So – I don't like stupid fish anyway," he said. "I want a puppy."

"I know, honey, but apartment buildings don't allow dogs. Maybe someday we can get our own house again and then we'll buy you a puppy. I promise."

"Why don't we buy a house now instead?" he asked.

"Houses cost a lot of money, and we don't have enough. Daddy's job paid for the one in California, but now I have to find a job to pay for things. I won't be making nearly as much money as Daddy did because I haven't worked for a long time, but we'll still have a nice home, and more importantly, we'll have each other." She slipped out of her chair and walked to the counter where Caleb sat stiffly, his lower lip trembling just a bit. She knew he didn't want her to see him cry, being all of seven years old now, but he finally broke down, turning his face into her chest as she stood beside him. His tears wet her silk blouse. She held him close and ran her hand soothingly over the golden blonde curls.

When he looked up, he sniffed and tried to wipe the tears away with the sleeve of his sweatshirt. "Why did Daddy go away? Doesn't he love us anymore?" he asked.

Riley stood quietly at their side through all of this with a worried expression on her face, but now she reached up and patted Caleb on the arm, a smile of confidence on her lips. "Course Daddy loves us, silly. Daddies don't stop loving kids. Do they, Mommy?"

Both of them looked at Ivy for confirmation as though she had all the answers to the world's problems, or at least to their small world. She swallowed down the bitter answer she felt in her heart – that Todd had never loved anyone but himself. They needed to believe their father loved them, and she wasn't going to thrust reality in their innocent faces.

"No, honey, they never stop loving their kids. Daddy loves both of you very much. He just won't be living with us anymore. Someday when you're older, you'll understand." She kissed them both on the forehead and earnestly wished *she* understood.

"Oh, look at the time! We've got to pick up Aunt Holly. Come on you two - back into the car." She opened the door to the garage, slung her purse over her shoulder, and herded them out the door. They jumped into the Honda, and Ivy was already pulling out of the driveway when she thought she heard the phone ringing in the kitchen again.

†††

"We got the judge to okay the tap on her line at the apartment, but they wouldn't give us the one on her sister's line. That really stinks. What if Winter calls her before she moves in tomorrow? Are we supposed to know what's going on through osmosis, or what?" Andy Timmons leaned on the edge of Samson's desk and crossed his arms, a frown of disapproval on his face. His suit jacket bulged as though the thread holding it together would break and unravel at any moment. Short and muscular, he looked like a professional wrestler someone had dropped an anvil on. His military buzz stood at attention over a ruddy face only a mother could love.

Samson looked up from the forms cluttering his desktop. "I doubt her husband is going to get in touch with her. He left her for another woman, remember?"

"Yeah, well maybe so, but look at the woman he left. What was he thinking? Besides, those are his kids too and he's bound to get in touch with them sooner or later." Timmons scratched his cheek where a five o'clock shadow steadily darkened, and yawned. "Which reminds me, I've got to get home and see my own brood. I promised I'd make it for dinner tonight."

Samson had a hard time imagining Timmons as a loving father and husband, but the family pictures on his desk provided tangible proof that couldn't be denied.

"Have a good night. I'm going to finish this up and then I'll be leaving too. See you in the morning."

Timmons waved and headed for the door. "I need a good hearty dinner if I have to do manual labor tomorrow," he grumbled. Timmons job in the morning was to pose as one of the movers and help unload furniture when Ivy's moving truck came.

Samson grinned. "I thought you were tough, Timmons. You work out in the gym every day. What's a little lifting to you?"

"There's a big difference between lifting for recreation and lifting for labor; one pumps you up and the other beats you down," he said, and pushed out the door.

Samson thought about the wiretap being put on Ivy's apartment phone. She would be extremely upset when she found out, and eventually she would find out because she was a very smart woman. He knew from their first meeting that there was a lot going on behind those beautiful green eyes. She seemed to look at the world with way too much cynicism for one so young. He wondered what she endured with Todd Winter to make her so distrustful of men. More importantly, he wondered what caused her to quit trusting in God.

He signed his name to three more forms, shuffled them all into a neat pile and placed them in his out box. Time to go home. He pushed back from the desk and stood, glanced around the open office area where a dozen similar desks filled the room, and realized there were only three agents still working. He grabbed his jacket from the back of the chair and shrugged into it. Two of the men called goodnight as he slipped out the door.

He rode the elevator down alone to the underground garage. His footsteps echoed eerily against concrete walls as he approached his car. Grey walls closed in on every side, making him feel isolated, almost like being buried alive. He'd had a dream like that a couple of times and it wasn't pleasant. He preferred to park on the street, but it wasn't always possible. Day or night, the garage was dark and dreary.

He drew his keys from his pocket and reached out to unlock the door but clumsily dropped them to the ground. Reaching to pick them up he spied a small silver object attached under the edge of the rear wheel well. He crouched to get a better look. A tracking device. Not an inexpensive one either. He slowly made his way around the car, checking for others before straightening and brushing his pants off. He had to report this to the captain. Why would anyone want to track his comings and goings? He took a quick look around the garage. It was quiet. He disconnected the small device and pushed it into his pocket.

†††

"The Winter case is the only one I'm working on, Sir. I don't know why anyone would want to follow me. I certainly don't go anywhere interesting," Samson said, keeping his tone light.

"Well I don't like the idea someone bugged your car right here in the FBI parking garage. I want you to be extra careful from now on. Take precautions until we find out why you were targeted. I don't see how the Winter case could put you in jeopardy. That woman doesn't know you're an agent, does she?" Captain Herndon raised his brows. The Captain's temper was legendary but lately it even scared the seasoned agents. With red hair that ran in a wide band around his head from ear to ear, leaving a smooth pate on top like Bozo the clown, he had a comical look that belied his lack of humor. Samson was not deceived.

"Of course not, Sir, but she certainly wouldn't be tracking my car if she did. Her husband is the criminal, not her."

His defense of Ivy brought a snort of derision from the Captain. "I wouldn't be so sure about that, Agent Sinclair. In my experience the innocent wife often turns out to be *not* so innocent nine times out of ten."

"Yes, Sir," Samson said, although he strongly disagreed and thought the Captain might be unduly prejudiced because of his recent divorce. The job he'd done for twenty-six years seemed to have sapped his likability, leaving him cold and distant, a man most people felt inclined to avoid. No wonder his wife left him.

"Go home now. I'll send Jack along behind you in case you're being followed."

Samson started to protest then clamped his lips shut and nodded. "Fine. Goodnight, Sir."

The drive home was uneventful, and he waved Jack away as he let himself into the apartment building. Samson rode the elevator up to his apartment, not meeting anyone along the way. He made a ham and cheese sandwich for dinner and sat out on the deck to eat it in the dark. He enjoyed listening to the sounds of people settling in for the night. It made him feel less alone in the world.

Exhaustion soon overtook him, and he went inside. He only had a few hours to sleep before he would get up and meet his new neighbor. He hated the thought that he was forced to deceive Ivy. He had to keep reminding himself that parts of his job were not always pleasant, but necessary. The question for him now was: How would he manage to make friends with the woman without getting personally involved?

"Lord," he prayed as he shut off the light and climbed into bed, "I can use all the strength you can give me for this one."

{4}

Ivy left the kids with Holly and went to meet the moving truck early the following morning. She felt like a kid getting a new toy. A fresh start for her and the children would certainly make all the difference in the world. Once they moved in and settled down, she would need to find a job, but she would worry about that later. First, she had to make a proper home for her children. A place they could feel safe and secure.

She opened the door and walked into the shadowy apartment. Glints of sunlight peeked around the edges of the closed drapes. She pulled them wide, letting in the morning sun to drench the bare living room with light.

In the kitchen, she checked the wall phone for a dial tone. The reassuring buzz confirmed a working line. She dialed Holly's number and waited for her to pick up.

"Hello?" Dishes clinked on Holly's end of the line.

"Hi. The phone's connected so if you need to get hold of me you can."

"Great! Since you seem to misplace your cell every time you turn around." There was a smile in her voice. "The kids are having oatmeal and watching cartoons. Did you want to talk to them?"

"No, that's okay. I better go watch for the truck. See you later."

"Wait a minute. There was an odd message on the answering machine for you. They didn't leave a name. They just said bring the disc to Dodge park today at three. What is that about, Ivy? Are you into disc golf now?"

Ivy cleared her throat and tried to speak normally, but fear gripped her insides. "I don't know. Maybe it was a wrong number," Ivy said. Who was doing this? And why did they believe she was hiding something? Should she go to the FBI? Or would they just assume she was working with Todd as well?

The doorbell rang.

"I'll call you later, Hol."

She hurried to open the door, expecting to find men carrying furniture, but Samson Sinclair stood there instead. In jeans and a T-shirt, he looked just as fit and thoroughly buff as she remembered. When he smiled she actually felt her heart flutter, which up until now she thought only happened in sappy romance novels. "Can I help you?" she asked, trying her best not to look interested.

"I hear you're moving in today and thought I'd give you a hand," he said.

"Why would you want to do that?" She knew from experience that nothing comes for free. She placed her hands on her hips and eyed him narrowly.

He shrugged and glanced away, obviously not accustomed to women refusing his help. "Just being neighborly."

"What do you mean, neighborly?" she asked, and then blew out a frustrated breath when she remembered Caleb waving up at him on the balcony the day before. "You live right next door to me, don't you? And you didn't bother to divulge that piece of information *before* I signed the contract?"

Samson backed up a step. "I'm sorry, I didn't know my occupancy in the same building would be a detriment to you choosing one place over another. I've never been accused of being a bad neighbor before." He actually sounded hurt by her words, and she felt a moment's qualm. Maybe she was being a little too hard on him. After all he was trying to be helpful and do the Christian thing. *That was the rub*, what really made her so mad. Couldn't he be helpful just because he liked her rather than because he felt some kind of obligation? Well, if *he* could be neighborly than so could she. She didn't have to believe in anything to have manners.

She backed up and grudgingly waved him in. "Forgive me for being abrupt, Mr. Sinclair. But you surprised me. I had no idea you lived next door. I'm a little nervous about moving in, you know?"

"I understand. I just want to help any way I can."

"The truck should be here any minute now. I need to go down and watch for them."

"Can I do that for you, Ivy? I'll bring them up when they get here." He stepped back out the door, then stopped and turned to meet her gaze, a crooked smile turning one side of his mouth up. "Would you please start calling me Samson again?"

"I'll try," she said, returning his smile. She watched him stride down the hall to the elevator, then closed the door and leaned against it. She needed to loosen up. Being on guard all the time made her feel paranoid.

†††

Timmons slowly climbed down from the truck when it pulled up. Samson waited until the other two men opened the back doors and started pulling out boxes before moving to stand beside his partner.

"Ivy's upstairs in the apartment," he said.

Timmons cocked his head to the side and raised his brows. "On a first name basis already, are you?"

Samson ignored his remark. "She agreed to let me help, so I guess I'll be around all day keeping an eye on your work, Timmons." He slapped the older man on the back.

"Watch it, kid," he said in a low voice that rumbled like a growl. "I don't get paid to have little twerps like you telling me what to do, even if I am undercover."

"I'll try not to boss you around too much then." Samson laughed and climbed up into the back of the truck.

They hauled boxes and furniture to the third floor and placed them where Ivy instructed. The rest of her things were to be unloaded at a storage facility. Her brother-in-law had agreed to meet the truck there and take care of things.

"Mind if I use your phone?" Samson asked three hours later after he had connected Ivy's stereo equipment on the entertainment center in the living room.

She glanced up from the box she was opening. "No, go ahead."

He dialed, and she overheard him order a large pizza to be delivered.

"What do you like on your pizza?" he called.

She made a face. "Anything but anchovies or onions."

He grinned and spoke into the receiver. "We'll have pepperoni and black olives. Oh, and two large colas. Thanks."

"Interesting tact, inviting yourself to lunch," Ivy teased, rifling through a box full of CDs.

"It was the neighborly thing to do. I knew you were going to be here all day unpacking, and you probably wouldn't stop for lunch unless someone reminded you. That's where I come in. I'm always good about remembering to eat."

Ivy laughed and lifted a CD from the stacks. She opened the case and put the disc in the machine.

"Do you like Chopin? It calms my nerves and helps me concentrate on the task at hand." She closed her eyes and imagined the music soothing her tension away.

"Why don't you sit down for a few minutes until the pizza gets here?" Samson suggested. "You deserve a break after all the work you've done."

"You too." Ivy motioned for him to sit in one of the recliners and she relaxed onto the couch with a sigh. "I love this set," she said, relaxing down into the thick softness. "I probably should have sold it and bought something cheaper. But one little luxury can't be a sin, can it?" She lifted her brows and gave him a grin.

"I don't think so. Everyone deserves creature comforts. Was it a bad divorce?" he asked.

"What do you mean?"

He shrugged. "Well, you moved here with the kids and no husband, so I naturally assumed you'd recently split up."

She tried to read his expression. Was it pity or just morbid curiosity in his eyes? He remained inscrutable. She sighed and stared out the window. Smoky white trails left from jets crisscrossing overhead marred the otherwise clear sky.

"My husband isn't someone you would like. He's a self-absorbed, money hungry, lying cheat. And those are his good qualities." She turned back and met a sympathetic gaze. "He embezzled money from the company he worked for and ran away to Acapulco with a blonde bimbo, leaving me to pick up my children and go home. So, I did. Omaha is where I grew up. I thought it might be a good place to start over again."

"I'm sorry."

Ivy blinked to keep the tears from flowing. She certainly didn't want to cry in front of Samson. She barely knew him. "What are *you* sorry for?"

"That you had to go through all of that alone."

"I suppose if I trusted in your God everything would be so much easier, right?" she asked, trying to get a rise out of him to keep herself from crying.

His lips turned up slightly and he shrugged. "I never said it would be easy. But it works for me. The Bible says you can cast all your care upon him, for he cares for you."

She remembered a similar lesson from her Sunday school days. Apparently, they still taught the same false promises. "It would be nice to be able to believe in that sort of thing."

"I'm not simple-minded just because I believe God cares about me and takes a hands-on interest in my day to day life."

"I didn't say you were."

"No?" He leaned forward, forearms resting on his knees. "Would you rather believe that everything happens by chance? With chance you can't rest in the knowledge that everything will work out for good, but with God you can, even if you can't see it now. That's all trust is – resting."

Ivy could see that he clearly believed what he said, and from what she'd seen of him, lived as though he did. Christianity wasn't just a robe he put on Sunday morning and pulled off during the week, but a real part of him; in the way he spoke, the way he acted, and the way he treated those around him. If everyone who professed to be a Christian lived that way, she wouldn't have such a hard time believing.

"I'm sorry. I certainly don't have all the answers. At least you have something to believe in. I respect that. It's just been so long since I've been able to trust anyone enough to put myself in his hands, that it's hard to imagine." She moved to the sliding glass doors and stared out into the bright afternoon. Children rode their bikes and skated on the asphalt path. Two women sat on a bench nearby keeping an eye on them.

"If your husband is half as bad as you described, I can see why trust doesn't come easily. But your skepticism goes back further than that, doesn't it?" he asked, his voice quiet and thoughtful.

She slowly turned, hands on her hips. He seemed to be able to see into her soul and she didn't like the idea. "Actually – a long way back. I was thirteen. I believed in God and the good in people then. Before..."

She never finished her sentence because the phone rang announcing the arrival of their pizza.

✝✝✝

Samson opened the pizza box on top of the small kitchen table and lifted out a slice. Ivy rummaged around until she found plates in a nearby box and handed him one.

He managed to grin with his mouth full. "Don't waste a plate on me. I'll just graze over the box."

She shrugged and set the plates down on the kitchen countertop. "Less work for me." She leaned over the table and picked up a slice. "We can sit out there. I trust you won't spill on my lovely beige carpet."

"I'll do my best."

She moved to the living room and sat in an overstuffed chair.

"Do you have a date to keep?" he asked after a couple minutes. He stuffed the last bite of a second piece into his mouth and leaned back against the wall with a satisfied sigh.

Ivy looked up. "What do you mean?"

"You keep looking at your watch. Am I keeping you from something?"

"No, not really." She pulled a black olive off the top of her slice and stuck it in her mouth. At this rate, she'd be done eating a piece by suppertime.

"You want me to help you unload any of these boxes?" He wiped his hands on a paper napkin and moved to open the flaps of the one nearest him. The box contained dozens of children's books. "You want these in the kids' room?"

"Sure."

He lifted the box easily and trudged down the hall.

The phone rang when he returned, and he snatched it up before Ivy could rise from her seat. "Hello?"

"Sinclair?" Timmons gravelly voice was not what he'd expected.

"Yes."

"They left a message on her sister's answering machine and set up a meeting with *Miss Innocent* to hand over the plans. I told you she knows more than she's letting on. Don't let her out of your sight, Sinclair." Timmons hung up before Samson could reply.

"Who was it?" Ivy asked.

He hung up the receiver and turned to wash his hands at the sink. Had she really been lying this whole time? Disappointment caught him by surprise. He had to get himself together. "Just a man from my office. I don't need to go in today, so I can help you out the rest of the afternoon." When he turned back around, there was a pensive look on her face. He hated feeding her half-truths, but it was his job. "Something wrong, Ivy?"

She nipped at her bottom lip. "I got a strange phone call yesterday. At first, I thought the FBI was harassing me about my husband again, but I don't think they would threaten my children."

"Someone threatened your children?" He moved to stand beside her. She looked worried. It was apparent the call had frightened her.

"The caller said if I didn't bring them this disc they want, my family would be in danger. I don't have any idea what they're talking about. How can I give them something I don't have? The FBI went through all of Todd's things. If this disc existed, wouldn't they have found it?" She leaned forward with her elbows on her knees and lowered her head into her hands. "I don't know what to do. I called my sister this morning and she told me someone left a message on the answering machine with instructions to bring this mystery disc to Dodge park at three o'clock." She shook her head. "I'm pretty sure there are at least two Dodge parks in this city. An East and a West. One is by my sister's house but the other is somewhere on this side of Dodge Boulevard."

"They obviously know you've been staying with your sister, so they're probably talking about the park by her house." Samson glanced at his watch; they had forty-five minutes. He could send a car, but they didn't know who they were looking for. If they were going to do a sting operation, they would need to use Ivy, and he didn't know if she would even cooperate once she learned that she was under surveillance. Captain Herndon and Timmons were both wrong. Ivy had no clue about the stolen weapon plans. She believed what she'd been told, and she'd been lied to by everyone, first her husband, then the FBI in California, and now him.

"Whatever," she said, a tinge of exasperation in her voice. "What does it matter? I'm not meeting them. This person is probably dangerous or deranged. And I don't have what they want."

"You're right. But you should call the FBI and report this, so they can protect you."

"Protect me? That's a laugh. You should have seen the way they treated me after Todd disappeared. You'd think I had stolen the money." She jumped up, strode to the stereo and shut it off. Slowly she turned to face him, arms crossed. "They probably wouldn't believe me anyway."

A wave of guilt washed over Samson. He got up and went to the kitchen, took the phone off the hook and held it out. He wished he could make the worry in her eyes go away, but he was under orders. "I want you to call and talk to them right now, Ivy. I promise they *will* listen and if they don't, I'll talk to them myself. You've got to trust someone. This is not something you can handle on your own."

She gazed across at him for a long moment before her eyes softened and she nodded. "Fine."

Samson watched her rummage through her purse looking for the number the FBI gave her in California. He noted the lines of tension on her face and the way she held the receiver clenched in her hand when she made the call. She was wound tighter than a broken music box.

After about five minutes of discussion she hung up and released a quiet sigh. "Well, they know everything I know, so hopefully they can find out who is doing this." She pulled a cold soda from the fridge. "Would you like one?"

"Sure, but would you mind if I run next door for a minute? I need to make a quick call to the office."

She smiled. "You can use my phone again. I won't charge you."

"Thanks, but I don't want to tie up your line. They might need to call you back."

††††

Samson opened the door of his apartment, self-recrimination eating away at his conscience. He hated not being able to come clean with Ivy and tell her everything. How could they expect cooperation from someone who didn't trust them, and for good reason? The Bureau certainly hadn't been above board with her. Instead of telling Ivy the truth – that her husband was in way over his head with espionage and likely to get himself killed – they'd lied to her. The type of people Todd Winter dealt with would not be played for fools. He may have managed to temporarily ensure his own safety by sending the bad guys after his wife, but they would soon realize it was a wild goose chase. And then they'd be gunning for him.

"Well, it's about time, Sinclair. I was wondering how long it would take you to get out of there and report in." Timmons sat on Samson's couch with a glass in one hand and the remote control for the TV in the other. He'd made himself right at home.

"What are you doing in my apartment?" Samson asked. He closed the door, strode across the room, and flipped the television off as he passed.

"Hey, I was watching that!" Timmons dropped the remote and stood up, stretching his muscular arms above his head. "This sitting around stuff is making me tired. What did you find out?" he asked.

"She told me about the phone call. She doesn't know what they're talking about. She really believes the line the bureau fed her. She's innocent! So, you can quit hoping to frisk and cuff her."

"You didn't tell her you're FBI, did you?" Timmons asked, hands on hips.

"No, I didn't, but someone threatened her kids, and she needs to know we're watching out for her. The impression she has of us so far isn't exactly cultivating trust."

"We aren't supposed to cultivate trust; we're supposed to get at the truth." Timmons strutted over to the sliding door, pulled it open and stepped out on the deck. "Hey, this is great. Wish we had one on our house. We could put the grill out there," he called through the open door.

Samson blew out a frustrated breath. "Look," he said, following Timmons through the screen door, "she told us the truth. She doesn't know anything. They think she has the disc, which I'm sure her husband implied. Maybe he's playing a game of double cross to get more money – who knows. But she's innocent, and she deserves to know what's going on." The phone rang, and he went back in the apartment to answer it. "Hello? Yeah, he's here." He held his hand over the mouthpiece and yelled, "Timmons!" He spoke hurriedly into the receiver. "Captain, before Timmons gets on the line I'd like to say something. Ivy Winter has told us everything she knows. Now she deserves the truth. She should know what her husband did, so she isn't completely in the dark."

"Fine, Sinclair, go ahead and tell her," the captain barked over the line, "but trust me she won't thank you for the information. In fact, she'll hate you for deceiving her this far. You think the truth is the best policy, but with women it's like letting a lion loose with a wounded buck. You don't stand a chance."

"Thanks for the insight, Captain," He handed the phone to his partner. "Don't forget to lock up when you let yourself out." He slid his gun into the ankle holster under the leg of his jeans, snatched up a small paper sack from the counter, and hurried out the door.

✝✝✝

Ivy watched Samson go, curious as to why he needed to call the office on a day he said he had off. She put his can of soda back in the fridge and went to change the CD. A lone Saxophone filled the room with a smoky blues tune that she loved. She went to the sliding door and slid the screen open. A gentle summer breeze blew the sound of children's laughter up from the pond. She stepped out onto the deck and let the sunshine warm her skin.

A man's voice carried from the deck next door. A privacy partition separated the decks and kept her from seeing who stood there. But it definitely wasn't Samson. Samson's voice was smooth and mellow, like the music she loved. This man's voice was more of a bellow with a little gravel thrown in. Did Samson have a roommate? She turned to go back in but stopped when she heard Samson say, "She's innocent, and she deserves to know what's going on." She edged closer to the side of the deck, but he'd apparently moved back inside and out of her hearing range.

Was he talking about her? What truth? She stepped back inside and banged the screen shut. Hugging her arms tightly around herself she paced the length of the living room and back again, dodging boxes and furniture. She thought

Samson was different, that because he was a Christian she could trust him, but here he was talking to a stranger about her private matters. She'd bared her soul, while he was holding something back.

Fueled by anger, she unpacked boxes with renewed energy. She was noisily shoving pots and pans into the lower kitchen cupboards when a soft knock came at the door. What was she going to say to him? Should she demand to know why he had been discussing her life with a stranger? Slowly she rose from the kitchen floor and opened the door. He leaned nonchalantly against the doorjamb, wearing a Cornhuskers baseball cap and holding a crumpled paper bag.

"How would you like to go for a walk?" he asked. She started to shake her head, but he cupped her chin with the palm of his hand and smiled. "You've been working way too hard this afternoon. It's time you took a break." He held up the sack and shook it. "I've got day old bread for the ducks, and we can walk the path to the park and back. I'd really like to talk to you if I could."

She pulled away and stepped out of his reach. She refused to feel susceptible to this man? She had gone through enough lies and deceit with Todd without repeating the same mistakes over again. Yet somehow, in the hidden recesses of her heart, she wanted to believe that Samson wasn't the same. There had to be a reasonable explanation for the conversation she'd overheard. She wouldn't jump to conclusions but give him a chance to explain. "Okay, let's walk," she agreed quickly before she changed her mind.

They took the back stairs to the outside door. Staying on the path that led down to the pond, they paused long enough for Samson to toss a few handfuls of dried bread to the eager ducks, who came right up within a few feet of them, greedily pushing one another out of the way to get the biggest tidbits.

"Here, you want to try?" he offered gallantly extending the bag toward her.

"No thanks." He didn't say anything as he fed the ducks but occasionally cast a furtive glance her way. She felt her cheeks grow warm beneath his scrutiny and turned to watch a group of children riding bikes.

"Shall we walk to the park? It's only about a quarter mile down the trail."

"Sure." She started off and he fell into step beside her.

The sun beat down warm on their heads so that when they reached the shadowy canopy of the wooded area, it was a refreshing change. Two mothers smiled as they passed, jog-walking behind their toddler's bikes. Soon they were far ahead, and only an occasional birdcall broke the stillness.

"Ivy," he cleared his throat and readjusted the cap on his head in a nervous motion, "I know you moved here to get away from the trouble your husband caused and I'm sorry you have to go through this. But it appears the trouble followed you. Until everything is settled and the people behind this thing are arrested, you could be in danger."

She stopped in the path and faced him. "What are you talking about? What people? Todd stole money from Monroe Industries; no one else was involved as far as I know."

Samson shook his head. "I hate to be the one to tell you this, but your husband didn't embezzle from his company. What he did was steal highly classified weapon plans under contract for the United States government. Someone paid him a lot of money to get them, but apparently he never handed over the disc he copied them on."

Ivy was pretty good at hiding her feelings, but she knew her face must register complete and utter shock. She felt tears near the surface and bit her lip until she tasted blood. Would Todd do something so despicable to his own children as to taint their name with *traitor*? She turned away and blinked rapidly. "How do you know all this?" she asked, not even bothering to deny the possibility that Todd would do such a thing.

"Because I'm FBI."

Everything came crashing in. Anger built in her chest and she clenched her fists at her sides. Samson Sinclair had played her for a fool, pretending to care about her and the children when in reality all he cared about was making a bust. She knew he seemed too good to be true. Didn't Mom always say that if something sounded too good, it probably was?

She spun around so fast it caught him by complete surprise when she slapped his face. Her palm stung with the force and fueled her anger. "How dare you pretend to be my friend with all your talk about God and faith, when all you really wanted to do was spy on me!" Before he could respond she turned and ran. She didn't know where she was going, but she had to get away. From Samson. From the mess Todd made. And from the shambles her life had become. She ran until her lungs felt ready to burst. Finally, she slowed to a walk, trying to catch her breath, and realized she had run at least a quarter mile past the park. She slowly retraced her steps, favoring a stitch in her side. Samson had dropped a bomb into her lap. It was bad enough when she thought her husband was a common thief. Now this. To top it all off, her next-door neighbor just happened to work for the FBI. She pushed sweaty bangs off her forehead and sighed. They probably tapped her phone too.

She reached the park and collapsed exhausted onto a wooden bench facing the playground area. A small boy climbed through a maze of jungle gym equipment, oblivious to her gaze. The sun still sat high in the sky, but the bench remained in the shade of a towering evergreen. The boy went down the slide headfirst and she cringed thinking he would fall off the end and get a mouthful of sand, but he stopped mid-slide and scooted back up. Her gaze shifted to the other side of the park. A man in dark slacks and shirt, a baseball cap pulled low over his eyes, leaned against a car on the street, staring at her. At least, he appeared to be staring at her. He held a folded newspaper in his hand, but he wasn't reading it. She glanced around expecting to see that he was waiting for someone, but there was no one else around. Even the boy had jumped from the swings and was riding his bike across the grass, probably on his way home. She looked back at the man, and he waved for her to join him. What kind of park was this? She suddenly felt defenseless. No one appeared on the bike path and across the park the street was empty of cars. She glanced through the trees and realized the path back to her apartment would be even more secluded. She stood up and looked around, hoping for another option.

The man continued to stare and gesture. When she didn't comply, he started across the field in her direction. Fear leaped into her throat, and her heart felt as though it was pounding in staccato. A Bible verse from her Sunday school days rushed through her mind. "*What time I am afraid, I will trust in thee.*"

"God help me," she breathed as the man drew nearer. Abruptly he stopped and pulled a gun from the paper, aiming the thing in her direction.

"Ivy, get down!" Samson yelled from somewhere behind her. Without hesitating, she threw herself onto the grass. Two shots rang out, sharp and horrifying in the quiet afternoon. She opened her eyes and saw the man running toward the car parked on the street. He leaped in and tore off, tires squealing in protest.

"Are you all right?" Samson called weakly from the other side of the bench.

She sat up, rubbing a scraped elbow. "I'm fine, I guess," she muttered as she stared off after the car.

She looked over her shoulder but didn't see him. "Samson?"

"Down here," he said, his voice unnaturally weak. "Could you call an ambulance? I've been shot."

"What?" Her anger forgotten in the moment, Ivy leaped up, skirted the bench between them, and flew to where he lay bleeding on the ground. She stared in horror at the red stain spreading slowly across his side but managed to keep her head and applied pressure to the wound. Her hair fell across her face as she knelt beside him, and he reached up and brushed it back. She went still at his touch. He smiled up at her as if to say everything was all right. Then he passed out.

{5}

Timmons strode into Samson's hospital room without knocking. He grinned as he let the door swing shut behind him. "Doc said the bullet passed right through. Didn't hit anything too important. You don't really need your gallbladder, do you?"

"Funny."

He shook his head, a look of amazement on his face. "I can't believe you've been shot at two times now. I've been in the FBI twenty years and only been shot at once. Think maybe somebody doesn't like you?"

"I know the nurses don't like me or they wouldn't have let *you* in here," Samson said, frowning at his partner's intrusion. "I've been shot – is harassment part of the healing process?"

His partner laughed loudly and pulled a plastic container out from behind his back. "Look here. My wife was so glad you were shot and not me, she baked you brownies." He placed the gift on Samson's lap.

"Tell her I said thanks. I'm sure I'll need them. They didn't even bring me dinner. Said I was late

61

checking in – can you believe that? If I'd known, I'd have gotten shot earlier."

"You've grown quite sarcastic since partnering with me, Sinclair. I like that." Timmons stepped over to the window overlooking the parking lot and stared into the gathering dusk. His bushy brows drew together. "So, I guess you assumed incorrectly about the park. They didn't mean East Dodge. They meant West Dodge. She has a strange coincidental connection to Dodge parks after just moving here, don't you think? Are you still positive she doesn't know anything about the disc? After all, she did run away from you and arrive at the park first. Maybe she intended to meet him all along."

"No," Samson ground out between clinched teeth as pain shot through his side when he tried to sit up. "She didn't know anything until I told her. She was understandably upset when she found out I worked for the FBI and ran off to get away from me – not to meet up with anyone." He pushed the button on the bed and waited as the motor slowly brought the head up to a comfortable position.

There was a knock at the door. Before he could respond the door pushed open and two blonde heads peered around the corner at him.

"He's awake!" announced Riley.

Ivy followed her young daughter into the room, a reticent smile curving her lips, while Caleb hung back by the door.

"I'm sorry," she apologized. "I told her to wait, but she was excited to see you."

Samson grinned, not in the least disturbed to have these visitors. He motioned for Riley to come closer and opened the container of brownies.

"Look what I got. You think maybe your brother would want one?" he asked conspiratorially. Riley wrinkled her nose in thought and then nodded.

"Why don't you go ask him," he said.

Timmons stood out of the way and watched the interaction with a speculative look.

"I don't believe you've met my partner, Andy Timmons," Samson began.

Timmons politely stuck out his hand, but Ivy ignored the offer and stared at him, her eyes slits of concentration. A moment later she nodded in recognition.

"Now I remember where I've seen you. You were with the movers this morning. So, I have two spies keeping track of me. How flattering to think that I'm so important. Tell me – is my phone tapped too?" she asked, her tone hard-edged enough that even the children seemed to sense trouble. They came forward with brownies in hand and stood close to their mother as though joining forces.

Timmons gave a slight nod and grinned at Samson before making a beeline for the door. "I really should get going. It's been nice meeting you, Mrs. Winter."

"Was it something I said?" she asked, her voice dripping with innocence.

Caleb stepped closer to the bed. He watched the slow drip of the IV going through the tube and into Samson's arm with great interest.

"Does it hurt?" he asked, his eyes wide. A Mickey Mouse cap covered his blonde head today, and with jeans and a monster truck T-shirt he looked every inch the seven-year-old he was.

Samson pointed to the needle in his arm. "You mean that – or this?" He pulled down the sheets and revealed his side wrapped in bandages.

"Wow!" Caleb said. Apparently, no other words would suffice. He gazed into Samson's face with something akin to hero worship. "Did you really get shot saving my Mom?"

Samson pulled the sheets back up to cover his chest, suddenly self-conscious. Ivy's expression had softened, and he smiled timidly.

"I wouldn't say that I saved her exactly. She dropped to the ground as soon as I yelled. That's a good lesson for you two," he said including Riley in the conversation. "When your Mom tells you to do something, you should always do it right away. You never know when obedience could save your life."

"Aw, come on. Mom just tells us stuff like clean up your room and don't watch so much TV. How can that save our lives?"

"Well, have you ever tripped over something in your room and fell and hurt yourself? Messy rooms can be very dangerous places. And we all know that television can suck your brain waves out and turn you into a zombie," he said, his expression serious.

Riley's eyes widened in horror. She moved to her mother's side and took hold of her hand.

"What's a zombie?" asked Caleb, in no way swayed by Samson's argument.

"A zombie is someone who watches too much TV and never reads a book," answered Ivy quickly. Samson raised his eyebrows at that, but she laughed and shook her head. "I have to put them to bed tonight – you don't," she said.

"Point taken." He patted Caleb's baseball cap and grinned at Riley, who hugged her Mother's side. "I'm sure glad you guys decided to come and see me tonight. I was getting pretty lonesome in here."

"I was in the hospital once, and I hated it," Caleb informed him importantly. "They took my tonsils out and put'em in a glass jar. It was gross!"

"Kids, Holly's waiting in the hall. Say goodnight to Mr. Sinclair and go on out now. I'll be there in a minute."

"Night, Mr. Sinclair." Caleb held out his hand and Samson shook it.

"Goodnight, Samson," said Riley before she darted out the door with Caleb right behind.

Samson laughed at Ivy's chagrin. "It's all right, she can't help being mischievous. She takes after you, doesn't she?"

Ivy glared playfully at him and then pulled up a chair and sat down, her expression suddenly serious. "I want to thank you for today. I know I've been downright nasty to you on occasion and I'm sorry. I'm still not too hip on the idea that you've been spying on me, but after today I'm glad *someone* was there watching out for me." She brushed a stray lock of hair back behind her ear. "I'm just so tired of all this. I moved here to get away from everything, and it seems I haven't gotten away from anything."

He reached out and touched her hand lying on the arm of the chair. She didn't move away but instead linked her fingers with his for a brief moment, then released him and stood to leave.

"The kids are waiting. I better go."

"Are you staying in the apartment tonight, Ivy?"

"No, we decided to stay with Holly tonight," she said as she started to open the door.

"I'm glad. I don't like you staying there by yourself with me in here."

Confusion clouded her green eyes.

What must she be thinking? His remark had come off sounding possessive. He cleared his throat and tried again. "I'm assigned to you after all."

Was it his imagination or did the look in her eyes turn to hurt? He wished he could take the words back, but she pulled open the door and was gone.

He relaxed against the pillows and closed his eyes. How was he supposed to stay close to this woman and protect her without giving in to feelings that had nothing to do with his assignment? He was being pulled in two different directions; his job and the attraction he felt for Ivy pulled him one way, while his love for God and wish to follow him pulled him the other. He needed to stand strong and trust God.

He reached over and picked up the Gideon Bible that lay on the bedside table and turned to Zechariah. He knew the passage by heart. *"Not by might, nor by power, but by my spirit, saith the Lord of hosts."* It was the only way he could do this job and stay pure in heart.

He closed his eyes against the bright florescent lights of the hospital room and prayed, "Give me guidance and strength to do what is right and make me a vessel that you can use to bring Ivy back to you. She needs you Lord; I see her searching. Help her to trust again."

†††

Ivy remained silent as they left the hospital and got into Holly's car. Her sister didn't try to intrude on her thoughts. Instead, she chatted with the children and asked them about the new apartment.

When they pulled out of the hospital parking lot Ivy kept her eye on the side mirror of the car, wondering if they were being followed. Would the FBI assign someone new to keep track of her, or would Samson Sinclair continue his job once he was released?

Holly turned onto the road, and another pair of headlights followed close behind. Ivy watched until the car pulled up along side them at the next light, the blinker on to turn right. She expelled a breath of relief when she realized the driver was an elderly woman. Just like them, she'd probably been visiting someone at the hospital.

Holly turned on the radio to a light jazz station. The kids were unusually quiet in the backseat and Ivy glanced back to check on them. Caleb was playing a handheld electronic game, earbuds in his ears, and Riley stared out the window. Ivy closed her eyes and leaned her head back.

The confrontation with the man in the park played again in her head. Seeing him coming toward her, the gun in his hand...there had been nothing she could do. She opened her eyes and stared through the window into the darkness. Where had those words come from? *God help me*! Like the automatic reflex actions of breathing and swallowing, she'd cried out to God. So many years had passed since she read the Bible or had anything to do with religion. She'd tried to forget everything she learned and everything she went through. But now the memories came crashing through and she leaned her head back against the headrest, closed her eyes, and let them come.

It had been a bright sunny day in August when Linda and she had walked the seven blocks to the little red brick building that served as church to about a hundred people. Linda was her best friend and the reason she began going to church. Her folks had no religious affiliations but were glad to have her go off for the morning and leave them to sleep in, for she was an early bird and would go about the house singing and playing while everyone else was in bed.

On this particular Sunday, Linda was excited because she was meeting with the pastor after the service. Pastor Benson always met with people before he would baptize them to make sure they understood that baptism was just the outward sign of their trust in Christ for salvation. Ivy wished she could be baptized too, but she needed to have her parents' permission and they wouldn't agree. They'd already had Ivy and Holly baptized as infants and felt they'd covered all their bases.

"I'm going to be baptized tonight if Pastor Benson says I can," Linda said, her eyes bright with anticipation. She wore a new pink ruffled dress and matching shoes. There wasn't a prettier girl around. Sometimes Ivy wished she had blonde hair and blue eyes instead of dull brown and green but then she would remember that Mrs. Adams, her Sunday school teacher, said that God made everyone different for a reason. She wondered sometimes what reason God could have for making her so drab and Linda so bright. Today she felt like a moth flitting next to a monarch butterfly.

"Do you have to stay very long?" She didn't want to walk home alone. She enjoyed their walks to church and back together. Usually they walked, but if it rained then they would go in the car with Linda's family.

"Mom said it wouldn't take more than a few minutes. If you wait for me, you can come out to dinner with us. We're going to a restaurant, and Dad said I could order anything I want." She twirled around on the sidewalk as nimbly as a ballerina and then grabbed Ivy's hand and pulled her along at a faster pace. "We better hurry, or we'll be late for Sunday school."

Sunday school classes were in the basement, and the children were separated into rooms by age and gender. At age thirteen they'd moved up to the teenage girl's class and were eager to fit in.

Mrs. Oleander wore a red dress with a white sweater around her shoulders and red and white high-heeled pumps. Her hair was dyed to an unnatural shade of black with hints of blue gleaming through. She wore bright crimson lipstick and false eyelashes that reminded Ivy of spider legs wiggling around.

"Get settled girls. We need to start class." She clapped her hands to hurry them into their chairs and waited for their chatter to still. "To those of you who are new to our class, welcome. I do want to say that you will have to sit still and listen without bothering with a lot of questions like you did in the junior class. We are young ladies in this class and naturally have already heard all those antiquated children's Bible stories; therefore, we deal more with deportment and social issues young ladies would find helpful and amusing."

Ivy bristled somewhat at the insinuation that Mrs. Adams wasted time answering questions and telling stories that were somehow old fashioned. How could Mrs. Oleander say that? Mrs. Adams was the best teacher she'd ever had. She really cared about each of the kids and answered their Bible questions as though each one was as important to her as if an adult had asked.

Perhaps Mrs. Oleander didn't really mean it that way at all.

But she spent the entire class telling about the two-week cruise that she and her husband took. She regaled them with stories about shipboard entertainment and described the lovely dresses the women wore and the way they fixed their hair.

Ivy was confused and naturally disappointed when class was dismissed. She expected another exciting Bible lesson. Last week Mrs. Adams had told of Daniel being thrown into the lion's den and how his faith and prayer kept the lions' mouths shut. He trusted in the Lord, and the Lord saved him. There were so many stories of God literally pulling people from the clutches of evil and she thrilled to every one. How could fashion and cruises compare to that?

After the service Linda and her parents went into the Pastor's study to discuss baptism, and Ivy sat in the pew waiting. She could hear the last people lingering outside the front door of the church and then finally calling their good-byes and driving away. The auditorium was quiet except for the occasional murmur of the pastor's deep voice coming from behind the door of his study, and the hum of a vacuum cleaner in the basement classrooms. Someone must have stayed behind to clean up.

She stood up and stretched. The hard, wooden pew made her back stiff and sore. She reached down to retrieve her Bible and realized she had forgotten her purse downstairs in the Sunday school classroom. She would hurry down and get it before Linda and her parents came out and wondered where she'd gone.

The stairs were dark, but a light was shining in the junior classroom down the hall, and she could hear the vacuum louder now. She stopped at the teenage girls' classroom and opened the door. The light switch wasn't where she thought it would be, so she stepped farther into the room, groping along the wall in the dark. She heard footsteps behind her, but before she could turn around someone shoved her into the dark room and slammed the door shut. A hand clamped over her mouth, another grabbed her wrist in a bruising grip and she was pushed clumsily to the floor. Hands groped her until she thought she'd scream, but when she tried to catch her breath, someone covered her mouth again. The air was thick with the heavy sweet scent of bubblegum. Two voices whispered and chuckled back in forth over her in the dark, and she realized there was more than one faceless monster doing these terrible things to her. She whimpered against the sweaty palm that held her mouth shut, and tears squeezed from the corners of her eyes, but still they continued to assault her.

Amid horror and fear she cried out in her mind to God, "Save me! Please don't let them do this to me!"

When she sobbed louder against the boy's hot palm, he muttered threats and swore at her to shut up. In the back of her mind she heard a constant hum. With each passing second, it seemed to grow louder and louder. Suddenly the door burst open and Mrs. Oleander stood there with purse in hand. An elderly man vacuumed the hallway behind her. The light spilled in around Ivy where she lay whimpering on the floor and she recognized the boys crouched over her as Mrs. Oleander's teenage sons Wallace and Grady.

"What is going on here?" Mrs. Oleander asked, her voice harsh with anger. "I knew you were a girl with little morals when I first laid eyes on you. What have you tempted my boys to do? Get up! Get up, I said! I want you out of this church building immediately, and you are never to set foot here again. Do you understand?" She took Ivy by the upper arms as she rose unsteadily to her feet and shook her as though she were a rag doll. Ivy thought she was going to throw up, but she drew a deep breath and pushed the feeling away. When Mrs. Oleander released her, she stumbled forward out the door. When she glanced back, the boys stood behind their mother with leering grins on their faces. Mrs. Oleander, hands on hips, glared such a look of hatred at Ivy that she couldn't stop the tears from coursing down her cheeks. She turned and fled up the stairs and out the front door before anyone should see her and accuse her again of the unspeakable.

She ran down the street and home, crept silently in the back door and up to her room before anyone realized she was back. Her sister must have heard her crying because she knocked on her door, but Ivy had ignored her and laid there on top her rumpled blankets until she'd cried herself to sleep.

✝✝✝

"We're home," Holly announced as she pulled into the driveway and pushed the button to the garage door opener. The door slowly came up, and she parked on her side of the empty space and shut off the engine.

Ivy opened her eyes and blinked away the dampness forming in the corners. She followed the kids inside as they argued about how many lightning bugs it took to fill up a coffee can and if it were full, could they use it for a flashlight? How did they come up with this stuff? She listened to them talk and laugh and giggle about silly things that didn't really matter and was glad. It took their minds off things that did matter. Like the fact that their father deserted them. They would have enough hard times and disappointments later in life. She wished she could spare them, but she knew she couldn't. Life was full of sorrow.

Mrs. Adams had told Bible stories about the times when God miraculously saved his people from evil, but she failed to tell of all the times He didn't. Admittedly, Samson's heroic arrival at the park earlier had seemed like an answer to her prayer. But thirteen years ago, there had been no hero to save her.

She could picture Samson's clear, probing gaze when he spoke about his faith. He probably believed every story in the Bible. Was he a fool to have such trust in God or had she been wrong all these years?

She put the kids to bed and joined Holly in the kitchen for a cup of decaffeinated coffee just as Bill got home. He wore baggy shorts and a sweatshirt with Nike emblazoned across the chest. He stank of beer and his eyes were tired and bloodshot.

"Hi ya, girls. Whatcha been doin?" He gave Holly a slip-and-miss kiss across the cheek as he passed and grinned at Ivy as he hung his keys on the pegboard by the phone. He then went directly to the fridge for another can of beer.

"Where have you been tonight, Bill?" Holly asked, an edge in her voice.

The tension went up ten notches in the room and Ivy wished she were anywhere else.

"Where do you think I've been, Babe? I've been working," he said. He popped open the can and took a big gulp. "One of us has to pay the bills. That little shop sure isn't raking in the dough."

Ivy could see her sister's neck begin to grow red with anger and knew she should either intervene or get out quickly. The phone rang but neither moved to answer it, so Ivy reached over and picked it up.

"Hello."

"Ivy?" The familiar voice sent a cold finger down her spine. She couldn't think of a thing to say to the man she'd lived with for the past eight years.

"Ivy?"

"I'm here." She waited for him to go on. What did he want now? He didn't really think she would take him back after all he'd done, did he?

"I need your help. There are some really bad people after me. They think I have something they want, but I don't. They said they'll kill me if I don't get it for them." The fear in his voice was real although she refused to feel sorry for him at this point.

"I think I've already served my purpose, Todd," she said, her voice brittle enough to shatter. "You used me as a decoy, didn't you? Apparently, the safety of your own family means nothing to you. They've already threatened the children and have shot at me."

She heard his quick intake of breath, and then a sob as he cried over the line like a broken man. "I'm sorry, Ivy. I didn't mean for any of this to happen. You've got to believe me. I just needed a little time to get squared away, so I told them you had the disc. They paid me half a million up-front, but Brenna took the money and ran off. I don't even have enough money to pay the hotel bill." He sniffed and blew his nose loudly.

Bill and Holly were watching her as though she might fall apart, but she had no intention of doing any such thing. Todd no longer pulled at her heartstrings no matter how hard he tried.

"I don't know what you expect me to do. I certainly don't have any money to send you. You didn't leave me any, remember? I have to go out now and get a job to support myself and the children." Her voice was cold, and he was silent on the other end for long seconds.

"Ivy, I just need enough money for a plane ticket. If I come back to the states and get the disc I'll be able to bargain with them," he explained.

"Todd, the only thing I can do is advise you to turn yourself in to the FBI. They're looking for you too. I think you'll have a better chance with them. I've got to go now. I'm tired." She started to hang up when she heard a loud pop, like a firecracker or maybe a car backfiring.

"Ivy, I wasn't really going to give it to them. I swear." His voice sounded thin and strained. Then the line went dead.

She replaced the receiver. Why did he end the conversation so abruptly? He sounded strange. She wondered if he were sick or something. Why should she care? The man had no thought for anyone but himself.

"Are you all right, Ivy?" Holly asked, concern creasing her brow. The argument with Bill had been forgotten in the drama of the moment. She reached out and touched Ivy's arm.

Ivy patted her hand and smiled although the smile never reached her eyes. "I'm fine. Todd's the one running for his life. I have the FBI protecting me."

"Have I missed something?" Bill picked up an apple from the fruit bowl on the table and shined it against his shirt.

Holly turned her attention back to her wayward husband. "Well, if you were ever home you'd know that Ivy was shot at today," she said, the bite in her words razor sharp.

"What? Why would someone shoot at Ivy?" His eyes gleamed with excitement at the prospect of a big story. Ivy knew someday he wanted to be more than just a sports columnist. When they got engaged, Holly had told everyone she was marrying a journalist. Obviously, his dreams had not yet come to fruition.

"It's a twisted story, but all tied to Todd's latest criminal fiasco. I'm sorry, but I've got to go to bed. I'm exhausted – it's been a rather long day." She kissed her sister's cheek and made her way to the guestroom she'd been using for the last few nights.

The children lay on the floor tucked snugly into sleeping bags, their breathing slow and even. She knelt beside them and pressed a kiss to each smooth forehead before trudging wearily to the bathroom to undress for the night.

Tomorrow they would move to the apartment, and Holly and Bill would be alone to hash out their problems, whatever they were. She certainly didn't want to be here in the middle of it all. She had more than enough of her own.

She splashed warm water onto her face and patted it dry with a towel. Her reflection in the mirror had a look of helplessness. How did she come to this point in her life? Everything seemed so bleak and unfixable. She felt like a boat at sea, adrift, with no way to get back to shore. She slid to the floor, leaned against the wall with her knees pulled up to her chin, and let the tears come. She cried quietly, not wanting the kids to hear and be afraid.

Long after the tears dried up she sat and thought about her life. In the past she blamed God whenever things didn't go her way even though she professed not to believe in him. Right now, looking back, she knew she had only herself to blame. As a rebellious teenager she married a boy with no scruples. Her parents had disapproved of him, but that didn't stop her. They had never been religious, but they had morals, which they believed Todd lacked, even then. She should have listened, but she didn't. What would her life have been like if she had married a man like Samson Sinclair? He was more than just handsome, he was dependable, honest, caring, and he had faith in something bigger than himself. Not long ago she would have smirked at that being a plus in a man. But in Samson it's what made him strong. His faith wasn't just what he believed; it was who he was.

Her feelings were hurt when he reminded her at the hospital tonight that she was just his assignment, but he wouldn't be the man he was if he didn't take his job as seriously as he did everything else. She imagined that being a man of such high principles, he wouldn't dream of getting involved with a married woman, even if she were separated.

She yawned. It had been a long day. She wouldn't be able to function tomorrow if she didn't get some rest. She finally crawled into bed around eleven o'clock but still lay awake for some time going over in her mind the conversation with Todd. What was that sound she'd heard right before he hung up? Had it been a car backfiring like she first thought or something more sinister? Eventually her thoughts blurred together, and she fell into a restless sleep, Todd's face haunting her dreams like a specter.

{6}

After his release from the hospital the next morning Samson stopped in the office on his way home for an update. He pulled a bottle of aspirin from the drawer of his desk while he waited. He hadn't yet filled the prescription for pain pills the doctor gave him. He shook two tablets into his palm and then on second thought added two more. He was too tired to walk down to the water fountain, so he chewed and swallowed them dry, grimacing at the bitter taste.

"Captain Herndon wants to see us right away. I figured you'd be in soon, so I waited," Timmons said, striding into the room.

Samson closed the desk drawer and held back a groan when he stood up. "I'm as ready as I'll ever be," he said.

Captain Herndon's office was a meager ten-foot square cubical with a door. It didn't have a view or even a window; just a few feet of private space he'd been allotted because of his title. He thought he deserved something fancier like some of the bigwigs upstairs, but he suffered in silence, mostly. On the wall behind his standard issue steel desk was a picture of the little remembered, twenty-first president of the United States, Chester A. Arthur. Believing that he was a direct descendant of the president, he made sure everyone knew of the connection. It was his claim to fame.

He leaned back in his chair, with his fingers laced behind his head; the yellow sweat stains under his arms like badges of honor for all to see.

"Boys, I've got the proverbial good news bad news situation," he announced as they sat in the straight back chairs facing him. Leaning forward with his arms on the desk, his expression was grim. "The good news is, we found Todd Winter. The bad news is – he's dead. Apparently, he lied to his wife again, because he was found on an island in the Bahamas, not anywhere near Acapulco. He was shot twice, once in the chest and the second in the temple. He didn't have any identification on him, but they traced his face and fingerprints through Interpol. We're assuming the disc is still out there somewhere, and the only lead we have is Mrs. Winter." He locked eyes with Samson and pointed a meaty finger at his wounded side. "Are you going to be able to cover her? Because I think she's in more danger now than before."

"I'm fine, Captain," Samson said, as the aspirin in his bloodstream was finally dulling the ache in his arm.

"Good. You're still the inside man, and Timmons will watch your back. Someone's already shot you once – don't let it happen again. I want you to pick that woman's brain for anything she may know, whether she knows she knows it or not. That disc has got to be somewhere – either in California or here with her. Either way she could lead us to it. If it falls into the wrong hands, I guarantee you can kiss any promotion you have in your minds goodbye."

"Has anyone told her about her husband yet?" Samson asked.

Captain Herndon shook his head. "You're it. I've got Matthews keeping an eye on her right now. So far, she hasn't left her sister's house. When she arrives at her apartment, you can take over from there and give her the news. Send Matthews home – he's been up all night."

"What do you want me to do, Captain?" asked Timmons, popping his knuckles restlessly.

Timmons couldn't sit around the office another day, thought Samson, without punching someone out of sheer boredom. His partner needed action of some kind all the time. He knew he was restless, but he didn't want him hanging out in his apartment again. The man had eaten nearly everything in his refrigerator.

The corners of Herndon's mouth turned sharply down as Timmons knuckle cracking continued. "Stake out the apartment building, and if she leaves I want you to tail her and don't let her out of your sight," he barked. "Now get out of here and find that disc!"

†††

Ivy packed up the last of their things in the minivan she'd leased and after making sure the kids had their seatbelts secured, she waved to Holly and drove away. A black SUV had been sitting across the street all night and was still there. As she drove slowly past, she could see the shadowy figure of a man sitting slouched behind the wheel with his head leaned back against the headrest. She made a left at the next corner but kept an eye on her rearview mirror. The car pulled away from the curb and followed. As she headed south on Dodge Boulevard her tail stayed two or three spaces back but never strayed from the lane she was in. She turned left at the next light, and then sped up hoping to lose him in traffic. Sure enough, the turn signal changed, and he had to stop and wait for the next light. She breathed a sigh of relief and drove the rest of the way to the apartment building second-guessing whether the car had really been following her or just on the way to the mall.

At the apartment building, she pulled into a parking space, shut off the engine and turned to speak to the kids in the back seat. "I want you two to stay in the car for a minute."

Ivy climbed out of the van, her gaze sweeping the parking lot. If she saw a suspicious man lurking in the area she wondered what she would do. Jump back in and speed off to her sister's house? A car was parked a few spaces over, the windows tinted so she couldn't tell if anyone was inside. It reminded her of the car that the man in the park had driven off in. With a jolt of fear, she turned to jump back in the van.

"Ivy!"

She turned and saw Samson Sinclair climb slowly out of the car. She stood immobile beside the minivan, waiting for her heart to stop pounding erratically. He walked briskly across the parking lot, although he seemed to be favoring his side.

"Are you all right, Samson?" she asked, a trace of tenderness in her voice that he couldn't miss.

He gave her a lopsided grin laced with pain. "I'm fine – just a little sore. I picked up my prescription for painkillers on the way over. I'll have to take one soon." He waved at the kids through the window. "Nice van. When did you get this?"

"I ordered it the other day, and they delivered it this morning. Pretty good service, huh?" She turned and slid the side door open to let the kids escape. "Okay, you two – I want everyone to carry something. Hopefully we can get everything in one trip and not have to come back."

"Here, I'll help you." Samson bent to pick up Ivy's suitcase, but she put a restraining hand over his.

"Hold on! You can't pick that up. You were just shot yesterday. I'll carry this one. You take the kids' overnight bags. They're not nearly as heavy. Caleb, grab your backpack. Riley, you carry the jackets. Let's go," she ordered, and they all made their way to the front door.

Once upstairs, Samson and the kids waited patiently outside the door of the new apartment while Ivy rifled through her purse for the key. She gave them all a smile of success as she stuck it in the lock and turned the deadbolt, then threw open the door and stepped inside. Out of the corner of her eye she saw movement by the sliding glass door. A slim figure dressed in black jumped from the deck.

"Samson!" She dropped the heavy bag and ran to the window. The end of a rope was tied to the metal banisters and dangled down the side of the building, but there was no sign of the intruder. She turned slowly back to the room and realized that her new home was completely ransacked.

"Mommy, somebody broke Buster." Riley stood in the hallway holding a stuffed rabbit, its head torn halfway off and most of the insides gone. Tears welled up in her blue eyes and her lower lip began to quiver. "Why would someone hurt my bunny?" she asked in a broken voice.

Ivy forgot about the five-thousand-dollar loveseat that was slashed, the pictures torn off the walls, the CD cases lying broken on the floor, and fell on her knees to comfort her little girl.

She pulled her into her arms and held her. "I'll fix Buster as soon as possible and make him as good as new again. I promise."

Riley rubbed her face against her Mother's pink cotton sweater, using her as a human tissue. Her lip still protruded but her sobs soon subsided.

"What happened to our house, Mommy?" asked Caleb, his eyes as round and bright as new quarters. He bent to pick up a book that lay by his feet, the cover torn nearly off.

"I've got to make a call." Samson glanced at Ivy and she nodded. He went to the phone and dialed the office, asking in a low voice to speak to Captain Herndon.

Ivy sighed. When would this be over? She thought that moving here would be a good thing for the children and for her. Would Todd's sins follow them for the rest of their lives? She put an arm around each of the children and sat down on the damaged couch with them by her sides. Riley clutched the pitiful looking rabbit to her breast with one hand and stuck her thumb in her mouth. Caleb pulled away and went to the sliding door to look out.

"Don't touch anything, Caleb. The police have to dust for fingerprints," called Samson from the kitchen. Fear showed in Caleb's face and he timidly returned to Ivy's side.

"A team will be here in a few minutes to get prints and look around." Samson said, joining them in the living room.

"When is this going to be over?" Ivy looked up into the face of the man who unconsciously had become her protector since she had returned to Nebraska.

He met her helpless look with a grim one of his own and shook his head. "Not yet. I need to talk to you in private, Ivy. Do you think the kids could go to my apartment with Agent Timmons?"

Ivy looked down at her babies snuggled under each arm. She nodded. Samson called on his cell and moments later Timmons knocked on the still open door and walked in. He gave a nod to Samson and Ivy. His eyes darted here and there taking in the total chaos of the room.

"Kids, Mr. Timmons is an FBI agent. He's going to take you to my apartment next door where you can watch TV while I talk to your mother for a few minutes," Samson explained, his voice calm and reassuring.

Riley still clung tightly to Ivy's arm, but she pulled gently away and smiled down into her daughter's frightened face.

"Go with Caleb and Agent Timmons. It will be all right. I need to talk to Samson alone, and then we'll get some lunch." She walked the kids to the door and watched them follow the agent down the hall and inside Samson's apartment. Then she turned and faced Samson, anger suddenly rising to the surface.

"Why are they doing this to us?" she demanded.

The forensic team soon showed up and Samson became all business, showing them the damage and the rope where the intruder had climbed down to make his escape. When they were busy dusting for prints and going over every room inch by inch, he motioned for Ivy to follow him out of the apartment and down the back stairs. Outside in the summer sun he paused and ran a hand through his hair, then reached in his back pocket and pulled out the cap he had stuck there. Ivy walked beside him, wondering if he was about to drop another bomb into her life. She didn't think she could take much more.

"Would you like to sit down?" He nodded toward the bench facing the pond. No children played nearby. The area was temporarily deserted except for the two of them. She guessed it must be about noon as the sun was hot overhead. The kids had probably gone inside for lunch. Ivy sat down on the bench and stared straight ahead. She didn't know if she was ready for what Samson was about to say. His expression had been serious earlier, but now he looked positively grim.

"There was news this morning from Interpol – about Todd."

Ivy felt her muscles turn to stone. She couldn't move, and she could barely breathe. Her conversation with Todd just a few short hours ago seemed like a figment of her imagination after she'd tossed and turned half the night with his face intruding in her dreams. She cleared her throat but was unable to ask the question that hung between them.

Samson took her hands, tensely clasped together, and held them very gently. "Todd was shot and killed last night. I'm sorry," he said, his voice soft with concern.

She felt sick at the news. She should have been able to do something. He had asked for her help, and she had turned him down cold. Maybe if she had wired him the money, he would still be alive. She closed her eyes against the memories, but one lone tear crept out from beneath her lashes; then Samson pulled her into his strong arms and held her as she let loose and sobbed against his white T-shirt, leaving damp splotches behind. Eventually she pulled away and drew a shaky breath, wiping at her eyes with the back of her hand.

"I should have called someone. It's my fault," she stated miserably.

"How can it be your fault?"

"Todd called me at Holly's about nine o'clock. Said he was in trouble. That people were after him. The woman he ran off with took all his money. He wanted me to wire him enough cash to get a flight back to the states. He thought he could retrieve the disc and use it as a bargaining chip again. I turned him down flat, but if I *had* sent him the money, maybe he could have gotten away before they killed him." Fresh tears coursed down her cheeks

Samson shook his head. He pulled a handkerchief from his pocket and handed it to her. "That's not true. It wouldn't have changed anything. He died before ten our time, shortly after talking to you. There was no way he could have flown out of the Bahamas that quickly. You are not to blame in any way for his death. He brought this on himself," he said, his voice suddenly stern and gruff.

Confusion filled her heart. "I know he wasn't the man I imagined I married when I was nineteen, but he was the father of my children. What am I going to tell them – that their father was a thief and got what he deserved?"

"I don't know, but I know someone who does. Someone who can heal broken hearts and bind up wounds."

Ivy knew he was talking about God again and probably quoting some verse in the Bible, but she didn't think God could help at a time like this. The bitterness of Todd's death was too new, and the ache of regret filled her heart. Regret that all those years were wasted instead of filled with love and happiness like marriage was supposed to be. Could it be that God *did* blame her for what had happened in that Sunday school room thirteen years ago and this is what she deserved? She shook that thought away by standing briskly to her feet and turning to look up at the building behind her. Even from here she could see the rope dangling down three stories from her balcony railing. A man knelt by the window, presumably dusting for prints.

"So, Todd is dead and now they're after me. Since I don't know where the disc is and they're not likely to believe me even if I told them so, what are we going to do?" she asked, her hands braced on her slim hips.

Samson reached out and gently pulled her back down to sit beside him. "Look, as far as the FBI is concerned, you are the only lead to finding that disc, so they're not going to let anything happen to you or the kids."

Ivy shrugged. "I can't say that's a confidence booster. What about you?" she asked, meeting his eyes.

"Me?"

She released an exasperated sigh. How could he not know what she was getting at? Men were so dense sometimes. "I don't trust the FBI, Samson. I trust you. Are *you* going to let anything happen to us?"

He stared at her for a second, his eyes narrowed, as though trying to decipher hieroglyphics, and then he reached out and cupped her cheek in a gentle caress.

"I promise to do everything in my power to keep you safe, Ivy. I'm glad you trust me, but I'm not infallible. You witnessed that first hand at the park."

"Having God on your side can't hurt," she said and smiled. "I may not have the faith that you do, but I believe you have enough for both of us."

He smiled. "That's a start."

†††

The forensics team was long gone, and Ivy and Samson picked up the worst of the mess by the time Agent Timmons returned with the children and a sack of groceries. At Samson's request, he had taken them out for pizza to give Ivy time to digest the news of her husband's death, and they had gone willingly, apparently having bonded with their new guardian. Then he had taken the kids grocery shopping and picked up a short list of items that Ivy had written out for him. Timmons was a regular teddy bear.

"I think they pretty much covered the entire apartment in their search, and since the suspect in question was still here when we walked in, we can assume they didn't find anything," Samson reasoned.

He sat on the floor, leaning back on his arms, his long legs stretched out before him. Timmons relaxed in the recliner closest to the window, his huge arms crossed, and his eyes closed. Ivy put the kids in her room to watch cartoons and shut the door, so they wouldn't overhear the adult conversation. She caught the last of Samson's statement as she came back down the hall.

"Does that mean they won't be back?" she asked.

Timmons snorted, not bothering to open his eyes. "They're not going to give up that easily. They may even start getting serious now."

"Timmons," Samson warned in a low voice.

"She needs to know. If they can't find the disc on their own, they could make it personal. We should be keeping her sister's house under surveillance as well as the apartment."

Ivy's eyes widened. "Do you think they would go after Holly to get to me?" She licked her lips nervously. "Maybe I should call her right now and see if she's all right."

"Not yet." Samson said. "Let's not worry her unnecessarily. I already called and requested someone watch your sister's house."

She sent him a grateful smile and sat down on the damaged couch she'd covered with a quilt.

Samson voiced the question in all their minds. "They've already searched this place – so what's their next move?"

"What about the stuff on the truck that went to the storage facility?" Timmons opened his eyes and ran a hand over his crew cut as though checking to see that it still stood at attention. "Someone should go through that, and since I've been there before and know where everything is – I'll go," he volunteered.

He pulled his beefy frame from the recliner and stepped over Samson's legs.

Samson grinned. "You seem to be in a hurry. Are you sure you don't want to stay and baby-sit the kids? We could go," he suggested good-naturedly.

Timmons picked up his suit jacket and struggled to pull it on. Finally, he gave up and tucked it under his arm. "I'll call the Captain from the car and get him up to date. Later," he called as he exited the apartment without a backward glance.

As soon as the door closed Samson burst out laughing and doubled over on the floor. Ivy had missed the show since she faced the other direction. She raised an eyebrow.

"That man has either got to quit lifting weights or get longer arms," he said, his laughter subsiding to a chuckle.

She smiled, but then her expression grew serious. "I've been thinking about where Todd might hide something. He had a safety deposit box in California. Do you think he would use such an obvious place?"

Samson stood and walked to the window. He could see some kids feeding the ducks and one girl with long blonde hair and a frog in her hand, chasing another child who ran away, screaming obligingly.

"Did the FBI get a search warrant for it?" he asked, turning back to the room and to the conversation.

"I don't think so. They never asked me about it. Maybe they didn't know he had a box. It was just for our personal papers – marriage certificate, the children's birth records, stuff like that. Since I have the key, I doubt he would hide something there. But it's possible he had a separate box I didn't know about. Is there some way to find out?"

"If we knew which bank he used, we could probably get the records but there are as many banks in the Los Angeles area as there are tourists. We could check out your box though." It was a long shot, but he wanted to give her hope.

"There's one person who might know exactly where the disc is." Ivy's voice had grown hard. "Did anyone bother to pick up the trail of the blonde my husband was traveling with? If she stole his money, perhaps she's going to retrieve the disc and try to sell that too."

"I haven't heard anything. But you could be right. If we locate her, she might lead us straight to the disc and to the people behind this." He turned back to the window and watched the antics of the children. They had slipped their shoes off now and were dipping their feet into the murky pond. He wrinkled his nose at the thought of how smelly they would be when they got home.

"Thanks, Samson," Ivy said. He wondered what she could be thanking him for and turned back to see her eyes shimmering with unshed tears. She quickly dashed them away as though ashamed of showing weakness in front of him.

"Thanks for what? I certainly haven't been much help. They threatened you on the phone, shot at you in the park, and now your apartment has been trashed." He was embarrassed that the list was growing. He had been assigned to watch her and so far, he'd been doing a bang-up job.

Ivy cocked her head to the side, her eyes still bright. "Thanks for staying here all day and helping me pick up. I know you didn't have to do that. I appreciate it – I really do."

He cleared his throat and nodded. "You're welcome. By the way, since you mentioned it, would you be willing to have me spend the night on your couch? I'd feel much better if I were here instead of next-door where I can't really hear what's going on. Not that they'll be back tonight but..." He let the rest of the thought hang between them.

"Yes, please stay. At least until they get that security system put on the sliding door. They said they could come out tomorrow morning." She'd called the security company earlier and requested emergency service, but apparently there had been a rash of burglaries in the area and that was the quickest they could come.

"I better collect my things from next door. I'll be right back but make sure you lock the door behind me just in case," he warned. He opened the door and scanned the hallway in both directions before going out and closing it firmly behind him.

Once in his own apartment he grabbed his overnight bag from under the bed and started throwing things in. He didn't need much but he took a change of clothes, his toiletries, and his Bible. He zipped it up and swung it over his shoulder before noticing that the answering machine light was blinking. The tiny screen said there were three messages. He pushed the button and listened.

"Samson, this is Hank. I was wondering if you could combine my class with yours tomorrow. Maggie has come down with the flu, and I think I should stay with her. She's been feeling mighty poorly."

Samson bit his bottom lip. How was he going to watch Ivy and the kids tomorrow? He didn't like to miss teaching his class and now they needed him for two classes. He had grave doubts as to whether she would agree to go with him. He sighed and listened to the next message.

"This is Hank again. Maggie wanted me to relay a message. She said to tell you she's praying for you and someone named Ivy. Talk to you later."

Samson smiled and shook his head. Maggie was home sick with the flu and yet not too sick to worry about him.

He waited for the third message. Just dead air. Apparently, someone was machine shy or had the wrong number. He deleted the messages and turned to go, when he remembered that he hadn't checked the lock on his sliding glass door. Since Ivy's break-in he couldn't be too careful. He pulled back the drapes. The lock was set and the bar in place, but as he looked out he saw a man staring up at the building.

He was medium build with short dark hair and sunglasses. He couldn't make out his features clearly from three stories up, especially as he stood in the shadow of the building, but Samson was sure it was the same man who shot him in the park. The man's gaze shifted, and he could have sworn he looked right at him. Then he turned and casually strolled away around the other end of the building. Samson's first instinct was to run after him, but he knew with his injured side that he could never get out of the building and catch up before he was gone.

He also knew now that he couldn't possibly leave Ivy and the children alone all morning while he was at church. The situation remained too dangerous and she said she didn't trust anyone but him. She wouldn't appreciate having Timmons around under foot. They didn't seem to like each other very much. Besides, Timmons was supposed to be off tomorrow too. He had a family, and Samson didn't want to take him away from them for the one full day they spent together. If Ivy wouldn't go to church with him, then he would just have to stay at the apartment to protect her.

He checked his gun, then slid it back in the side holster under his arm and grabbed a light jacket to conceal the bulge. Better safe than sorry. He reached for his bag and went out, locking the door behind him.

{7}

"Everything's all right, Holly. We're safe. I just wanted you to know that the man out front is FBI. He's there for your protection, so don't try to lose him." Ivy spoke from experience. She didn't want her sister becoming unnerved at the thought that she was being followed.

"I don't think you should stay there. It's not safe. The place has already been broken into and you haven't even spent the night." Her sister's voice rang shrill with worry, reminding Ivy of Riley when she got excited. She pulled the phone about four inches away from her ear to protect her hearing.

"Agent Sinclair is going to spend the night on my couch, so we'll be well protected," she said, trying to sound calm and collected for Holly's benefit.

"You mean the man who rented you the apartment and just happens to live next door? Are you sure you can trust him?"

Ivy smiled. One thing she *was* sure of was her trust in Samson Sinclair. She wasn't sure why, but she was willing to put her life in his hands if need be.

"Yes, I'm sure. Now please don't worry anymore." There was a soft knock at the door. "I've got to go. Talk to you later." She hung up and stepped to the door to look out the peephole.

"It's me," Samson announced quietly from the other side.

She opened the door and he gave her a crooked smile. He clutched a pillow under one arm and an overnight bag in his other hand. She quickly turned away and hurried back to the kitchen to hide the grin that stretched her lips. The notion of a sleepover with Mr. Sinclair was suddenly very funny and she had to stifle a laugh behind a pretend coughing fit.

She started chopping vegetables but continued to watch him. He set his bag in the corner of the living room and started to take off his jacket, but hesitated, and pulled it back on. He looked up quickly to see if she had noticed, and she blushed as he caught her watching him. She turned away to wash the celery at the sink. When she went to open the refrigerator, he stood in the doorway with a goofy look on his face, one of her newly sliced carrot sticks in his hand. He took a bite and crunched loudly before doing the worst imitation of Bugs Bunny she'd ever heard.

"What's up Doc?"

"That's terrible. It's a good thing you have a paying job," she teased.

"You really think so?" he asked, his brows lifted incredulously. "The boys in my Sunday school class think I'm a master."

She laughed. "Well of course they do. They're only seven years old! If I'm not mistaken, at that age they also think making gross sounds in their armpits is entertaining."

Ivy could still feel his eyes on her when she turned her back and continued chopping. She felt self-conscious and wasn't paying as close attention as she should have been. She mistook her finger for celery and cut a nice slash in the side.

"Ow!" She jerked back. "I don't believe this!" She turned the faucet on and stuck her finger under cold water to wash away the blood.

Samson came up from behind and took her hand in his, turning her about to face him. He nudged tenderly at the cut to gauge the depth and wrapped a clean tissue around it. "Do you have a bandage? I don't think you need stitches, but you don't want to be doing anymore slicing today. I'll finish that." He released her hand and picked up the knife on the cutting board, rinsed it under the water and resumed chopping.

Ivy backed away and fled to the bathroom to get a bandage and get herself under control. The touch of his hand on hers shouldn't make her feel all tingly inside. She'd just found out her husband had been killed. What was wrong with her? She was shaking like a leaf. It must be the shock of cutting her finger. The gash wasn't very deep, but it hurt a lot. Samson was her bodyguard for heaven's sake, not her date. He didn't mean anything personal by the way he treated her. He would probably treat anyone he watched over the very same way. Trouble was, she didn't want him to treat everyone else the same. That realization came with a sudden jolt of fear. She was *not* going to fall in love. It was the last thing she needed at a time like this. Todd wasn't even cold in his grave, and here she was mooning after a man she barely knew.

Samson had chopped all the celery that she set out and was waiting for her to tell him the next step when she reappeared. She started mixing her ingredients for salad and turned on the oven to toast the French bread she'd had Timmons buy that morning. He stood back out of the way and watched, not saying anything.

"Why don't you go sit down while I finish getting dinner ready," she suggested firmly. He made her nervous, standing there hovering. What she really needed was another kitchen accident, so he could tend to her wounds. That thought brought a smile to her lips. She shook it away and began buttering the already-sliced bread. Garlic Salt shaker in hand, she hesitated but then started pouring. "Garlic is our friend," she mumbled to herself. Hopefully, vampires weren't the only things it warded off. Perhaps it would also keep her friendly bodyguard at bay, so she could think straight.

"I hope you like garlic bread," she called.

"Love it." He glanced up from the newspaper he was reading. "You sure you don't want some help in there?"

Ivy shook her head. "I have everything under control. Thanks anyway."

She checked the pasta and poured it in the colander. Then she put the bread in the oven and turned on the timer. Next, she opened the jar of spaghetti sauce to heat in the microwave. Hopefully he wouldn't mind store bought sauce because she didn't have ingredients for homemade.

"I'm hungry." Caleb trudged into the kitchen, rubbing his eyes and scratching his scalp.

The kids had fallen asleep watching Scooby Doo earlier and when she went in to check on them, they had been sprawled across her bed, snoring softly. She'd spread a blanket over them both and decided to let them sleep a while longer.

She bent now and kissed him on the top of the head. "Dinner's just about ready. Is Riley awake?"

"She's watching Dora the Explorer. I told her it was time to eat because I could smell the food, but she wouldn't come," he said, eyeing the cooked pasta.

Ivy set a bowl of black olives on the small table and went to pull the television addict from the clutches of her addiction. Riley still lay across the bed in her previous position except now awake and staring at the screen.

"What do you think you're doing, girlie? You're going to melt your eyes watching so much television," she threatened, then bent over her daughter and gave her a good tickling. Riley giggled so hard she nearly fell off the bed. Ivy caught her and hugged her soft, little body close before setting her on her feet and marching her toward the kitchen.

"Wash your hands and we'll eat." The kids both went into the bathroom at the same time, and she could hear water running and splashing and giggling going on. Finally, they reappeared looking wetter and more awake.

"We have company, so we'll have to chew with our mouths closed," she warned them as they sat at the table.

Samson tried to look shocked. "You mean you don't usually eat with your mouths closed?" he asked, his eyes wide.

"Nope," Caleb said and Riley grinned.

"Neither do I!" Samson announced, and he stuck a noodle in his mouth and began to chew, his mouth wide open. The children laughed, and Ivy shook her head in amazement.

"Wait a minute," said Samson. "We can't eat with our mouths open until we thank God for the food."

Riley and Caleb both looked at Ivy, their bewilderment obvious. Samson waited expectantly as though for permission. Ivy met his eyes across the small table and nodded. He bowed his head and closed his eyes, and the children followed suit not wanting to be out of Samson's good graces.

"Lord, thank you for the food we are about to enjoy, and thank you for the woman who prepared it. Also, thank you for Riley and Caleb, my new friends. Amen."

Ivy opened her eyes and peeked during Samson's prayer. She couldn't believe that she sat in a small apartment in Omaha, Nebraska with an FBI agent at her table saying grace. This moment was such a long way from where she had been just a few short days ago. Everything seemed unreal. But when Samson lifted his head and smiled across at her, she couldn't imagine being anywhere else.

They ate in companionable silence for a few minutes until the kids got wound up once again and began to chatter. Ivy let the conversation drift over her as she ate, while Samson answered Caleb and Riley's questions with the patience of a saint.

"Mommy said that going to school here will be a lot more fun than California because sometimes you get off for snow days," Caleb said. "That's when the snow is so deep the school buses can't even drive through it. Wouldn't that be cool! Then we could build a big snowman and stuff." Caleb had lived in California since he turned four and didn't really remember what having snow was like, but his imagination always worked overtime.

Samson nodded. "Oh yeah, blizzards are great. I remember once when I was a boy the snow was so deep we couldn't get out our front door. My father had to crawl out a window and shovel a path."

Caleb's eyes widened, "Wow!"

"Yes, I'd agree with that," commented Ivy wryly. "Anyone for desert? I've got some chocolate cookies that Aunt Holly sent along."

The kids both grabbed a cookie in each hand and went off to put their boxes of toys away in their room. Ivy started clearing the dishes and Samson tried to give her a hand, but she shooed him back to the living room, out of the way. The kitchen was too small for two people to clean up without bumping into each other every other step.

"I know you said that you didn't go to church, but would you consider changing your mind for tomorrow?" Samson called from the next room. "I'm supposed to teach two Sunday school classes. Hank is staying home to nurse Maggie because she's sick with the flu, and he wanted me to combine my class with his. I don't want to leave you and the kids here alone for that long, but if you tagged along you could help me out. It's just little boys between the ages of seven and ten. They don't bite – often." He leaned his elbows on the ledge cutout that separated the kitchen from the living room, a teasing half smile on his face that no doubt had melted many a Delilah's heart. But she wasn't one of them, and she wouldn't be manipulated so easily.

She turned back to the sink full of dishes soaking in soapy water. "I don't think that would be a very good idea," she said.

She heard the crinkling of cellophane as Samson snagged a cookie from the bag. "What are you afraid of, Ivy? God isn't going to hurt you."

Her back stiffened but she didn't turn. She started washing the first plate, scrubbing so hard the design was in danger of coming off. "Well, he's never helped me either."

She didn't want to speak of it again. The only time she had bared her soul was when Todd and she were first married. He merely laughed at her fear and told her she was making too much of the incident. Boys would be boys after all. Besides, it showed her how silly she was to believe in an all-powerful God. Believing in yourself was what got you through life, he had informed her. She stared down at the soapy water as tears welled up in her eyes, but she refused to let them fall, while remembering the faces of those two boys as they sneered at her behind their mother's back.

Samson moved quietly to stand behind her. She could feel his breath, warm on her neck, as he gently touched her arm and turned her to face him. She hesitated for just an instant and then sank her face against his chest. His arms closed around her like a warm blanket, and she leaned there feeling protected. She didn't know if government protocol prohibited agents from comforting emotional women, but it felt good to have someone strong to lean on, if only for a moment.

"What happened?" he asked, although she didn't think he really expected an answer. She let out a shaky sigh and his chin came down to rest on the top of her head in a way that reminded her of being held as a small child. She hadn't felt this safe in a long time.

She pulled reluctantly away and drew a deep breath. Avoiding his eyes, she turned back to the dishes that still needed washing. "Let's just say that I have a long-standing phobia of church."

"All right. You don't have to tell me anything. Your past is none of my business after all. But if you ever change your mind – I'm here." He turned and left the room.

Ivy mechanically went through the motions of washing the few plates and glasses, all the while listening to Samson playing with Caleb and Riley. Riley's high-pitched giggle followed Samson's hilarious imitation of a gorilla. She smiled at the children's happy voices. Caleb was apparently getting into the action too. He roared like a lion and soon they were all roaring. It sounded like a zoo full of sick animals.

She pulled the plug and let the water drain away. It was time to make some changes in her life. She wasn't going to let the past affect the present anymore. Samson had been good to the kids and to her. He'd asked the simple favor of going with him to Sunday school so that he wouldn't worry about her being home alone, and she freaked. Well, no more! She lifted her chin.

"Caleb! Riley!" she called out, "Could you both come in here a minute?"

They came running, Samson bringing up the rear. He appeared to be having as much fun as they were. They stopped in the kitchen doorway.

"What, Mom?" Caleb asked as though he were in a hurry to be back playing.

"Would you two like to go to Sunday school with Samson tomorrow morning?" she asked quickly before she had time to change her mind.

"Yeah! That would be great!" Caleb said, although he had never been to church before and had no idea what Sunday school was all about.

Over the clamor of the children's happy voices, Ivy heard the beating of her own heart, thumping a ragged tattoo. Her gaze was drawn to Samson like a magnet. He smiled happily, and she smiled back despite her misgivings.

{8}

"What was I supposed to do? He told me his wife had the disc, but he wouldn't say where. There was really no point in my sticking around. He was starting to get suspicious. So, I took the money and left." Brenna sat back in the limousine, her legs crossed, causing her short black skirt to ride up mid-thigh. Her silky, red, blouse was low-cut, form fitting, and matched the three-inch heels she wore. She ran a hand through spiky cut black hair and sighed. She was dying for a smoke. She opened a little silver case and pulled out a cigarette. Placing it between her lips, she leaned forward as the man facing her held a lighter. She smiled and blew a plume of smoke off to the side.

"So why did you kill him? He could have led us to the disc. He just needed a little incentive. That's why I took the money, to give him a reason to come out of hiding and retrieve it." She drew once more on the cigarette, then crushed it out in the ashtray. "I'm trying to quit," she said in answer to his wry expression.

He slipped his hand inside his suit coat and slipped out a photograph. "This is his wife. I want you to meet her."

She took the picture and tapped a long red fingernail on the woman's image. "So, this is his ball and chain. From the way he talked, you'd think she was a step down from Phyllis Diller. She's actually pretty, in an understated kind of way," she conceded grudgingly.

"Get close to her. I want this resolved." He picked up the phone and pressed redial.

"How close? You know I'm really not that good at doing the girlfriend thing. Men are my specialty. Can I just work on the FBI guy?" she asked with a practiced pout.

He spoke into the phone. "Has she left the apartment yet? All right, keep me informed." He replaced the receiver and met Brenna's eyes. "Very close. Close enough to be invited into her home and her confidence. Can you do that?" he asked. "We're running out of time, and I'm running out of patience. I have a lot of money riding on this. Don't let me down, Bree. You don't want to end up like Mr. Winter now, do you?"

The lines in his face looked deeper and harsher than she remembered. Ace Anderson was not a man to dally with, and she valued her life enough to take his threats seriously.

"Face down in a phone booth? I don't think so. I'll get what you want," she promised.

"Good. They just left the apartment with Agent Sinclair. Lionel is following them. When we learn where they're going, we'll drop you off." He leaned back and folded his arms across his chest, a pleased expression on his normally stern face.

His gray hair was cut short to keep the natural curl from having a mind of its own. Brenna noticed that he liked his *things* kept in line as well as people. The slightest scuff on his highly polished shoes and he would flip out. Absently stroking his mustache with a well-manicured finger, he watched Brenna through half closed lids. Under his scrutiny she realized that he regarded *her* as one of his things. The look in his eye was definitely possessive. She never thought of herself that way before, but now with recent threats still fresh in her mind and the way he watched her as though he were weighing her possibilities, she felt an edge of fear creep into her soul. Was she also expendable, as Todd had been? She hadn't expected them to kill him. Sure, he had been playing a game of his own, but she was confident that in the end he would have given them what they wanted without having to shoot him. Todd was arrogant and cocky, but he would have come around. He just needed to be squeezed a bit tighter, made to feel the pressure of not cooperating. She took his money, so he would have no recourse but to retrieve the disc. But Ace Anderson had eliminated Todd before he'd had a chance. Would she have been another causality of the game if she hadn't flown back to the states that morning?

"Lionel has no idea where they're headed?" she asked, breaking the silence that stretched awkwardly between them.

"They were dressed up. Perhaps they're going out for brunch." Ace adjusted the air conditioning and leaned back to let the air hit him full in the face.

The phone rang, and he quickly picked it up and listened. He stared across at her, a definite smirk on his thin lips.

"When's the last time you attended church, Bree?"

†††

It had been a long night for Ivy. She had tossed and turned hour after hour thinking about Todd and how she was going to tell the children about their father's death. His body was being shipped back to the states and they would have to have some sort of memorial service, but she was going to keep it as small and private as possible. The children had never attended a funeral before and although Todd had not been a model father, he was still their daddy, and attending his funeral would likely be devastating.

Morning came too soon, and Ivy pulled herself from bed with the realization that she had promised Samson they would go to church with him today. As the time drew nearer, she developed a case of cold feet, but she wouldn't admit it for the world. She had already told the kids they were going, and she couldn't back out now.

When Agent Matthews pulled the car around to the front door, they all climbed in, and Ivy felt her heart begin to pound. The young agent got out and let Samson take the wheel. Ivy stared out the passenger side window, not wanting him to see misgivings in her eyes. She chided herself for acting this way, but no matter what she thought logically, the fear in her heart just grew.

The feel of Samson's hand covering hers jerked her back to reality, and she turned to find him watching her anxiously.

"Are you all right?" he asked softly under cover of the children's chatter in the back seat.

Ivy nodded but she felt closer to a panic attack than all right. She tried to breathe normally and slow down the racing of her heart. The roads were fairly empty at this hour of the morning. The malls hadn't opened yet, which definitely cut back on traffic. She supposed most people were sleeping in, which is what she would be doing right now on a normal Sunday. But this was anything but normal.

"Agent Matthews is going to take care of the security people when they come this morning to replace your locks and wire your new system. It should be installed by the time we return," Samson informed her.

She had completely forgotten the appointment. "Thank you."

"We're almost there," he said as he turned off onto a side street. "Only a couple more blocks."

The streets were lined with houses that had obviously been built in the late fifties and were all very similar to one another except for the choice of paint, which differed only by a shade of tan or gray. Most were small ramblers with unattached garages set back from the house and apparently unoccupied, for the streets and driveways were littered with vehicles. Trees that had been left to grow for decades, trimmed only when they interfered with electric lines, shaded the avenue and kept out much of the sun's morning rays.

Samson drove slowly as though offering Ivy a few extra moments to pull herself together. She drew a deep breath and let it slowly out when they pulled up outside the church at last. He carefully parallel-parked the car along the street between an old van and a Buick. Ivy looked up at the building and felt a bit of relief that it didn't in any way resemble the church from her past. Instead of brick it was covered in white siding with frosted windows that would keep the occupants' minds from wandering outside during a lengthy sermon. The double door on the front was painted brown and stood open, welcoming anyone who wished to enter. Two little boys played on the steps, scuffling back and forth until she feared one would fall on the cement and get injured.

Samson, apparently on the same wavelength, opened his door and yelled up at them, "Billy! Roger! Cut that out before somebody gets hurt."

He went around and opened the door for Ivy while the kids climbed out of the back and stood looking nervously around. "Well, this is it," he said.

Ivy noticed a black limousine drive slowly by as they made their way up the steps and into the building. It seemed rather out of place in this neighborhood.

"I'd like you to meet our Pastor," Samson said, lowering his voice so only she would hear. Ivy paused inside the door and looked around.

A man in a dark pin-stripe suit was speaking with an elderly woman. He smiled politely.

"You need new songbooks in the pews with large print lettering. I can't be expected to see something that small at ninety-four years old," she said, shaking a finger at him. She pushed her glasses up on her nose and shuffled away to the sanctuary.

The man turned to greet them next.

Samson shook his hand, smiling. "Pastor Nichols, how are you? I want to introduce you to a friend of mine. This is Ivy Thompson and her children, Caleb and Riley.

Ivy cringed at the use of her maiden name. Now that Todd was dead she felt guilty for dropping his name. Perhaps she'd been too unforgiving, wanting to escape his memory so completely. She wondered if the children noticed and what they thought of it.

Pastor Nichols extended his hand to Ivy. His eyes reflected the blue of his tie when he smiled. "It 's nice to meet you. Welcome to our church. We're always excited to have visitors." He nodded in the direction the elderly woman had disappeared. "Our adult Sunday school class meets right in there, and Samson can show the children where theirs will be."

"I've asked Ivy to help in my class today, Pastor. As you probably know, Maggie is sick, and Hank stayed home to take care of her, so I have two classes to teach."

Pastor Nichols looked puzzled for a moment but then nodded. "Well you be careful," he said looking back at Ivy, his eyes crinkling at the corners, "those boys can be a handful."

She nodded and smiled politely. More people filed through the door and shook the Pastor's hand on their way to join their morning classes. Children scurried off to the basement while adults wandered into the auditorium. She felt a tug on her arm, and Samson led the way down the back stairs to the room where he taught. Four boys sat on folding chairs watching while two others wrestled on the carpeted floor. They jumped up at the sight of Samson coming through the door and quickly found a chair to plop into, grins plastered on their faces. He grinned back. Soon the chairs were full, and a bell rang down the hall when it was time for class to start.

"Good morning, boys," he began. "I want to introduce some friends of mine. This is Mrs. Thompson, and this is Caleb and Riley. They are going to stay in our class today and help out."

Caleb and Riley sat on the front row with Ivy and listened with great interest as Samson told about the upcoming church activity. They were going to a park where they would play games and have a cookout. There would be prizes and ribbons, and everyone was invited to come. Ivy could feel her kids looking at her for reassurance that they would be included. She stubbornly ignored their silent plea and kept her eyes on Samson.

The story was one that she remembered from her early days of Sunday school in Mrs. Adams' classroom. It was about Jonah, a man who tried to run away from God, but God wouldn't let him. A giant fish swallowed Jonah until he repented and obeyed God, and then the fish spit him out onto dry land.

The children sat in silence as Samson finished the story, and then hands started going up all around the room. He answered questions until the bell rang and Sunday school was over. The boys filed out amid good-natured pushing and laughing. Samson turned and began peeling pictures from the flannel board, placing them carefully in a file folder marked with the name of the Bible story.

Caleb stood up and went to watch. He had been quiet during class, but Ivy could tell he really wanted to ask Samson a question. He fidgeted with a songbook that lay on the chair beside him, pretending to be absorbed by it.

"So how did you two like Sunday school?" asked Samson. He peeled the last picture and tucked it away in the confines of the folder.

"I liked it," Riley said with her usual agreeableness.

"What about you, Caleb?" He turned and put a hand on Caleb's small shoulder.

Caleb looked up at him, his eyes alive with questions. "It was cool! But I wonder if Jonah got seasick inside the fish. Do you think he puked in there? 'Cause if he did, he would have to smell it for three days."

Ivy rolled her eyes when Samson looked at her and burst out laughing. Caleb just grinned as though he'd told a very funny joke but wasn't sure what it was.

Riley tugged on Ivy's sleeve at last and pulled until she was down to her level. She whispered in her ear, loud enough for Samson and Caleb to hear, "Can we go eat now? I'm starving."

Ivy was glad of any excuse to escape and not have to go upstairs and mingle with people she didn't know, then sit through a sermon she felt sure would be her undoing. Samson's lesson had been enough for one day. It brought her face to face with the girl she had been thirteen years ago. That girl had run away from God just as surely as Jonah had done, but she didn't want to think about that now.

"Sure. We can go." Samson nodded and picked up his brown leather Bible on the chair.

Ivy met his eyes. He seemed to know what she was feeling even without an explanation. He turned out the light and waited for them to go out the door. The children ran out, but Ivy stood paralyzed. Her legs felt weak, and they almost folded under her as her mind returned to a dark classroom on a Sunday long ago. A low moan escaped her lips. The sound of a wounded animal. Samson reached out for her just as her legs buckled and she slumped against him, pressing her face into his shoulder.

He quickly put her down on one of the folding chairs and sat beside her with his arms enclosing her body like a shield. The children trooped back in, wondering why they hadn't been followed. They watched Samson comfort Ivy with soothing words and loving pats. Tears coursed down her cheeks as the dam finally burst inside.

Riley came and patted her arm, not knowing what else to do in a situation like this. Caleb just stood by the door, a flashing billboard of emotions playing over his young features.

"It 's all right, kids," Samson said to ease their worry. "Your mom's just tired and sad about a lot of things. We'll get her home and into bed and she'll be as good as new," he promised.

They could hear the piano playing in the auditorium as they slipped out the back door. They didn't see anyone on their way to the car, not even the dark-haired young woman in the short skirt who entered the church and looked furtively around before taking a seat in the last row.

✝✝✝

Brenna looked over the small auditorium but didn't catch even a glimpse of Ivy Winter or the handsome FBI man. Maybe they were still in another part of the building. She hadn't seen them leave, so they must be here somewhere. She took a seat in the back row, next to a young couple with two small children. They glanced up with a smile of welcome as she sat down, although the woman cast furtive glances her way, as though she didn't quite fit in. Well, wasn't that what church was all about – welcoming individuals from all walks of life? She looked around at the people and realized that in comparison to her they were all dressed rather conservatively. Her skirt was riding up her thighs again and she tried unobtrusively to tug it down with one hand as she held the songbook with the other. She hated feeling out of place, and usually dressed to fit in to any given situation, although in her line of work it had never entailed attending church. Anderson hadn't given her that option. He dropped her off and expected her to perform.

Finally, the singing was over, and the preacher stood up to give his sermon. Brenna shifted nervously in her seat. Where were Ivy Winters and her agent friend? She turned again to look back at the open door, but no one else had come in since she sat down except for two little boys who had gone out to the bathroom earlier.

"This morning I want to talk to you about love," the preacher said. "Jesus said that we should love one another. He encouraged us to love those that hate us and despitefully use us. Sometimes loving someone is a chore. Sometimes the people we need to love are so hardened toward kindness that they make it nearly impossible to love them. But Jesus said to love those people. He also said that he wouldn't give us anything too hard to bear. On our own it's impossible to love someone who hates us, but with God nothing is impossible." He paused and looked slowly around the room, his gaze seeming to rest on each face as though he were trying to read their souls. Brenna squirmed uncomfortably on the hard, wooden pew and recrossed her legs. She was beginning to think this was one of the worst ideas Anderson had ever come up with. She was sure that he was getting a real good laugh out of the whole situation.

"I'm sure every one of us has someone in our lives that on our own is hard or impossible to love. He or she may have done something to you that seems beyond forgiveness."

Brenna bit her lower lip, probably messing up her perfect ruby lined lips. She began to tap her fingernails on the arm of the pew, causing the young couple to glance irritably her way again. She sent them a frigid smile and crossed her arms. This was getting her nowhere fast. Ivy Winter and the FBI agent were a no-show, and she was left to stew in a room full of goody-two-shoes who apparently had never had anyone really cross them or they wouldn't be able to nod and shout those amen's as the pastor talked this love and forgiveness fantasy. It was time for her to make her exit before he was done, and she had to play nice with all the inmates.

The pastor smiled a sad smile and for just a moment stared down at his Bible lying across the pulpit. When he looked back up he seemed to be looking directly at Brenna.

"When my wife, Isabel, was shot this past year standing in line at the 7-Eleven, I went through something that I hope none of you will ever have to experience." He wiped at his eyes with a white handkerchief.

Brenna stopped thinking about escape and listened.

"I don't just mean the experience of losing a loved one, for many of you have lost those dear to you. I mean that I hope none of you have to experience *hate* the way I did. I hated the man who had done this to my wife and to me." He ran a hand through his thinning hair and drew a deep, cleansing breath.

"I hated him so completely that I couldn't feel the presence of my Savior, Jesus Christ. I know He lives within me and I could never do anything to change that, but I couldn't feel it anymore. Hate had taken over my spirit. Until one day a man came to see me. A man you all know. I didn't want to speak to him because I knew what he would say. But I let him in anyway. Samson sat me down and shared with me his love for God. He read these verses from Matthew." He glanced down at the passage in his worn Bible. *"But I tell you love your enemies, bless those who curse you, do good to those who hate you, pray for those who mistreat you and persecute you."* He looked up, and his gaze was unwavering. "I told him that I couldn't. That man had taken what I loved most in this world – my wife. Then Samson reminded me that God had freely given His own Son for us. Jesus died for the whole world and that meant He'd died for that man also. He died for the murderer as well as the child who lies to his parents about taking a cookie. He died for the rapist as well as the woman who cheated on her husband. He died for the bank robber as well as the man who falsified information on his tax return. He died for sinners."

Brenna realized she was listening so intently that she was holding her breath. She wondered how any man could forgive something like that. It was the true nature of people to exact revenge. She had seen it done many times in her short life.

"I know you're thinking that it's only human nature to hate a man like that, and it is. But God wants us to lose our old nature and take on a new nature when we accept Christ as our Savior. He died that we might be free of sin's bondage and death. It took me a long time to reconcile my heart back to God, but when I finally let it go and let him have his way, true peace flooded my soul. I believe that everything works together for good to them that love God, and even through this tragedy I have seen good come. Last week, I visited jail and talked with the man who shot my wife. His name is Dirk. I told Dirk about Jesus. How he died on the cross and washed away our sin with his own precious blood. I told him that I forgave him for what he did and more importantly that Jesus forgave him and wanted him in the family of God."

Pastor Nichols stopped as tears spilled down his cheeks, and he couldn't go on for a moment. He wiped his face again with the handkerchief and smiled. "Dirk fell down on his knees right there and asked Jesus into his heart to be his Savior."

Hallelujahs broke out across the room amid sniffling and wiping of eyes. Pastor Nichols raised his closed Bible into the air. "I am here to tell you *that all things do work together for good to them that are called according to his purpose.* My wife was a Christian, and I know that she is in heaven this moment with God, but that man may never have heard the salvation story if this tragedy had never taken place. I believe that Isabel, along with the angels of heaven, are rejoicing over Dirk's salvation."

Brenna wiped self-consciously at her own eyes, touched by his story of forgiveness, although she had a hard time understanding such a concept.

They began to sing again, and the Pastor invited those who wished to come forward and he would pray with them. She felt a tug on her heart to do just that but instead pressed her lips firmly together and slipped from the pew and out the door before she could change her mind.

{9}

"I feel like a fool to let the past have such a hold on me," Ivy murmured quietly as she sat on the grass watching the children play on the playground equipment nearby.

Caleb and Riley had insisted on having McDonalds for lunch, so they picked hamburgers up on their way home. After eating and changing clothes, they all walked to the park.

Samson leaned back on the palms of his hands beside her and shook his head. "You can't help but be affected by something like that. I only wish I'd known before I had you go down into that Sunday school room."

Ivy had finally told him everything. It spilled out, along with a few more tears, while they watched the children play. She had been holding it in for so long that it was actually a relief to share it with a friend. And he *was* becoming a friend despite her misgivings about letting him into her life. He had listened until she was done and then squeezed her hand gently as it lay in the grass between them.

"It's not your fault, Samson. I've been pushing this down inside me for so long, it had to come out sometime. I'm glad you were there when it did." She managed a watery smile for his benefit.

Caleb waved at them from the top of the slide and then let loose and slid to the bottom with a jungle call that would have rivaled Tarzan's. Samson gave him a thumbs-up, and he quickly ran to do it again. Riley was on the swings talking to another little girl about her age. They seemed to be having quite a conversation going as they swung slowly back and forth.

Samson turned his attention back to Ivy. She met his gaze and felt a blush on her cheeks. She couldn't help but notice the way his hair curled at the back of his neck and around his ears and could almost imagine the feel of it beneath her fingers. His dark eyes, with long lashes tipped golden at the ends, drew her in and wouldn't let her go.

With an audible sigh she pulled her gaze away and lay back in the grass, closing her eyes against the sun. It was warm on her skin and left her with a feeling of lethargy in her limbs as she lay soaking up rays.

"Are you tired?" he asked.

Ivy didn't bother to open her eyes but merely shook her head. "The sun just feels good," she said. She didn't want him to know she was daydreaming about him. After all, she had probably imagined the way he looked at her. She was just interpreting things all wrong. He would protect her out of duty, and he had proven to be a friend, but it would never go any further than that.

"Maybe we should get back. I don't want to put you and the children in jeopardy. I know you said you didn't want to feel like you were prisoners, but until we find the disc, we need to be careful." He signaled the kids with an ear-piercing whistle, and they both came running.

"Do we have to go home now?" asked Caleb, a frown between his brows. He was the outdoors type and would spend all day out there if he could. With his blonde hair and tanned skin, he already looked like a miniature California surfer dude.

Samson nodded and helped Ivy to her feet. Caleb ran ahead while Ivy, Samson, and Riley followed along behind.

Walking back to the apartment, Ivy's thoughts flew in circles. How was she going to tell the children about Todd? She had procrastinated long enough. She watched Caleb running along ahead of them and knew he would take it the hardest. No matter how poor of a father Todd had been, his son loved him. Riley was young enough that the concept of death was still a little too hard to grasp and hang on to for long, but Caleb would be crushed. Ivy knew he had always believed Todd was coming back, and now that was not only improbable but impossible as well.

†††

Ivy sat the kids down on the couch and explained with as little detail as possible that their father had been killed while on a trip to the Bahamas.

"Daddy loved you both very much," she said without a moment's hesitation, "and I know that you'll miss him."

Caleb began to cry and buried his face in her lap where his sobs were muffled against her body. He didn't barrage her with endless questions as she thought he would but seemed to accept the fact that Todd was gone for good. Although she guessed he would want to know more when his pain lessened, it was enough for now.

Riley stayed close, patting Caleb's back every once in a while, as though reminding him that she was there. She didn't cry but wore the serious expression of someone much older who was trying to be brave for others.

Samson stayed in the background, trying not to infringe on their privacy, but giving Ivy a kind smile when she glanced up. As usual he seemed to know what she was feeling. She wanted to be alone with the children at this time, but she also needed him within easy reach for moral support.

The three of them spent the rest of the day inside curled up on the big king-sized bed watching cartoons. The children snuggled close, needing to feel that physical connection to the only parent they had left. Riley's head rested in Ivy's lap, and Caleb leaned against her shoulder as she lay propped up with pillows against the headboard. The only thing that broke the stillness of the room was the high voices of the little, blue cartoon characters frolicking on the screen.

She could hear the sounds of rattling pots and pans in the kitchen where Samson was no doubt trying to fix dinner. She smiled to herself as she pictured him with an apron around his waist and hot mitts on his hands, pulling a casserole out of the oven. The vivid picture brought a giggle to her lips, and the children both turned to look at her in surprise as though laughing was an unheard-of commodity in their lives. She smiled, and they relaxed by degrees until they too were laughing naturally at the antics of the blue guys.

†††

"I want to go with you. Caleb and Riley can stay with Holly for a couple of days." Ivy stood with her arms crossed and determination in every line of her body.

Samson had waited until the kids were in bed for the night and asleep before he sprung the news that he was flying to California in the morning.

"There's no need for you to be there. The bank will release the contents of the box as long as we have your signature," Samson told her again. He eased around her as she stood blocking his escape in the hallway and picked up the newspaper from off the counter to end the conversation.

"I'm *not* giving you my signature. I'll release the contents to you myself, but only after I open it myself," she said, following him to the living room.

Samson sighed and put down the paper on the arm of the chair he sat in. He looked up, obviously annoyance. "We can get a court order if we have to. Why are you arguing about this? I told you I would take care of it. You and the kids will be safe here with Timmons. There's no need for you to be involved."

Ivy's mouth dropped open, and she shook her head. "What do you mean? I have been involved ever since Todd left me in this situation. Now I want to go with you to California but if you don't wish to travel with me, I'll go on my own." She turned and walked away before he could argue the point.

She came out of the bedroom minutes later with a basket piled high with dirty laundry and dug some quarters out of her purse. Before he knew what she was doing, she had tugged the door open. Samson jumped up and grabbed his two-way radio from the pocket of his jacket.

"Wait a minute. I want Dan to stand outside the laundry room while you're in there and walk you back. You shouldn't go out alone, even down the hall." He turned up his radio.

"Dan, could you come in here a minute?" The radio crackled, and the other agent gave an affirmative reply.

Within three minutes he was standing outside the door. He was tall and slim with thinning blonde hair and wire-rimmed glasses. He wore a pair of khaki slacks and a blue polo shirt that hung on his thin frame like borrowed clothes. Ivy thought if anyone tried to attack her she would have to protect herself as well as Dan. He didn't look strong enough to defend anyone, but perhaps his looks were deceiving. After all, Samson wouldn't entrust her to Dan unless he were capable of doing the job.

Samson held the door wide and then stood watching as Dan and she walked down the hall to the elevator. She could feel his gaze boring into her back and knew that he was still stewing over her ultimatum from before.

The laundry room was on the first floor at the far end of the building. Ivy walked self-consciously with Dan at her side. It seemed very weird to have a bodyguard just to do laundry, but on the other hand, he could be a godsend if she ran out of quarters. She went in, leaving Dan to wait out in the hall. The room was small and stuffy. There were six washers and six dryers but by the look of it most of them were already taken. Apparently, Sunday was washday. One other woman occupied the room. She was bent over an open washing machine, pouring granular soap over the clothes inside.

"It works better if you run the water over the soap first and add the clothes last," Ivy volunteered with a friendly smile. She hated it when her clothes got that white, crusty soap embedded in the fabric and it never washed out.

The woman turned and stared at her for a moment. She wore black Lycra biking shorts and a cut off white T-shirt that revealed a flat stomach with a diamond belly button ring on display. Her hair was cut very short and styled in a wild, spiky fashion that only a very confident woman would dare to sport.

"Thanks. I'm not used to washing my own clothes," she admitted as she turned back to the machine and tried to shake the soap down before putting quarters in and shutting the lid.

Ivy picked the only two empty machines left and filled them with the clothes from her laundry basket. She poured in the soap and closed the lid.

"Hey, I thought you were supposed to put the soap in first," the young woman reminded her.

"I have liquid soap." She held up the bottle.

"Oh."

Ivy smiled again and held out her hand. "I'm Ivy."

"Raven. Raven Black."

Ivy raised an eyebrow. "I guess your parents named you appropriately," she said.

"Oh, that." Raven ran a hand through her wild tresses. "I've tried other colors, but I always come back to the one I was born with."

"Have you lived here long?" Ivy asked, trying to be neighborly. She might as well get to know people if she were going to live here for a while.

Raven shook her head. "No. Not long at all. With my job it's hard to stay in one place for long. It would be nice to settle down and meet my neighbors for once," she said, a wistful look in her pale blue eyes.

"What do you do that keeps you on the move?" Ivy set the soap bottle in her now empty basket.

The young woman seemed to have lost her train of thought for a moment and just stood there with a blank look on her face. Ivy wondered if she were on drugs or something. She was sort of pale, dark smudges under her well-lined eyes. Her lips were frosted a shade of burgundy that gave her that vampirish look of having just had dinner. She was a pretty girl but way too made up to be in exercise shorts washing towels.

"I'm in a rock band," she said at last. "I sing lead. We got a gig to play regular for a while, so we took it. It sure beats one-night stands." She jumped up to sit on the washer and crossed her slim legs. Her tennis shoes were gleaming white as if they'd never been worn. Ivy wondered what she did to keep in shape. She certainly wasn't a runner from the state of her shoes. Maybe jumping around on a stage and screaming out lyrics did a body good.

"I've never met anyone in a band before." Ivy glanced at the sign on the door. It read, *We are not responsible for stolen articles*. She bit her lip.

"If you want to go, I'll keep an eye on your stuff till you get back. I was planning to stay here anyway," Raven said. She rolled her shoulders back in a stretch, then jumped down from the machine and strolled over to the bulletin board affixed to the wall.

"Look at this," she said reading from the advertisements posted there. "Someone has a perfectly good, nearly new, free hamster with cage. You can't beat that kind of a deal now, can you?"

"No, I guess not." Ivy walked over to look at the ads for herself. It couldn't hurt. After all, they were in a new city, with new people. You could learn a lot from the ads in a building. She read an ad for a woman companion and laughed.

"What?"

"This one." She tapped the three-by-five card tacked to the wall. "White male seeks woman 25-30. Must have blonde hair, enjoy watching wrestling, and love Chinese food."

"That leaves me out," Raven said with a pout. "Unless I change my hair to blonde again."

"Don't tell me that you like wrestling."

"Doesn't everyone?"

There was a knock at the door and then Dan pushed it open and poked his head in. His gaze moved over the room, landing momentarily on Raven with an appraising glance before locking with Ivy.

"Just checking to see if everything is all right. Did you want to go back to the apartment?" he asked.

Ivy could see that standing outside of a laundry room was not Dan's idea of the perfect assignment. She nodded and turned to pick up her basket, placing it on the washer where her clothes were now swooshing.

"I'll be right out."

"Wow, your husband's really protective, huh?" Raven's brows drew together.

"He's not my husband," Ivy said and then stopped. She probably shouldn't tell everyone she met that the FBI was protecting her. So, she just smiled and turned to go. "I'll be back soon."

"I'll be here," Raven said as she hopped back up on the top of the washer and began tapping the heels of her tennis shoes against the machine to a beat inside her head.

†††

Brenna slid off the washing machine. How was she going to get close to Ivy Winter when an FBI puppy dog was following her around all day? She went to the door and peered out. The hallway was clear in both directions. Of course, someone could come to collect his clothes at any moment and then where would she be? She had pretended those towels were hers when in fact someone had left them in the dryer. She wouldn't be caught dead washing her own clothes. But over the years she had learned to improvise when a situation called for it. She had been listening in on the radio frequency that Sinclair was using to communicate between Ivy's apartment and the FBI car parked out front when she heard the message that the bodyguard was needed. She listened at the open elevator doors until she saw they were headed to the laundry and then went down ahead of them.

Ivy's visit to the Laundromat was the first chance she'd had to observe her up close. She wasn't anything like Todd said she was. That didn't necessarily surprise her. She'd known what kind of man Todd was from the beginning: a womanizer who would use blatant lies and deception to get what he wanted. She had played him so easily – simply because she was better at it than he was. He hadn't seen that coming.

Brenna released a heavy sigh and returned to the bulletin board. With hands on her hips and her chin thrust forward, she looked over the remaining ads pinned to the cork. She wished she had brought her iPod. The sound of gurgling, swishing, and spinning was getting on her nerves.

The door pushed inward, and a young man breezed in. He looked old enough to be drafted but too young to drink. He was dressed in the mode of the day, baggy khakis, T-shirt, and a long-sleeved shirt with the tails hanging out. Brown hair hung limply to his shoulders, and he absently pushed it back behind his ears as he opened the lid of a dryer and checked the dampness of his clothes. He quickly shut the door and added another quarter before looking up and meeting Brenna's eyes.

"Hey," he said.

He seemed embarrassed at her noncommittal stare and turned quickly away. He opened the next dryer and repeated his earlier actions before straightening and heading for the door.

"Excuse me," Brenna called after him.

He turned back with a puzzled but still hopeful frown as though unsure why she would be addressing him after giving him the cold shoulder.

"You live on this floor?"

"No, I'm on two," he said, his tone wary.

Brenna gave him her warmest smile and watched him melt. It was so easy to topple them when they were young and naïve. She crossed the room to close the few feet of space between them.

"Do you live with a girlfriend?"

He really started to look all hot and flustered now. He shook his scraggly hair and grinned, showing a set of uneven teeth that protruded just a bit in front. She tried not to be distracted by his inadequacies. He was a man after all, and that's all that mattered.

"I moved in with my brother, but he got married last month and I've been looking for a roommate. The rent is kind of high for one guy."

"Really," she said. "I just happen to be in the market for a new place. My roommate and I don't get along very well. Would you consider letting me look at your apartment?" she asked, subtly placing a hand on his arm as she spoke.

He grinned again, a little too eagerly. He reminded her of *Dumb & Dumber*, the buck-toothed bumpkin befuddled by a beautiful woman.

"Sure! You want to come up right now?"

Brenna shook her head and pointed back at the washer. "I have to keep an eye on my clothes. But I could come up in – say an hour?"

"Great!" He turned to go and then spun back around with a flustered shake of his head. "Oh yeah, I forgot. I'm Nathan, and my apartment is 210."

Brenna ran a hand through her short spikes and nodded. "You look like a Nathan. I'm Raven. See you in an hour." Turning her back, she dismissed him from her mind.

When Nathan had disappeared down the hall and back up the elevator, Brenna reached into the garbage can at the end of the row of machines and pulled out the two-way radio she had hidden in there. She turned it on and listened, hoping to hear another exchange between Sinclair and the other agent, but there was only static.

✝✝✝

"How'd it go?" Samson pulled open the door before Ivy could knock. Apparently, he had been watching for her. Dan handed her off and turned to leave.

"Great! Didn't you know Laundromats are the number one place to meet men? That and the fresh fruit section of a grocery store. They love to squeeze those grapefruits," she said as she whipped past him with a small smile on her lips. He slowly closed the door and turned the dead bolt into place.

"So, how're the kids? Are they still sleeping?" she asked and plopped down on the couch. After what they'd been through today she didn't know if they'd be able to sleep.

Samson crossed the room and stood awkwardly beside the couch, his hands on his hips. "The kids are fine. I haven't heard a thing out of them since they went to bed." He scratched his chin and tried to appear nonchalant. "What men did you meet in the laundry room? Dan stayed with you the entire time, didn't he?"

Ivy pillowed her arms behind her head and grinned up at him. "If you get me a soda, I might tell you."

He shot her a dirty look before turning on his heel and striding to the refrigerator. He pulled out a can of diet cola and popped the top. "Your highness," he said, returning with the drink in hand.

Ivy couldn't help but laugh at his expression. She had to sit up to keep the soda from spilling down her shirt. "I'm just pulling your chain. There were no men. I did meet a young woman though. She seemed to have been born with absolutely no natural laundry abilities. Can you believe it? Some things just have to be learned."

Samson seemed relieved at the admission that there were no men in the laundry. He sat in the chair across from her, visibly relaxed from his previous stance. His hair was mussed from running his fingers through it, and there were dark lines under his eyes that were no doubt from lack of sleep since being assigned to her. Ivy felt a sliver of remorse for giving him a hard time, especially since he'd taken a bullet for her and was still recovering, but she still had no intention of backing down on her decision to go with him to California.

"Our flight leaves at 7:35 so you'll have to make plans with your sister to watch the kids while we're gone. Will that be a problem?" he asked.

His announcement took her by complete surprise, and she choked on a mouthful of soda, beginning a coughing jag that didn't want to let up. Samson jumped up and tried to help by pounding on her back, but that only made her drop the can which was still half full. It landed on the beige carpet, and a puddle of fizzy brown liquid pooled out. He ran to the kitchen and grabbed a towel, while she stood there trying to catch her breath. He returned, picked up the can and soaked up the mess as she moved out of the way.

"Are you all right?" he asked, looking up from his cleaning job.

"Yeah, sure."

Ivy's coughing subsided, and she stepped out on the deck to get a breath of fresh air. Darkness had settled around the pond, but there were still a few lights reflecting off the surface of the water. The moon glowed full in a cloudless sky, and Ivy was sure that tonight she could make out the holes in the cheese. She smiled and turned to find that Samson had followed her out.

"The temperature's dropped about twenty degrees since the sun went down," he said. "Feels good."

"Yes, it does," she agreed. The deck was small but felt even smaller with Samson beside her. His close proximity heightened her sense of awareness, and she caught the scent of spearmint mingled with the light intoxicating smell of his aftershave.

"Thank you for agreeing to take me with you tomorrow," she said. "I promise not to be any trouble. I just need to be there – to see an end to all of this."

She turned back toward the darkness and rested her hands on the wrought iron banister. The cold metal felt good to the touch.

Samson moved beside her. "I don't want you to get your hopes up, Ivy. We're just checking the box on the off-hand chance that he couldn't think of anywhere better to hide the disc. I doubt it will be there. It 's too obvious. He would have known that we'd think of it."

"But you didn't," she reminded him. "Perhaps he knew it would be so obvious that you wouldn't think of it."

"That's funny," he said. "I hope you know that the FBI takes a very dim view of teasing their agents."

Ivy laughed lightly. "Well if you can't take teasing, you shouldn't be in the profession. There's a lot to tease about."

He turned his head, and she smiled up at him, caught up in the feeling of camaraderie. The smile in his eyes dimmed as he lowered his lips to hers. Later she would believe it was the work of the full moon but in the moment, it felt as though his eyes were magnets drawing her closer. She met his kiss with lips, soft and willing. He drew her close, and her arms moved up around his neck where her fingers found their way into the hair at the top of his collar.

The telephone rang, and they drew apart, staring at each other as though unsure of what just happened. Samson pulled back the curtain and disappeared inside to answer the phone while Ivy stood shivering in the moonlight. It suddenly felt much colder without his arms around her.

He was still on the phone when she got the courage to go inside. She glanced his way, but he was standing at the sink, speaking in a low voice.

"I'm going down to put the clothes in the dryer," she called out. She snatched up her keys and nearly ran out the door.

She knew Samson would probably be mad that she didn't wait for Dan, but she had to get out of there and be by herself for a while. Everything was complicated now. A kiss could make or break a good friendship, and she wasn't sure she wanted anything more than friendship at this point. Her life was full of problems as it was.

She pushed through the laundry room door expecting to see Raven, but she was gone. She must have finished her washing and left for the night, despite what she'd said about watching her things. Ivy hoped her clothes were still where she'd left them.

She pulled them out of the washer and placed them in the dryer, all the while thinking of the way his mouth felt on hers. She couldn't get it out of her mind. Was it wrong to feel this way so soon? She added quarters and pushed the ON button, then leaned weakly against the machine with her eyes closed and her hands pressed against her temples.

"You're back," Raven said as she breezed through the door, startling Ivy out of her reverie and nearly giving her a heart attack.

Ivy tried to smile a welcome, but she really didn't feel like being chatty at the moment. She waited while Raven switched her towels to a dryer and hoped she would go away. But there didn't seem to be any chance of that.

"I didn't see your boyfriend outside. Did he decide to let you come by yourself this time?" she asked.

Ivy detected more than idle curiosity in her voice. "He's around somewhere," she said off-hand. Deciding she'd rather be back in the apartment with

Samson than here making small talk with a stranger, she turned to go.

"Are you leaving already? I was hoping you'd stay and keep me company while the clothes dry. I'll buy you a soda," Raven offered, nodding at the pop machine in the corner of the room.

Ivy hesitated, not wanting to appear rude to a neighbor. She shrugged and reluctantly set down the basket. "Sure. Why not?"

Raven put a crisp dollar bill into the machine. She looked back over her shoulder, a hand poised over the buttons.

"What do you want?"

"Diet cola."

"Sounds good to me." Raven purchased two and handed one to Ivy. "So, what do you do for a living? You wouldn't happen to be in the music business would you, because our band really needs a new manager?" Raven pulled a cigarette from the pocket of her T-shirt and glanced around the room with a wistful expression. "S'pose this is a no smoking area," she said darkly.

Ivy pointed at the big red and white sign above the dryers. "You could say that. Those things will kill you, you know."

"I've heard. I'm actually trying to quit. I just carry one with me in case of emergency."

"Doing laundry is that bad, huh?" Ivy took a swallow of cola and smiled.

"No, it's not that. It's just been one of those days."

"I know what you mean. I've had one of those weeks. I just hope the end is in sight."

"Did you have problems moving in? Every time I go to a new place, something goes wrong."

Ivy shook her head. "Moving went fine. It 's everything else that's screwed up. It's a long story not worth repeating. You wouldn't believe me if I told you." She watched the clothes through the little window as they tumbled around in the dryer and noticed that one of Samson's shirts had gotten mixed in with her things.

"Sounds intriguing," Raven prompted. She set her can of Coke down and waited for Ivy to continue.

The door opened, and Ivy turned to see Samson enter. His eyes weren't a warm brown anymore but rather dark and stormy. He crossed the room in three strides, his gaze piercing. "Need some help carrying the basket?"

It didn't take a genius to see that he was angry. Ivy felt her own temper rise at his attitude. She wasn't his prisoner, and she wouldn't be treated like one. She ignored him and stubbornly pulled still damp clothes from the dryer, folding each one slowly and carefully as she did so.

"Hi." Raven said.

Samson's abrupt reply was anything but. "Look, we can do this in the apartment," he said firmly. He took the folded piles and placed them in the basket.

Rather than create a bigger scene, she gave in and set the rest of the clothes on top of the basket. When she looked up, she saw Raven's eyes full of questions. But she didn't have any answers for her. Samson carried the basket to the door and she followed. She looked back and shot Raven an apologetic smile. "See you around the building. Good luck with the band."

"Thanks." Raven said, her eyes wide with interest as Samson hurried Ivy out of the laundry room.

Once the door closed and they were out of Raven's hearing, Ivy sent Samson a scathing look. "Who do you think you are? You can't come and tell me what to do. I am not your prisoner. Did you really think I was in danger in the laundry room, talking to a neighbor? So, you left my children alone to fend for themselves?"

Samson waited to respond until they were safely inside the elevator, heading for the third floor. "Dan is waiting in the apartment. I wouldn't leave the kids alone even for a few minutes," he said in a calm voice that belied the stormy look in his eyes.

Ivy felt her anger drain slowly away. Samson was trying to protect them and keep them safe, and she was acting like a spoiled child. She knew her reaction had more to do with the kiss they'd shared than it did with his coming to take her back to the apartment. She dropped her gaze and stared at the closed metal doors reflecting them as two shadowy figures.

Back in the apartment, she checked on the kids while Samson sent Dan home for the night. She could hear him moving quietly around, checking the security system, getting a drink, and fixing his bed on the couch.

When she came down the hall he was at the window looking out into the dark night. All the lights were off in the living room and kitchen except for the small nightlight above the stove.

She wore a comfy, old flannel robe that used to belong to Todd. It fell well below her knees and belted at the waist. Her hair, just brushed, fell soft and shining around her shoulders. Her bare feet made no sound on the thick carpet, but he turned when she approached as though he had a sixth sense.

She stood before him with her hands in the pockets of the over-sized robe and tried to smile as she met his eyes across the few feet that separated them. The small space seemed much farther than it had earlier in the evening. There was no anger in his eyes now, but neither was there warmth. He was holding himself aloof again as though she were only an assignment. She dropped her gaze and drew a heavy sigh, feeling that something special had been taken from her. Then she squared her shoulders and met his eyes.

"I want to apologize, Samson. I shouldn't have left the apartment without Dan. It won't happen again. I just wanted to say that before I turn in for the night." Her voice grew wistful. "My mom always said you should never go to bed angry." She didn't wait for a response but quickly escaped to the safety of her room at the end of the hall and shut the door.

{10}

They were on their way to the airport early the next morning. They left Timmons in charge of the kids until Holly could come and pick them up. Samson sat up front with Agent Bob Davenport, who'd been assigned to drive them. The men made small talk while Ivy slumped against the window in the back with her eyes closed. At the airport Bob pulled up to the curb in front of their airline drop off.

Samson had already pulled the two overnight bags from the trunk before Ivy stepped out onto the sidewalk with her purse slung over her shoulder. She straightened the collar of the yellow polo shirt she wore beneath a navy-blue blazer. She looked tired as though she'd slept little the night before. The morning sun brought out copper highlights in her hair, and he remembered the feel of it beneath his hands when he kissed her. He pushed the memory away and headed into the airport.

After going through security, they hurried through the terminal toward the gate where they would board. Eppley Airfield was busy this morning with people scurrying from one place to the next, some shopping for reading material or snacks, others just killing time until a boarding call. It was a small airport compared to most. People were a little more laid back here, not worried about missing their flights due to crowds or getting lost somewhere in a maze of subways.

Ivy tried to keep up with his long stride but finally fell behind. He glanced back and saw that she had stopped to help a little boy who was lost. A moment later a young woman with bright red hair, wearing a tank top and shorts, came running up and hugged the little boy fiercely.

"I told you to stay by me, Aiden!" she exclaimed in a terrified voice. "Thank you, ma'am. I appreciate your looking after him."

Ivy nodded. "No problem. I have kids too," she said as though that explained it all.

Samson waited for her to catch up, and they headed off again. He glanced at her from time to time as they walked down the long terminal, people passing on every side. She was quiet, keeping her thoughts to herself today.

They arrived at the gate with time to spare and checked in. The flight attendant allowed them to be seated first after Samson showed them his credentials. They boarded the plane, stowed the bags in the overhead compartments, and took their seats.

Since no one else was seated near them yet, Samson tried to break the ice that had formed between them. "That was nice what you did for that little boy. Making him feel safe till his mother got there."

Ivy gave him a sidelong look and shook her head. "It wasn't done out of the goodness of my heart. It was a selfish act," she said, her voice soft.

Her eyes glistened, and she blinked the tears away. He covered her hand with his on the armrest between them. "How so?"

She drew a shaky breath. "You wouldn't understand."

"I could try."

"I guess I'm still making deals with God." Her voice was thoughtful as though she were trying to understand it herself. "If he'll take care of my kids while I'm gone, I'll take care of someone else's."

Her confession made him tighten his grip on her hand. Fear reverberated through her like a live wire. She stared out the window of the plane, her lips pressed tightly together.

"You don't have anything to worry about. There will be agents watching the house around the clock. The kids will be fine, and we'll be back in time to tuck them into bed," he promised. She pulled her hand away and bent to retrieve a tissue from her purse.

Samson watched as flight attendants greeted passengers at the door, showing them to their seats if they needed help. Soon the plane was full, and they taxied out to the runway. Ivy had closed her eyes again and appeared to be sleeping. The jet lumbered down the runway, engines roaring, and against all odds the huge bird took flight and headed for California.

Ivy's head crept slowly down until it rested against his shoulder. She was breathing softly, and he was glad she could sleep since she seemed to need it so desperately. The feel of her cheek against his arm was reassuring somehow. She trusted him enough to fall asleep against him. Maybe someday she would have faith enough to trust God again and not just make deals with him as if he were a loan shark.

The rest of the flight was routine. They got a
bag of peanuts and a soft drink and then the line at the
bathroom lengthened. Ivy woke up about halfway
there and sat up to look around with the expression of
an owl blinking in the daylight. She rubbed her hands
over her face and leaned back, stretching her cramped
legs out as far as they would go. They wouldn't go far
since they were flying coach. Captain Herndon said it
was a waste of taxpayer money to fly first class and
they would get there just as quickly in economy.
Samson shot her a commiserating smile. He gingerly
adjusted his seating position. His side had been
aching for the last hour or so, but he hadn't wanted to
wake her by moving.

"Was I leaning on your stitches?" she asked,
placing her hand lightly on his arm. "I'm sorry. You
should have pushed me over."

"Don't worry about it. You were tired. You
needed the rest. It didn't really bother me. In fact, it
was nice," he admitted.

She blushed, and he couldn't help thinking how
beautiful she looked with color in her cheeks and her
green eyes heavy lidded from sleep. He wanted to
kiss her again, but this wasn't the time or place.
Besides, he was jumping ahead of God's plan again.
So far nothing had really changed except him. He had
become personally attached to a woman he was
supposed to be protecting. Taking her with him to
California was probably a big mistake. He was going
to have to work very hard to keep things strictly
professional.

†††

Brenna stretched beneath the blankets and
slowly rolled to her side to peer at the lighted dial of

the little clock radio beside the bed. It glared the time in neon red digits. She blinked and pulled the blankets down to her waist, looked slowly around. The room was windowless, completely dark except for a strip of light coming from the crack at the bottom of the closed door. She sat up and planted her feet on carpeted floor. Nothing looked remotely familiar except for the small backpack she'd brought with her the night before. It lay on the table by the clock. She stood up and looked down. She'd apparently slept in her panties and bra. Where were her clothes?

Someone turned up a stereo in the next room and rap music blared through the thin walls. She grimaced at the beginnings of a migraine coming on.

She opened the door and peered out. The room facing hers was a bathroom, and it was unoccupied, so she ducked inside. She looked around the small space and decided it could probably be considered a serious health hazard. There were dirty clothes piled in the corner, and the vanity was cluttered with a razor and shaving cream, shampoo, a dirty washcloth, a box of bandages, and a well-used toothbrush. Whoever lived here was a slob. The bathroom fixtures looked as though they'd never had contact with a bottle of cleanser. She splashed water on her face and looked up into a grime-streaked mirror. Unable to find a clean towel, she dried her face on a robe that hung from the back of the door and wrinkled her nose at the musty smell.

She cautiously opened the door and started down the hall when she remembered her state of undress. Her clothes must be here somewhere. She ducked back in the bedroom, flipped the light switch, and searched the floor. She finally came up with her black shorts and T-shirt under the blankets at the end of the bed. She pulled them on and checked the

Barbara Ellen Brink

mirror above the small dresser. She was a mess. Her hair stuck out in some places and was flattened down in others. Mascara was smeared beneath her eyes giving her that nice zombie look. To make matters worse, one of her diamond stud earrings was missing.

She turned and began searching the bed again, looking under the pillows and blankets. Just as she came across it, there was a knock on the door.

"You up in there?" a male voice called through the crack. It sounded familiar, but she couldn't place it. In fact, she couldn't remember much of anything from the night before after leaving the laundry room.

"Raven?"

She pulled open the door and came face to face with the eager, young, buck-toothed male. He grinned at her. She leaned against the wall for support, her head pounding now.

"You feel any better this morning?" he asked.

It all came back to her. The night before she came here to con a place to stay so she could keep an eye on Ivy Winter. In the process she had drunk a bottle of wine with this kid and fell asleep. Apparently, he had put her to bed himself. She remembered what she'd been wearing and raised her eyebrows, wondering just how helpful he had been.

"I'll live. Do you happen to have any Ibuprofen in there somewhere?" she asked pointing toward the bathroom.

"Sorry. I might have some aspirin, though." He went in and started rummaging through drawers and cupboards, his long hair falling down around his face.

She decided not to wait and see. While the coast was clear, she snatched up her bag and made a beeline for the door, quietly letting herself out. She needed to get herself in order and then contact Ivy.

She had to find that disc before Mr. Anderson got tired of waiting.

††††

An hour later, dressed in a yellow and orange flowered cotton top and a pair of matching Capri's, Brenna looked like an ad for the softer side of Sears. She ran a hand through her hair, waiting outside the door of Ivy's apartment. Just when she'd decided to knock and see if anyone was home before she could pick the lock, she heard the elevator doors open and footsteps approaching.

"Can I help you?" asked a woman, stopping a few feet away.

Brenna turned and met the gaze of a younger version of Ivy. She was blonder than Ivy but with the same widow's peak, and her eyes were blue rather than green.

"I was looking for Ivy. I'm a neighbor." She gestured vaguely down the hallway. "Do you know where she might be?" She asked and smiled brightly.

The woman stared at her for a moment as though she didn't know what to think about Ivy having a visitor. Finally, she held out her hand. "I'm sorry. I'm Holly, Ivy's sister. You surprised me. She just moved in. I didn't realize she'd met anyone yet."

"That's all right." Brenna shook her hand. "I haven't lived here very long either."

Holly moved toward the door, and Brenna stepped back out of the way. "She went out of town. She should be back tomorrow. I'll tell her you stopped by." She paused with her hand on the knob. "What was your name?"

"That's right! I completely forgot she was leaving this morning." Brenna shook her head and watched Ivy's sister fall, hook, line, and sinker.

"She told you she was flying to California?" she asked, eyes narrowed warily.

"Yeah. We were talking about where we used to live. I'm from Montana, and she said she was from California and that she was flying there in the morning. I guess I spaced it off. I was going to ask her if she wanted to come over for lunch. I've got lasagna in the oven. Better go take it out." She gave a quick wave of her hand and headed back toward the elevators. She heard the woman knock on the door behind her and the thump of a deadbolt sliding open. Brenna could feel Holly watching, making sure she left. Some people were just so paranoid. She didn't dare turn around to see who opened the door. She got into the elevator and rode down to the ground floor. She had to get on a plane to California before Ace Anderson realized that she'd lost Ivy.

She pushed through the front doors and hurried down the sidewalk to where her convertible was parked in the lot. She pulled the key fob from her pocket and unlocked the doors before she felt the presence of Mr. Anderson's shadow.

She turned around. Sure enough, Lionel stood a few feet behind her, watching. The man gave her the creeps. He was short and wiry with dark hair combed straight back. He must have used gel or something because Brenna had never seen it move, even on a windy day. His eyes were nearly black and held no warmth, although she had seen a spark of enjoyment when his job entailed violence. He worked solely for Mr. Anderson and was always close by his side. Which meant his boss probably wasn't far behind.

Raven looked for the limo but didn't see it – yet. Her gaze came back to Lionel. Did they already know about Ivy's trip to California? If so, would she soon be expendable, as Todd had been? If Ivy retrieved the disc from wherever Todd hid it, then they would need to get it from her before she handed it over to the FBI.

"Hey, Lionel. What's up?"

He smiled, revealing the gap between his front teeth. He had the crooked smile of a stroke victim where only the left side of his face moved. He clinched and unclenched his hands at his sides as though contemplating the feel of them around her neck. "Mr. Anderson wants to see you, Ms. Blackman," he said in his raspy voice that barely rose above a whisper. The rumor was that he drank Drano when he was a boy. She didn't know if it was true, but it added to the nasty mystique surrounding him.

"I'm on my way to the airport, Lionel. Tell him I'll call when I get there." Raven opened the door of her car and slipped inside.

He moved forward and grasped the door, keeping her from shutting it in his face. She turned the key in the ignition instead. The motor revved up, and she gave him a cold hard stare.

"Does Mr. Anderson want me to lose Ivy Winter? She's on her way to California, and that's where I plan to be if you will just shut my door," she ground out between clenched teeth.

Lionel stared back at her for several seconds and then abruptly slammed the door and walked away. Raven watched him in her rear-view mirror. He strode purposefully toward a dark brown Plymouth with rust working its way up the sides. He got in and sped off before she had time to back up and take her own route to the airport.

What was that all about? He hadn't known Ivy left for California. That meant Mr. Anderson didn't know yet. She still had a chance to retrieve the disc and finish the job before they decided she wasn't worth the hundred grand they promised.

Ivy had a head start but not a big one. She could catch up. It was a good thing she kept a bag of extra clothes and necessary items in the trunk of her car because she didn't have time to stop at the motel to retrieve anything. She flew down the highway, her fingers crossed that she would get a seat on the same flight as Ivy Winter. Staying one step ahead of Mr. Anderson and his little henchman was the only way to survive.

✝✝✝

Samson drove the little, rented Mazda straight from the airport to the First National Bank and Trust of Glendale, a suburb of Los Angeles. It was eleven-thirty in the afternoon here. They had gained two hours traveling west. The streets were bustling with business suits going to and from lunch. A parking space finally opened up after they drove around the block three times.

They stepped out onto the curb and looked around. The sun beat down hot on city sidewalks, and Ivy wished she had worn something lighter. She waited for Samson to lock the doors and put coins in the meter. Then they crossed the street and went into the bank.

The air-conditioned building felt like an icebox after the heat outdoors. Their footsteps on the marble floor echoed against vaulted ceilings. Ivy glanced up as they crossed the open traffic area. Surveillance cameras monitored every corner of the bank. Two burly guards were stationed at the big, double-glass front doors and another guard stood outside the hallway that led into the vault. She had been with Todd when he opened their account and rented the box, but she hadn't been back since. Todd had always handed her cash when she needed it, and she never had to deal with banking matters. Now she wondered why she never questioned that.

Samson headed toward a group of desks strategically placed across the bank from the tellers. Carpeting in this area evoked a hushed *important banking business going on* feeling. He stopped at the first desk. A young, black man in a double-breasted suit and red silk tie leaned back in a leather desk chair talking on the telephone. He held up one finger to acknowledge he would be right with them. Quickly ending the conversation, he nodded toward two chairs facing his desk.

"Please, have a seat. I'm Nate Johnson. How can I be of service?"

Samson waited for Ivy to initiate the conversation since it was her box they needed access to. There was no point in getting into the details of the case with this man unless their initial search proved fruitless.

She proffered her hand across the width of the desk. "Ivy Winter, and this is my friend Samson Sinclair."

"What can I do for you, Ms. Winter?" he asked, as he sat forward in his swivel chair, placed his elbows on the desk, and steepled his fingers beneath his chin.

Ivy flashed him a quick smile and drew her key from the pocket of her jacket, holding it up for him see. "We need to get into my safe-deposit box," she said.

He led them through the bank toward the vault. The guard nodded as they passed by.

"How are you, Bob?" Mr. Johnson greeted the elderly man in uniform.

The process of unlocking the safe-deposit box from the wall with the bank's key and her key didn't take long, and then he left them alone to look through the contents privately.

Ivy turned the key in the lock and slowly lifted the metal lid. There was a brown manila envelope that contained Caleb and Riley's birth certificates. She set that aside and picked up a white envelope with her name written on the front in Todd's handwriting.

"I don't remember putting this in here," she said. She turned it over in her hands.

Samson lifted the remaining item in the box. A small, black, felt pouch. He pulled open the string at the top and poured a few dozen gold coins into his palm. They were about the size of a thin nickel and were a strange currency he wasn't familiar with. A folded paper fell out last. He opened it and gave a low whistle.

"Well, there's no disc here, but you have a nice stash for a rainy day. It says here that he bought most of these coins about seven years ago, estimated value was fifteen thousand dollars. With the price of gold now I'd say you've got a good sixty thousand dollars right here. Was Todd a serious collector?"

Ivy shook her head, still clasping the envelope in her hand. She didn't want to read it in front of Samson. If Todd wrote something for her before he left, it would probably be hurtful. She folded it in half and stuffed it in the pocket of her jacket to be read later when she was alone.

"No, Todd bought a few at a time until he had what he called, an emergency fund. In case everything in America collapses – the banks, stock market, etc. He said everything would lose its value but gold. He liked to think that he would be ready in any scenario," she said. She sighed and picked up the remaining papers, stuffing them all inside the brown manila envelope. Her marriage certificate poked its head out of the stack, and she slowly slid it from the rest. She read the words in black typeset and the two signatures at the bottom. It was a contract of permanency that nothing but death was supposed to break. Which is what had happened in the end.

Samson handed Ivy the bag of coins, and she opened her purse and put them inside. It was quite heavy, and she thought wryly if someone tried to mug her, it would make a powerful weapon.

"I guess this was a wasted trip, huh?"

Samson shook his head. "No, not wasted. We needed to check it out just in case and besides, you had a chance to collect your things."

"I didn't even think about the bank when I left town."

Samson gave her a puzzled, sidelong look. "You didn't clear out your bank accounts?" he asked.

"I never wrote checks. Todd paid the bills. I used credit cards if there was something big that I needed, or Todd gave me cash for things like groceries and walking around money. I guess since I never dealt with the bank, I didn't think of the accounts as mine, although they were opened in both of our names."

He raised his brows. "Well, they're all yours now, and we should take care of it while we're here. Believe me, long distance relationships never work, especially banking."

They took the empty box back to Mr. Johnson, and he collected her key and asked if there was anything else he could do for them.

"Why, yes there is," Ivy said.

{1 1}

Ivy and Samson left the bank and walked across the street to their car. She wore a pleasantly surprised expression. When the teller placed a cashier's check for $117,423.56 in her hand and told her it was the total of the three different accounts at their bank, she started to laugh, thinking it was a joke. Then she looked up into the woman's face and realized she was quite serious. The money was really hers. There was no mistake. Todd had apparently been better at saving than she imagined.

Samson opened the car door for her and she slipped inside, still wearing a Cheshire grin that no amount of serious thoughts would wipe away. At the moment she didn't even regret that they hadn't found the disc tucked away in the safe-deposit box.

Samson pulled away from the curb and began to weave his way through traffic. He stopped at the corner to let pedestrians cross and then turned right and headed out toward the airport.

Glancing her way, he couldn't help but smile too. "If I didn't know better I'd think you swallowed a canary."

Ivy grinned. "I feel like I just won the lottery. I'm not a gambler, but I think I know what it feels like to win big." She couldn't keep a giggle from escaping, and then she shook her head. "I can't believe Todd had this amount of money just sitting in checking accounts. He always talked about investing everything."

She turned on the radio to an oldies channel and sang along. The old song was upbeat and lighthearted. It's what she felt right now – on top of the world.

"I'm happy for you and the kids. At least now you won't have to worry about making ends meet." He turned onto the freeway and melted into the traffic.

Had she heard a *but* in his voice? She turned to watch him. He was biting his bottom lip. She reached out and snapped off the radio when the DJ started going on about politics.

"But what?" she asked.

"Huh?"

"There was a but, in your voice, just now. Do you think Todd got this money illegally too? He worked hard at Monroe and got paid very well for what he did."

He raised his shoulders. "I never said any differently."

"Yes, but you were thinking it, weren't you?"

He kept his eyes on the road and let the silence speak for him.

She refused to believe that Todd would have ill-gotten gains tucked away innocently in the bank. She glared out the side window of the car and watched smoke stacks in the distance spewing a cloud of pollution into an already gray sky. She felt like a bright blue sky being overtaken by a rolling cloud of smog. It wasn't fair. Samson had ruined everything with his moralizing attitude.

"Just so you know," Samson said in an overly calm voice, "we have a tail." He glanced in the rearview mirror, put his blinker on and moved to take the next off ramp. Four lanes of traffic whizzed past on every side as he switched lanes and left the freeway.

Ivy tried to twist around to see if they were still being followed, but Samson placed his hand over hers.

"Don't turn around. We don't want them to know we spotted them."

She reached out to make sure the doors were locked when she noticed the neighborhood Samson was driving through. "Do you know what you're doing? This is not a safe part of the city. I thought we were going to the airport. Can't we lose them there?" she asked, glancing nervously around.

Many of the buildings in this part of town looked as though they were set for demolition. Every available inch of space, walls and windows, was covered in graffiti. The few open businesses had bars on the windows to prevent everything they owned from being stolen. A group of young men stood on a corner playing their boom box so loudly that it vibrated through the car when they drove past. Ivy could see the resentment in their eyes as they stared coldly back at them.

"You'd think they'd never seen anyone from Nebraska before," Samson said as he turned left at the next corner and accelerated.

Ivy laughed in spite of herself. She knew he was trying to lighten the mood, so she wouldn't be afraid, and she appreciated it, but things didn't seem to be getting better. She could see the car in her side mirror still tailing them, although the driver stayed far enough back to remain incognito.

Ivy slipped off her sunglasses and squinted at the car's reflection in the mirror. The driver appeared to be female, and unless there were midgets that couldn't be seen over the dashboard, she was alone.

"Are we going to get to the airport before our flight leaves? If we miss it, I won't be home in time to tuck the kids in bed like you promised," she said, starting to seriously worry about their predicament.

Samson sighed, and combed his fingers through his hair. "I can't believe you're going to hold me to that. I just helped you recover over a hundred thousand dollars that you didn't even know you had and how do you repay me? You want to hurry up and get home." His voice was teasing, but his eyes were all business when he glanced her way.

He stopped at a red light and looked slowly around. There were no other cars in sight. Their tail stayed far enough back that they still couldn't make out a face behind the wheel.

"Check your seatbelt, Ivy. We don't want to miss our flight," he said.

Suddenly she was thrown back against the seat as he gunned the car into the intersection and spun around, tires squealing. Ivy gasped and hung on for dear life. Had he gone completely crazy? He hit the gas again heading back the way they'd come, slammed on the brakes, and pulled directly into the path of the car following them. Brakes screeched madly, and the car came to a stop within inches of Ivy's door. Their tail was a woman. Ivy didn't have time to get a good look at the woman's face before she threw the car into reverse, spun around, tires smoking, and roared away down the street. Samson didn't try to follow. He slowly pulled back into his own lane and headed toward the freeway.

"I can't believe you just did that," Ivy said, once her heart got out of her throat. "Are you insane? We could have been killed!"

"Seatbelts save lives, haven't you heard?" He started to whistle *Oh Happy Day*, took the freeway on ramp and blended with traffic again.

Ivy glared at him. This was not the considerate Samson Sinclair she thought she knew. What was he thinking, putting them both in danger?

"Did you get a good look at the driver of the car?" he asked. "She seemed familiar."

Ivy shook her head, righteous anger adding bite to her words. "I was too afraid for my life to notice much more than the color of her hair. Red."

Samson was silent for a minute, and then he cleared his throat. "I'm sorry you were frightened. I needed to get a look at our tail and get the upper hand. I don't like being followed."

"Now you know how I feel, Mr. FBI. But I guess it worked. She tore away like a bat out of…oh, sorry." She grinned.

"Yeah, she did, didn't she?" He grinned back.

The exit for the airport came up sooner than they expected, and Ivy felt a little bit sad that their time alone was ending. She reached in her pocket, absently fingering the envelope Todd left her. She would read it after they got back home, when she was alone.

"Not going to share the letter with me?" Samson asked. He found a place to pull over out of traffic and put the car in park. He turned with his arm across the back of the seat, his fingers coming to rest just shy of her neck. His nearness sent a tingle down her spine even though he never touched her.

"I'm afraid to open it. Todd is gone, but I'm sure his words of rejection will still hurt. I heard them from him once – I don't know if I'm ready to read them in front of you."

Samson reached out and brushed his fingers softly along her cheek in a tender caress. She caught them and held them there for a moment, before reluctantly letting go.

"You are the most unconventional FBI agent," she said with a smile and shake of her head. She reached into her pocket and pulled out the folded envelope. The stiff paper crackled as she opened it and smoothed it out across her lap.

Ivy,

If you are reading this, it probably means that my plan to live forever failed. I know you're angry, but you can't hate me completely because I did leave you and the kids enough to get by. As you probably know by now, I also hid something certain people are looking for. It's a treasure that lies under the sea. Buried treasure is always so much fun to discover, don't you think? Good luck!

Todd

She finished reading and passed it to Samson who stared at the last line with a puzzled frown. Ivy leaned back and closed her eyes. How could Todd be so selfish that he chose to put his family in jeopardy even after he was gone? Or was this his way of making sure the disc was returned and she could clean up his mess for him? She rubbed slow circles into her temples with the pads of her fingers. When she opened her eyes, Samson was still staring at the letter.

"You have any idea what he's talking about?" he asked. He handed it back, pointing out the line about the sea. "Do you own a beach house?"

Ivy shook her head, an amused smile on her lips. "Not that I know of, but then I didn't know about the money in the bank either. Maybe I'm not the one to ask."

She folded the letter and pushed it back inside the envelope. It wasn't going in quite right and she pulled it out again to refold it. Along with the letter, a little stream of colored sand poured out onto her navy-blue slacks. She stared down, frowning, and then started to laugh. She poured the remaining granules into the palm of her hand and held them out for Samson to see.

"Have you ever seen green sand?" she asked.

He picked some up between his fingers and examined it closely, then lifted his brows, "You know something I don't know?"

"I don't own a cottage on a green sand beach, if that's what you mean. But I did own an aquarium of fish with green sand and blue and purple rocks. The only problem is – I gave it away."

†††

Brenna sat outside the pet store in a blue firebird that she'd conveniently borrowed and waited for Ivy and the FBI man to come back out. They had been in there for over fifteen minutes, and she was getting antsy.

Since they caught her following them, she had to switch vehicles immediately. It didn't take long to find an unlocked car she could hot-wire. Luckily, she'd already put a tag on their car while they were in the bank or she never would have found them again. She figured they were heading back to the airport, so she drove straight there. The closer she got, the stronger the signal. She passed them parked along the road. She waited a few minutes and when they turned around and headed away from the airport again, she followed, although this time she stayed well back. She also threw away the red wig and pulled a baseball cap over her dark hair instead.

She wanted to go see what they were up to, but she couldn't chance that they would recognize her. It was doubtful they were looking for the disc at a pet store, but they had been in there for quite some time. She glanced at her watch. Maybe they had decided to buy the kids a turtle or something. Kids always wanted presents when their parents came back from a trip.

She didn't have any kids of her own, but she was an expert on airport *guilt* gifts. Her father traveled for business most of her growing up years. He was gone so much that when he was home it seemed like he was just visiting. Whenever he came home she would receive something. Sometimes it was a snow globe, a music box, or a pretty necklace, but it was never what she really wanted. She just wanted a father who spent time with her because he loved her. Instead he spent his time working and left her to grow up on her own.

She pulled her thoughts back from the past and glanced up as the door of the store opened. Ivy and the FBI agent headed toward their rental car, deep in conversation. Brenna opened her window, hoping to hear something when they passed.

"We're just going to have to get a warrant," the agent said.

Brenna ducked her head as though she was looking for something on the floor of the car, then hurriedly rolled up the window and prepared to follow them. Wherever they were heading had something to do with the disc. Why did they need a warrant?

Their car pulled out and turned left across traffic. They stopped at the light and then turned right, blending into the busy street. Brenna stayed far enough behind that they wouldn't know she was there but kept her eye on the blip on the screen of her handheld tracking device. She wouldn't lose them again. She knew exactly where they were and which way they were headed.

She pulled the cap off her head and ran a hand through her hair, flipped on the air-conditioning and waited for the cool air to fill the small space. She liked California, but the summer heat was getting to her.

She preferred places that had a change of seasons. Skiing in Colorado was her idea of a vacation. Not where all the ritzy people stayed but at a secluded, little known spot where she could enjoy the weather in solitude. After a day of skiing she'd sit by the fire listening to mellow tunes coming from a nearly empty bar and feel as close to happy and content as she ever did.

The last time she stayed there she met Thomas. He said he came to be alone as well. Funny thing…they ended up together instead. For three solid days they spent every waking moment together.

She could just be Brenna Blackman with him. She didn't have to pretend to be someone she wasn't or play games. But she knew it could never last because of what she was. If he knew what she did for a living, what her past included, he wouldn't look at her the same way again. She couldn't bear that. So, she left without saying goodbye; no regrets. She still had the memory of their time together, and sometimes like now, she brought it out and daydreamed about what might have been. If she were still the innocent, young Brenna Blackman she left behind so long ago.

Was it really possible that God could forgive her? She longed for forgiveness and a clean slate if only to be the kind of woman Thomas deserved. But she would never be worthy. She had gotten herself into a mess and right now there was no way out. She had to finish this job, or her life wouldn't be worth spit. Afterward she would worry about God and whether or not he thought she was worth saving.

The blip on the screen stopped. She pulled into a parking space and watched them get out of their car and jaywalk to a tall office building across the street. She smiled. The Federal Bureau of Investigations.

"Well, well, well. I guess you found something," she said softly.

What did the pet store have to do with the disc? If they got a warrant, then they would return to the store and the disc would be out of her reach. She needed to beat them to it. Of course, she didn't have to play by the rules like they did. Which made the game much easier.

She pulled away from the curb and made a U-turn on her way to visit The Pet Emporium.

✝✝✝

Ivy followed Samson into the crowded elevator. The tight space made her think of cattle herded into a tiny corral. Luckily, they were first off, and she breathed a breath of fresh air. She followed Samson down the hall to a large reception area. He stepped up to the receptionist's desk and pulled out his credentials.

"We need to see Agent Reynolds. Is he available?"

The woman wore a jade green skirt and jacket offset with a print blouse that tied into a huge bow beneath a double chin. She peered at them over reading glasses perched on the end of her nose. Calmly she reached up and pulled them off, letting them hang loose on a silver chain around her neck.

"I'll check and see," she said in a voice husky enough to put Kathleen Turner to shame. She picked up the phone and turned away to speak to the man in question. After a moment of muttered conversation, she faced them again and smiled stiffly.

"He's available now." She indicated the hallway to their left. "Second door on the right."

"Thank you, Ma'am," Samson said.

Ivy hesitated, and Samson turned back. He gently took her arm and pulled her aside, out of the woman's hearing. "Do you want to stay out here while I talk to him?"

Her experience with the FBI in Los Angeles had been a nightmare. They'd treated her as though she were guilty by association. Reynolds, the agent in charge of the case, set the tone of the investigation. Ivy had good reason to be uncomfortable around him. "Do you mind? I doubt he would want me in there anyway," she said.

Samson gently squeezed her arm and smiled. "He's just a hard case. I'll take care of it." He pointed to a cart laden with a pot of coffee and a stack of Styrofoam cups. "Why don't you get some coffee and relax? It shouldn't take long."

†††

Reynolds sat behind a cheap, metal desk speaking on the phone. He was a large man, obviously with a large appetite. The garbage can beside the desk was full to overflowing with candy wrappers and fast food bags. He raised his brows when Samson hesitated in the doorway, then waved him in and abruptly hung up without saying goodbye.

"You must be Sinclair, from the big town of Omaha. Where's the broad? From Maude's description it sounds like you have Winter's wife with you. Is that right?" he asked.

Samson ignored the man's smirk. "I need a search warrant for the Pet Emporium. We have reason to believe the disc is in the Winter's aquarium. The aquarium was sold back to the store, and in turn sold to another customer. We need that sales information. Can you get the warrant or not?"

"So, after all our searching for that disc, she knew where it was all the time," he accused. He drummed fingers on the desktop, anger brewing in hooded eyes.

Samson rose up from the flimsy folding chair and placed the palms of his hands on the big man's desk, glaring back at him. "You don't know what you're talking about. Mrs. Winter has been nothing but helpful in our investigation. We need a warrant – now. If you don't want to get it, we can always call on someone else. That disc is still out there. If it falls into the wrong hands…" He let the thought hang. "Do you want to be responsible for losing it again?"

Reynolds pushed himself up from behind the desk with a grunt. He glared defiantly, then snatched up the phone and buzzed Maude.

"Get me Judge Kraft on the horn," he bellowed.

The call came through from the judge and Reynold's smug expression returned. "We got it. The judge said he'd send it over by courier, then we can be on our way."

"I don't think so. You dropped the ball back when Ivy Winter was still living here. You could have gotten into their safe-deposit box at any time, but you didn't even check to see if they had one. Now I'm in charge, and I don't think it would be a very good idea for you to come along. Mrs. Winter believes you think she's guilty of something. The right lawyer might consider that harassment. The bureau doesn't need that kind of trouble." He stepped into the hall but paused and turned back. "Thanks so much for your cooperation. Have a nice day, Reynolds.

"That's *Special* Agent Reynolds to you!" he said, hands clenched at his sides.

Samson lifted his shoulders. "Whatever."

†††

Brenna pulled into the Pet Emporium's parking lot and shut off the engine. She reached across the seat and opened the duffel bag she had brought along. It had everything a girl could need: surveillance equipment, makeup, cash, fake ID's, and a short black skirt that would work well with the tube top and sheer blouse she was wearing.

She scooted out of her jeans and into the skirt, applied a fresh coat of lipstick and mascara, and slipped her feet into a pair of black, high-heeled sandals. That ought to do it.

The Pet Emporium was the largest pet food store she had ever seen or ever wanted to see. There were collars, toys, medicines, cleaning and bathing supplies, and of course every description of pet imaginable. She didn't even know the names of half these animals.

The store was busy with customers. A young couple debated the quality of a rubber mouse in one aisle and a woman was buying crickets for a reptile's dinner in another. Two kids stared into a large fish tank, their lips making those funny kissing motions, while their parents chose the perfect dietary needs for their little rat-sized dog they had with them on a leash.

A young man came down the aisle toward her as she stood gazing absently at a stack of kennels. Some were so large *she* could sleep in them comfortably. She'd definitely slept in worse places.

"Can I help you?"

She looked up and met his eyes. They were so blue they looked like sapphires. Tinted contact lenses. His hair was also an unnatural shade of blonde, the roots showing dark where it parted on the side. He looked about twenty, but his nametag said MANAGER.

"Hello, Bob," she read from his tag. "I'm Agent Samuels. I believe you have something for me." She quickly opened and shut her fake FBI badge.

"Come on then," he said with a sigh. "I was just getting ready to look up the records when I saw you come in. I thought you were a customer. The agents that were in here before said *they'd* be back for the address."

He led her to the back room where boxes of supplies stood ready to be unpacked and arranged in their designated aisles. Bob sat down at the computer terminal by the wall and clicked on the screen. A list of some kind came up. He turned his head and frowned.

"Oh yeah, where is it? My boss said I can't give you anything until I have it in my hand." He held out his hand, palm up.

"They didn't call?"

"I got a call about five minutes before you came in. Dude said they'd be here within the hour and to have the address available, so they didn't have to wait." He turned in his chair and eyed her curiously. "You have a warrant, don't you?

"Actually, I need the address right now. They'll show you the warrant when they get here. Time is very important at this point. You wouldn't want the bad guys to get away, would you?" she said. She stepped close and laid her hand on his shoulder, long nails digging in as she turned him back toward the screen.

"Now give me the address before I get upset," she whispered into his ear.

He turned beet red like a child who had been reprimanded at school and started typing furiously. An address came up on the screen.

"That's it. That's who we sold the aquarium to. As is – we didn't even have to change the water. They bought it the day it came in and we delivered."

"Great. You've been a really big help, Bob. Now make sure that information is printed out and ready when the *dudes* get here, ok?" She spun his chair back around, bent down and kissed him, leaving him with a bewildered, happy look on his face.

†††

Ivy and Samson hurried through the store, looking for the young manager they had talked to earlier. He was nowhere in sight, but a woman in pink spandex stopped them to ask where the hamsters were kept.

"Do I look like I work here?" Samson asked Ivy after the woman had gone on her way in search of small rodents.

"I don't know about that, but you do have that special something that's the mark of a good dog food salesman."

"There he is." He pointed down an aisle.

The manager was headed toward the registers at the front of the store. They intercepted him when he stopped to pick up a bottle of dog shampoo that had been knocked from a display.

When he saw them approaching he reached in his pocket and pulled out a folded piece of paper. "That was fast. Agent Samuels just left, and you're already here. I'm glad I printed it out right away. Here you go." He paused and drew his hand back a fraction. "You do have the warrant, don't you?"

Samson pulled the document from his pocket and held it out in exchange for the address.

"Who is Agent Samuels?" Ivy asked.

Manager Bob looked up from the warrant. "The woman you sent to make sure the address was printed out and ready to go. She said you didn't want to waste any time when you got here."

Samson felt his heart thud in his chest as he realized they weren't the only ones to get a hold of this address. He met Ivy's eyes and saw dread and confusion. How could anyone know they were getting a warrant for the Pet Emporium? Only Agent Reynolds had that information. "What did the agent look like?"

Bob's face fell. "You mean you don't know her? She said you sent her. I never would have showed her the address if –."

"What did she look like, Bob?" Samson asked again.

"She was hot – real hot, with short black hair and I think she was wearing a black skirt and maybe a red shirt...or was it pink? I'm not really sure. But she was a real babe."

Ivy had to run to catch up with Samson, already moving toward the door. "What now?" she called after him.

"She already has a head start. But we can call ahead and make sure these people don't hand anything over to her."

"Sorry dudes!" Bob called out from aisle four.

Ivy dialed the number on Samson's cell phone as he drove through traffic like a madman. The phone rang ten times before she gave up.

"They aren't picking up, and they don't have an answering machine." Ivy laid her head back and closed her eyes in frustration. "How can this woman be one step ahead of us? Unless she's..."

"Your husband's accomplice. She traveled under an alias: Brenna Ballard. Agent Samuels must be another of her aliases. That woman sure has a lot of tricks up her sleeve." He shook his head. "What I don't understand is how she knew we were getting a warrant."

"What about the redhead tailing us earlier? Must be the same woman. Somehow she followed us to the pet store even after you thought you lost her." She stared blindly as buildings flew past. Samson cut in and out of traffic in a mad rush to overtake their opponent. A simple plan to check out her safe-deposit box had morphed into a full-fledged chase scene like something out of a Hollywood movie. "First, she's blonde, then a redhead, and now apparently brunette. It's going to be a little hard to know what to look for."

"Watch for the street. I think we're getting close," he said. He switched lanes and passed a Volkswagen going five miles under the speed limit.

"There." Ivy pointed. "Turn left at this light."

Samson moved into the turn lane and stopped behind a blue Firebird when the light turned red. He drew an impatient sigh and tapped his fingers on the steering wheel in time with the blinker.

"Will you stop that please? You're making me crazy," Ivy muttered.

"Sorry." He stopped tapping but his left leg started jumping nervously. The light changed, and they took off again. The Firebird left them in the dust, apparently in a bigger hurry than they were.

"It should be the next block," Ivy said momentarily.

She watched the house numbers as Samson drove slowly down the block. The homes were new, predominately brick and stucco structures with long, winding drives laid out in brick to match the homes. Baby-sized orange and lemon trees dotted many yards as well as virgin beds of earth newly planted with flowers of every hue. Ivy was reminded of her own home up for sale not far from here.

"Isn't that the car we were behind at the light?" Samson asked. He slowed to a crawl and pulled over to the curb, waiting to see who got out.

The car was parked in the driveway of a large, white stucco home and partially concealed by a six-foot high windbreak that rose between neighbors.

"What's the house number?" he asked. He kept his eyes on the tail of the car.

"17563."

"That's the house we're looking for. It would be an awful big coincidence if that car turned out to be the owners just arrived home, don't you think?" He opened his door and got out.

"What are you doing?" Ivy quickly unbuckled her seatbelt and started to follow.

"Stay here." He pulled the gun from his holster, held it down by his side, and walked quickly toward the windbreak.

Ivy watched him go; fear inched down her spine like the tip of an icy finger. Her lips moved in a silent prayer for protection as he moved stealthily across the grass and around the end of the windbreak. Soon he was out of her sight. She waited for a minute or two, then opened her door and got out. It was too nerve-wracking to sit here not knowing what was happening. What if he were hurt or in trouble? She should be ready to help.

She closed the car door as quietly as she could and retraced his steps to the Firebird. The car was empty except for a black duffel bag on the front seat. She glanced furtively around, made sure the owner was nowhere in sight and then opened the door and unzipped the bag. It was filled with a strange assortment of things. Along with clothing were a set of handcuffs, a small laptop commuter, and a stack of phony ID's. On the top of the pile was an FBI badge. She picked it up and examined it. It looked real enough to her. She put it back and zipped up the bag, feeling almost guilty for looking through this woman's belongings, although under the circumstances she had every reason.

The bang of a door startled her. She looked up and caught a flash of red out of the corner of her eye. She turned toward the house and saw Samson running after the woman. The suspect fled across the neighbor's yard and through a newly planted flowerbed. Samson closed the space between them very quickly. The woman's tight skirt impeded her progress and was no match for Samson's long stride. An apricot colored poodle came bounding around the corner of the large brick home and joined in the chase, barking ferociously.

Ivy watched in amazement and with a touch of amusement as Samson caught the woman around the waist and pulled her to the ground. She lay there, unmoving, probably had the wind knocked out of her. He slowly pulled himself to his feet, holding a hand on his injured side, and stood over her, breathing heavily.

Ivy ran to Samson. "Are you all right?"

He nodded, his mouth grim.

She looked down at the woman who she believed was responsible for what happened to Todd. He may have stolen the information, but someone had put him up to it and that someone now lay at her feet. The woman hadn't moved since Samson landed on her but was still face down in the grass trying to catch her breath.

Samson reached down, took hold of her shoulder, and pushed her onto her back. Pale blue eyes stared up at them defiantly.

{12}

"Raven?" Ivy gasped, not quite believing her eyes. How could her new neighbor have anything to do with this?

"You know this woman?" Samson asked, frowning. Then his expression changed as realization dawned. "From the laundry room. I knew there was something familiar about you. It's the hair that threw me. You were blonde when you accompanied Winter at the airport."

He reached down and grabbed her wrist, yanking her to her feet. She had lost one high-heeled sandal in the sprint across the yard, so she kicked off the other one, and sank her bare toes into the thick grass.

"What's going on here?" an elderly man called out as he rounded the corner of the house, brandishing a baseball bat.

"It's all right, sir," Samson said. He pulled his badge out of his wallet. "I'm with the FBI."

"Is that your dog, mister?" Raven asked, her voice cross. "Because if it is, I expect to be reimbursed for the fifty-dollar shoe he's chewing up."

Ivy looked back and saw that the poodle had stopped in his pursuit and was eagerly tearing Raven's high-heeled sandal to smithereens.

"That's too bad. But you were trespassing on his territory," she said, and smiled.

"Who's going to pay for the damage to my flowerbeds?" the man asked, pointing to the section of trampled plants they had just cut a path through.

Samson reached back in his wallet and pulled out a business card. He handed it to the irate man. "Just send the bill here. I'll make sure it's taken care of. We're sorry for the trouble." He turned and took Raven by the elbow and led her back to the car.

"Well, *Agent Samuels*. I wasn't expecting to run into you here. I forgot to pack my handcuffs," he said amiably. "So, what are we going to do with you?"

"You could always let me go," she said batting her eyes at him.

"I have a better idea," Ivy said. She ran to the Firebird and pulled out the duffel bag, then walked calmly back, a smile of victory on her face. "You could use these," she said, twirling Raven's handcuffs on one finger.

Samson secured Raven's wrists behind her back and put her in the backseat. Ivy stood patiently, still gripping the handle of the bag.

"How did you know those were in the car? I thought I told you to stay put."

Ivy handed him the bag and climbed into the front seat. She heard him chuckle as he walked around the front of the car. He climbed in the driver's seat and set the bag between them. He rifled through it and pulled out the stack of ID's she had glanced at earlier. His eyebrows went up a notch when he flipped open the FBI badge, but he set it aside and dug around some more. He held up an electronic device with a small screen that looked similar to the handheld games kids play. He pushed a button, and the screen lit up. A little light blinked steadily accompanied by an intermittent beep.

"Now I know how you beat us to the Pet Emporium. You've been following us ever since the airport," Samson said, glancing back over his shoulder at their reluctant passenger.

"Is that some sort of tracking system?" asked Ivy. She reached out to take it in her hand.

Samson pointed to the blip blinking on the small screen. "That's us. We seem to have a bug on board. And I don't mean our guest here," he said.

"So, what are you going to do with me – bore me to death?" Raven tossed her head and slouched back in the seat.

"Good question. I still need to get in that house and find the disc," he said, speaking to Ivy. "No one's home right now, and I can't break in like she was going to do."

"Guess you should have waited another couple minutes. I would have done the breaking and entering for you. Made your job a whole lot easier."

Samson ignored Raven's taunt and started the car.

"You could stay here and wait for the owners to show up and I could drive miss congeniality back to Agent Reynolds," Ivy offered. "He's probably feeling left out since he wasn't invited. I bet he'd love to have custody of this one." She knew Samson would never go along with it, but she would enjoy a few unsupervised moments alone with the woman, exacting revenge for being played a fool.

"She's a criminal, Ivy, and you are not a member of law enforcement. If something should happen to you, I'd be responsible."

"And so you should, Mr. Lawman," Raven spoke up. "But I doubt your girlfriend's plans involve relinquishing me to that jerk Reynolds. She wants to get her pound of flesh first. Isn't that right, Ivy? You don't agree with the preacher's theory of forgiveness he talked about in church Sunday, do you?" When they both looked back surprised, she shrugged. "I was following you, but you disappeared on me and I got stuck sitting beside Mary Poppins and her brood of small children."

"Forgiveness and punishment aren't necessarily related. All things can be forgiven, but all things can't go unpunished," Samson said, lifting her stack of ID's.

"I don't think all things can be forgiven either," Ivy said, her voice barely above a whisper. She stared down at the wedding band she wore. She didn't know what it symbolized anymore. A circle of lies? Certainly not trust and fidelity. She'd kept wearing it because it was easier than admitting defeat.

Samson reached out and touched her arm. "I know it's hard, nearly impossible when we've been hurt by someone, but we don't have to do it in our own strength. With God all things are possible. If he can forgive us, it's only right that we forgive others."

"That's a sweet concept," said Raven, "but when you actually have to do it, it's a different story, isn't it Ivy?"

Ivy turned to face Raven, anger seething to the surface. "Don't call me Ivy! You don't know me, and you're certainly not my friend. As to my pound of flesh – I don't need it. The law can have mine too.

You'll be in prison for a very long time. You know what they do to traitors in prison?"

Raven sat up as straight as she could with her hands cuffed behind her. "What are you talking about? Traitor to what?"

"Oh, didn't anyone tell you stealing classified weapon plans from the government and selling them was considered espionage? How naïve do you think I am? My husband may have had an affair with you, but you weren't the first and you wouldn't have been the last if you hadn't gotten him killed. I knew what he was; I didn't leave because I refused to hurt my children more than *he* already had. That doesn't make me stupid or naïve!"

She faced forward, hands clinched in her lap. She hadn't meant to say any of that; it just came pouring out in a torrent. So much had happened in a short amount of time that she hadn't had time to really deal with anything. Getting through one day at a time was all she could handle. Face to face with the woman who ran off with her husband was a bit too much.

"I don't think you're naïve or stupid," Raven said, her voice subdued. "But I guess I am. I truly had no idea what we were stealing." She slumped into the corner of the seat and turned her face to the window.

"Have you told anyone else where the disc is?" Samson asked, watching her through the rearview mirror.

She shrugged. "Someone may have followed me from Omaha. They don't trust me all that much. Not that we're best friends or anything. It's just a job."

"I think we better all stay put for now." Samson shut off the car.

They only had to wait twenty minutes before a black BMW pulled carefully around the Firebird parked in the driveway. The garage door went up, and the car disappeared inside. Moments later a woman came out on the steps to stare at the unfamiliar car parked on her property like a wart on an otherwise smooth complexion.

Samson hopped out of the car and was already on his way up the walkway, his hand lifted in greeting. The woman backed up a step and waited. He showed his badge, and she visibly relaxed. He pointed to the car and seemed to be explaining the situation, then he followed the woman into the house.

"I hope it's still there," Raven said.

Ivy refused to speak but gritted her teeth and closed her eyes. She prayed that Samson would find the disc and her life could get back to normal. Whatever that was.

"I don't mean to be annoying, but we *are* stuck in this car together. You can't just ignore me. I'm sorry your husband was a jerk, but apparently he was one long before I met him." Raven's words were soft, but they held a trace of sarcasm.

Ivy opened her mouth to respond, then clamped it shut and counted to ten. Her mother always said if she waited to speak, she wouldn't have as many words to take back in the end. She drew a deep breath and turned around.

Raven sat hunched in the corner of the car, her eyes glued to the door of the house. Her hair was mussed and there was dirt on her cheek from Samson tackling her to the ground earlier. Ivy suddenly felt sorry for the young woman. She shook her head, not knowing what to say.

"I know you hate me, and I don't blame you," Raven said. "If I were you, I would probably feel the same."

"It's not a matter of hate. I don't know you well enough to hate you," Ivy conceded. "I'm angry at the way you manipulated my husband and how you tried to manipulate me last night. You put my family in jeopardy by your actions. What do you want me to say – that I forgive you? It's a little too soon for me. I'd just like my life to get back to normal and feel that my children and I are safe from whatever games you and your cohorts are playing."

"Honestly, I don't know their plans. But I am sorry for the part I've played. Your husband didn't deserve to die like that." Raven shook her head, her eyes slanting away.

Ivy watched her, looking for deceit but although she was obviously a professional liar, she tended to believe her.

"Why did they kill Todd?" she asked.

"I don't know. There was really no logical reason to kill him. But then I didn't know the whole story. I was told we were spying for a rival company, not another government. I never would have gone along with that. I may be a thief, among other things, but I draw the line at selling out my own country."

"I believe you. But it doesn't change the facts." Ivy glanced back at the house. What was taking him so long? Had he found the disc in the fish tank or didn't the woman want to cooperate without a search warrant? "If Samson can't find the disc, you'll be in worse trouble than now."

A car drove slowly past, windows tinted so they couldn't see the driver's face clearly, but Ivy noticed he didn't even glance their way.

"I hate to contradict you," Raven said, her eyes following the receding car, "but it looks as though I'm in deep trouble whether or not Samson finds the disc."

Samson approached the car, a satisfied grin on his handsome face. "Well ladies," he said, opening the door. "Looks like this case is about to be closed."

He tucked his hand into his inside jacket pocket, pulled out a small plastic case, and clicked it open. It held a shiny disc about half the size of a music CD. "This is what all the fuss was about," he said and handed it to Ivy, so he could start the car. "Once we get it back into the proper hands everything should sort it self out."

"I hope you're right," Raven muttered and leaned her cheek against the cool glass of the windowpane.

Ivy would definitely breathe a lot easier with the disc back in the right hands. "Where to now?" she asked.

"The Federal building. We'll let Agent Reynolds take it from here. I don't want to be responsible for this thing any longer than necessary."

Samson turned the car around in the nearest driveway and headed back. The affluent neighborhood melted away as they drove downtown. It took them over half an hour to drive back through afternoon traffic. Road noise and the occasional beep of a horn pushed by an irate driver were the only things that broke the silence inside the vehicle.

They parked across from the Federal building. He flashed Ivy a reassuring smile. Before they could get out, a cell phone rang from the depths of Raven's duffel bag stuffed on the floor of the car next to Ivy's feet.

Samson met Raven's eyes in the rearview mirror. "Are you expecting a call?"

"Not exactly, but I have a feeling I should answer that." She scooted to the edge of the seat and waited. Samson reached in the bag and pulled out the phone. He hesitated, then flipped it open and held it to her ear.

"Yeah? No, I can't. I'm tied up at the moment. I'm sorry it didn't work out, but sometimes you win and sometimes you lose," she drawled. She listened for a moment and her whole demeanor suddenly changed. She lost the sarcasm in her voice. "You what? You can't do that! They don't have anything to do with this!" The caller must have hung up because she leaned back and expelled a frustrated breath.

Samson flipped the phone closed.

"I'm sorry," Raven said. "I'm really sorry. I never thought they would go this far."

Samson set the phone on the dash and looked up and down the street. "Someone's been following you?"

Raven nodded. Wisps of black hair along her cheekbones accentuated the paleness of her face and her eyes had lost their spark. "They know you found the disc and they want it back."

"That's not going to happen. We're already here, and there's nothing they can do about it. Besides, if you're willing to testify against these people, I'm sure the FBI will make a deal. You'll be protected," Samson reassured her.

"You don't understand," she shook her head. "They have Ivy's children. We only have forty-eight hours to get the disc back to them or they will..." She left the threat hanging, unable to finish the thought out loud.

†††

Samson didn't know which was worse, the look of absolute terror on Ivy's face or the remorse he felt for letting her down by allowing her children to fall into danger. In the short amount of time he'd known them, he'd grown to care about Caleb and Riley and he didn't want anything to happen to them. He sent up a silent prayer for their safety and picked up Raven's phone. He dialed Holly's home phone number. There was still a chance that it was a bluff. After all, an agent had been assigned to watch them. He squeezed Ivy's hand gently.

"Hello?" The voice on the other end was so tense and fraught with anxiety that his hope was immediately dashed. The threat was real.

"Holly? This is Agent Samson Sinclair. What's happening there?"

"Let me talk to her," Ivy said, her voice thick with unshed tears. Her eyes pleaded with him and he reluctantly placed the phone in her hand. "Holly, this is Ivy," she choked out. Her face bore a gray pallor of despair as she listened.

Samson waited, praying for God's strength to sustain her through this crisis.

"Agent Timmons wants to speak with you." She handed back the phone and began to sob.

More than anything Samson wanted to take Ivy into his arms and comfort her. Instead he got out of the car and shut the door. He didn't want Ivy to hear fear in his own voice when he spoke with Timmons.

"Andy, what's going on there? I thought we had Holly and the children covered. How could something like this have happened?" he demanded.

"I'm sorry Samson. The kids took off for the park without letting anyone know. Must have gone out the back door. We had a car out front and Mrs. Jameson was supposed to let us know before she took them anywhere. The kids surprised her too. She didn't know they were missing for half an hour. She's really beating herself up over it." There was a trace of sympathy in his gruff voice, and Samson knew his partner wasn't as tough on the inside as he appeared on the outside.

"How do you know where they were going?" he asked, a puzzled frown between his brows.

"They asked their aunt earlier if they could go to the park. She was too busy and put'em off. When she realized they were missing we searched the park and found the little girl's jacket on the ground. Right now, we're just waiting for the call. By the way – how did you find out so quickly? It just happened. Officially it's not even an abduction. They could still turn up."

Samson debated telling Timmons that they'd already received a ransom call and that the caller demanded the disc in exchange for the safety of the children. It would take the question of whether or not to go through with the trade out of his hands and into the hands of the Bureau. The information on the disc would be safe because the bureau's policy would never allow bartering. They would try to set up a sting operation to get the children back but without the disc it could blow up in their faces. And then what? Would the children just disappear, never to be heard from again? Ivy wouldn't be able to bear another loss. Her children were her whole life.

"Is there something you're not telling me, Sinclair?" Timmons asked. "Look – I know you're attached to those two kids and their mother, but we've got to do this thing by the numbers."

Samson walked around the front of the car and stepped up onto the sidewalk before he spoke. His grip tightened on the small phone as he fought the urge to lie. He knew he had to act responsibly in the position God had placed him. He was an FBI agent and that meant doing his job to the best of his abilities and obeying his superiors.

He rubbed the back of his neck. "They know we have the disc, and they want to trade it for the children."

Timmons expletive was lost in the rev of the car's engine. Ivy was behind the wheel. Before Samson had a chance to stop her, she pulled away from the curb, tires squealing against pavement as she made a tight u-turn and sped off. He stared after the rental car, his mouth hanging open, and realized he'd just lost the three things he needed most – the disc, his prisoner, and the woman he was falling in love with. Not necessarily in that order.

"Sinclair! Sinclair, are you there?" Timmons yelled.

He lifted the phone back to his ear. "I'm in deep trouble, Timmons," he said as the dust from the tires settled around him and the car disappeared from sight.

{13}

"You'd better slow down or you're going to have the LAPD after you as well as the FBI."

Ivy glanced in the rearview mirror and met the younger woman's eyes. In her mad flight to get away she'd actually forgotten about her passenger. She checked her speed. She wasn't thinking of the consequences when she climbed into the driver's seat and took off. She was just reacting. Caleb and Riley were in trouble, and she had to help them. She had the disc, and they had her children. What else was there to think about?

"You better ditch this car, or they'll find you real fast. That is, if Hercules back there has come out of shock yet." Raven leaned forward, watching the road ahead.

"His name is Samson," Ivy corrected. "And I can't ditch the car because I won't be able to get to the airport." She stopped for a red light.

"I can get you another car if you take these handcuffs off me."

Ivy didn't answer but tapped her fingers along the steering wheel, watching the turn lanes go. She was between a rock and a hard place. Without Raven's help she would probably get stopped before she made it to the airport. With her help she would be riding around in a stolen vehicle and possibly get arrested for grand theft auto. What kind of a choice was that?

"If you don't trust your personal FBI agent to get your kids back, I'm your only option. I can find a car faster than you can say rock and roll."

"It's not that I don't trust Samson. I do," Ivy said. "I just know he'll have to do whatever he's told, and I can't see the FBI handing over the disc no matter who's held hostage. Certainly not the children of a criminal."

"Oh, I see. He's a by-the-book kind of guy. He seemed like a straight arrow all right. Goes to church and everything." Raven's comment was snide, but Ivy thought she detected a hint of admiration in there.

She pulled into the parking lot of a corner drugstore. Time was running out, and she needed to trust someone. She *knew* this young woman wasn't the best choice, but right now she was her only choice.

"Samson's a good man. But he can't help me now. If I let you out of those cuffs, are you going to help me or run off to save your own skin?"

A slow smile spread across her face. Twisting around as far as she could, she held out her hands to be released. "You'll find the key in that little coin purse in the side pocket of my bag," she said, eager to be free.

Ivy hesitated for just an instant, then grabbed the purse and quickly opened the handcuffs before she lost her nerve.

Raven shook them off with a satisfied sigh. "I know this sounds cliché, but you don't know how much you value your freedom until you lose it." Looking in the rearview mirror, she combed fingers through mussed hair and wiped the dirt off her face. She dug in her bag and pulled out a pair of tennis shoes. After slipping them on she climbed out of the car.

"Wait here. I'll be back in less than five minutes," she promised with a wink.

Ivy watched her through the car's side mirror as she strolled away and hoped that she hadn't just done a really stupid thing by letting her loose. She saw her cross the street before she disappeared from view.

The electronic door of the drugstore swung open and shut numerous times as customers went in and out. It was a busy place. Ivy watched cars come and go as though the parking lot had a revolving door. She was beginning to grow restless when a tap on the driver's side window nearly made her jump out of her skin. Raven stood beside the car, a mischievous grin on her face and a set of car keys dangling from her hand. She opened the door and stood back while Ivy reached in for the duffel bag and her purse.

"There's always someone who forgets he lives in a dangerous city. Actually, left his keys above the visor. I'll never understand why people make it so easy for people like me - but I appreciate it." She laughed and led the way to a dark green minivan parked one row back.

"Do you want to drive, or do you trust me yet?" she asked, holding out the keys.

Ivy shook her head and opened the passenger side door. "I wouldn't go that far, but you drive. You have experience driving stolen vehicles."

"All right. Let's get to the airport before the big boys do." She slid behind the wheel. "I wish I had my cell phone. I could contact Anderson and smooth over the exchange for you."

"Wait!" Ivy yanked open her door and nearly fell out when Raven threw the car into gear. "Samson's phone! I think it dropped under the seat." She ran back to the car and retrieved the phone.

Raven moved to the passenger seat. "Give it to me," she said. "I'll dial. You drive. I don't think I can maneuver through traffic and deal with this creep at the same time."

Ivy got in and pulled out onto the street, headed toward the airport. She glanced at her watch. Would they be able to get a flight to Omaha as soon as they arrived? She was sure they wouldn't have much time before agents or police showed up to stop them. They were barely ahead of them as it was. If Samson stalled just a little while, maybe they could make it. If not, she'd find another way. Her children would not be at the mercy of cold-blooded killers. Not if she could help it. She drove on, praying that God would keep her babies safe.

Raven dialed Anderson's cell.

†††

"I'll call the Captain and fill him in. I can't believe this, Sinclair. How could you let that woman take off with the disc and your prisoner?" asked Timmons.

Samson shook his head at the rhetorical question and clicked the phone shut. Sticking it in his pocket, he looked up at the office building before him and sighed. He did not want to go into that building and report his loss of the disc. And he certainly didn't want Reynolds to know Ivy was the one who drove off with it. He would have to eat crow at Agent Reynold's invitation. Gloating was something he was sure Reynolds would excel in.

They would go after Ivy like she was some kind of criminal. But there was nothing he could do. The disc could not be handed over to a group of terrorists. They had no guarantee that Caleb and Riley would be safe even if it were. All he could do was work with Reynolds and make sure he didn't go after Ivy with weapons drawn. She was just a mother trying to rescue her children.

Maude wasn't at her post when he stepped out of the elevator. In fact, no one seemed to be around. The cubicles he passed were empty. He heard voices down the hallway and came face to face with Maude, bustling back to the reception room.

"Agent Sinclair!" she exclaimed, her surprise quickly turned to gloating. Samson knew the proverbial cat was already out of the bag.

"Is Agent Reynolds in his office?" he asked, although he heard the man's voice booming behind the closed door.

"I believe he's waiting for you," she said in her husky voice.

Samson raised his hand to knock when the door jerked open, and he was face to face with the big man. Reynold's whole face stretched into a grin. He glanced over his shoulder at the two men behind him.

"Here he is, fellas. Omaha's top agent! Good thing they don't have a lot of crime in the Midwest, huh?" The men laughed loudly, and Reynolds poked a finger in Samson's chest. "I just got a call from your boss, Sinclair. Sounds like you might need our help after all. Is that right?"

Reynolds was not going to let him off easily. He would rub his nose in this for as long as possible. He might as well get started. "Captain Herndon certainly didn't waste any time." He cleared his throat. "You should call the LAPD and put an APB out on my rental. They can't have gotten far. I'm sure they're heading for the airport. At least Mrs. Winter is. Her children are her first priority, and she'll be trying to get to them as quickly as possible." He calmly pulled the rental car contract from his pocket. It had the needed information of make, model, and license plate number.

Reynolds took the proffered papers, his mouth hardening into a thin line. He backed away from the door letting Samson step inside and dismissed the other two agents with a jerk of his head. He kicked the door shut and regarded Samson with enough venom in his gaze to kill a cobra.

"How dare you come in here and suggest to me how to go about finding what you lost! You are an incompetent agent who should have his badge taken away. I am in charge of this office. Is that understood, Sinclair?" He used his large bulk as threateningly as possible in the small confines of the office, but Samson was not intimidated, and Reynolds could see that. With a snort of disgust, he turned and retreated to the chair behind his desk.

"I told you that woman couldn't be trusted, and I was right. I don't suppose you've even considered the possibility those two are working together?"

"Ivy Winter and the woman her husband had an affair with? You've got to be kidding. Definitely not."

"Luckily, I'm not as naïve as you. As I discussed with your Captain, there is reason to believe those two planned this whole thing and her children's kidnapping is a ruse. I plan to proceed on that assumption."

There was nothing Samson could say to change the man's pig-headed stance, so he held his tongue and waited for the punch line. Obviously, Reynolds wasn't through yet.

He leaned forward with his elbows on his desk and regarded Samson from across the scratched surface. His thick neck and ever-darkening beard reminded Samson of Popeye's nemesis, Bluto. "I want you to get your butt on a plane and fly back to Omaha where you belong because I have no intention of allowing you to participate in this operation from here on in. Personally, I don't like you, and professionally I don't think you've got what it takes."

"I'm sorry you feel that way, Agent Reynolds, but I know more about the two women in question and what they might do than you do. You can't afford to keep me out of the loop. I can find them."

Reynolds stared through him, his hands clenched on the desktop.

Samson saw there was no persuading him. He'd already closed his mind and nailed it shut. So, he turned toward the door. "I guess I'll just have to go over your head."

"You go right ahead, boy. I already spoke to your captain, and he said to send you straight home." The smile on Reynold's face was malicious as well as victorious. He pulled the phone from the cradle and began to dial, summarily dismissing Samson from his office and the case.

†††

"Mr. Anderson. I have Mrs. Winter and the disc." At Ivy's look of shock, she raised a finger for silence. "It's a long story, but as usual the FBI screwed up. I'm a free woman. Since I have the disc, you have no more need for the children. Why don't you let them go, and I'll meet you wherever you say? I just want my money."

Ivy listened to the one-sided conversation, every nerve in her body strained to hear the man on the other end. She wished she could speak to the children and know they were all right, but it was better that Raven deal with this man and keep personal feelings out of it. She'd probably just break down and sob and that would help nothing. He was a cold-hearted creature to kidnap two small children in the first place, so an emotional plea would get her nowhere.

"Ok. We'll be there." Raven pressed *end* and leaned her head back.

"What did he say? Are Caleb and Riley all right? Did he hurt them?" Ivy's questions tumbled over one another as she glanced quickly back and forth between the road and Raven. "What's wrong?" she asked. Hysteria grew in her breast and she could barely breathe.

Raven unzipped an inside pocket of her duffel bag and pulled out a gun. She checked that it was loaded and placed it under the seat. Ivy watched, renewed fear inching down her spine. What had she gotten herself into?

Raven met her eyes. "Calm down, Ivy. As far as we know the kids are fine. He said he'd release them as soon as he has the disc in his hands."

She dug through the bag again and pulled out a pair of jeans and t-shirt. Without a care to whether anyone was watching, she pulled her blouse off and replaced it with the clean shirt then scooted out of her skirt and slid the jeans up her long legs, fastening them at the waist. She threw the discarded clothes into the back of the van and pulled the visor mirror down to touch up her makeup.

"When and where? Did he set up a time and place? Are we going to be able to get there in time?" Ivy asked. She imagined Riley and Caleb locked away in some dark, dank basement, shivering with cold and fear.

Traffic inched along as they neared the airport. Ivy hit the steering wheel with the palm of her hand and swore under her breath when a car suddenly stopped in front of her and she had to jam her brakes on to keep from a rear-end collision. Raven was holding something back, and she didn't like it. It was her children on the line, and she needed to know everything. Secrets would only get them hurt – or worse.

"What aren't you telling me, Raven?" she asked tersely, slamming the brakes on once again.

Raven was in the middle of freshening up her lipstick, and the sudden stop gave her lips a new shape. She glared at Ivy and wiped the long red streak from her mouth with a tissue. "Could you maybe pay more attention to your driving skills and less on me? I'm trying to put on makeup here."

"I can't believe you can act so calmly. My children have been kidnapped by the man who murdered their father! Don't you get that? And you're upset about makeup application?"

"There's nothing I can do about your children right this minute, but I can look my best if you would learn to drive," Raven said with her familiar sarcasm. "By the way, pull off at the next exit. We need to fill up with gas. It's on empty, and we've still got a long way to go."

Ivy looked down at the gauge. It was low, but they ought to have enough to get to the airport. "But the airport is only…"

Raven snapped up the visor mirror. "We aren't going to the airport. I checked the flights on your boyfriend's phone. There's no way we'd get out of there before they showed up to throw us both in jail."

Ivy didn't ask any more questions. The last thing she wanted was the FBI to grab them before she could save her children. She quickly put her blinker on and exited the freeway to find the nearest gas station.

Raven hopped out at the Texaco to fill the Van.

"That's it. Tanks full. Do you have thirty-four sixty?" asked Raven through the open window.

Ivy shook her head. "I don't carry cash when I travel. I've just got my cards."

"That should work. I doubt they've put a credit trace on us yet. They probably haven't even decided who's in charge." She laughed and reached in the window for the card.

While Raven went in to pay and buy some snacks, Ivy propped her arms around the steering wheel and let her forehead drop forward to rest there. She was emotionally drained. Not only were Caleb and Riley in the hands of a killer, but she'd broken trust with the one man who wanted to help her. Would Samson forgive her when and if this all became resolved? The last thing she wanted was for Samson's professional reputation to be damaged because of her decision, but the disc was her only means of rescuing the children. The fate of the world would have to rest in someone else's hands because hers were full with just her own problems.

Her weary thoughts turned to God. Did he really care for her the way Mrs. Adams taught all those years ago? Samson believed God was an active force in his life, a loving God he could trust with his cares. Tears filled her eyes. She felt as if she'd been blowing against the wind most of her life. She tried to keep God out of her life for so many years, believing she didn't need him, when in reality he had never left. She remembered praying as a child, asking for God's forgiveness and salvation. Mrs. Adams said God would never leave her or forsake her. From that day forth she was a child of His. Ivy wiped tears away with the back of her hand. If Mrs. Adams were to be believed, God kept His promises. Which meant that she had turned her back on him. All she had to do was put her trust in him again. Could she do that? Did she have a choice? The life she was living without him was empty. Not because Todd was a bad husband and she had been stuck in a loveless marriage, but because she didn't have God to turn to in those times. She didn't have the joy in her heart that she had felt the day she prayed that prayer.

The phone on the seat beside her began to ring, and she lifted her head in surprise. Samson's phone. Should she answer it or ignore it? On the third ring she picked it up.

"Hello?"

"Ivy? Are you all right?" Samson's deep voice warmed her heart and brought a smile to her lips.

"I'm fine, Samson. I'm sorry I took off, but I have to get to Caleb and Riley. I hope you're not going to be in trouble because of me. I wish there were another way, but I don't trust the FBI to put the welfare of my children first, so I have to," she said. She could see Raven inside the station standing at the register.

"I understand why you did it. I wish I could help, but I've been taken off the case. Thought you should know that Reynolds is on his way to the airport. They found the rental car and know you switched vehicles. Actually, I'm on my way to the airport now too. I've been ordered to return to Omaha."

"I'm sorry. I didn't mean for any of this to happen."

"I know that, Ivy."

She rubbed a hand over her face. "Samson, I've been thinking about God a lot lately. I've decided life is too short and too hard to live without him. But I'm not sure how to get back to him again."

Samson didn't say anything for a moment. When he finally spoke, his voice was husky. "Ivy, he never left. Just pray and ask him for the fellowship you once had. He's faithful to forgive."

Ivy smiled and sniffed. Her silent prayer went up to God and the sounds of traffic outside the car faded away as peace filled her soul.

"Ivy?"

"I'm here. Thank you. I think I can deal with this mess a little better now." She looked up and saw Raven walking toward the car. She carried a sack of groceries and a small Styrofoam cooler.

"I better go. I'll call you if I need you."

"Wait." Samson said before she could hang up. "You can't trust that woman, Ivy. She's a criminal."

"I know and now so am I," she laughed. "Just pray, Samson. Pray like you never have before," she pleaded. She pushed *end* and slipped the phone into the cubby.

Raven pulled open the side door and placed the cooler full of ice on the floor. She filled it with cans of pop, candy bars, and a couple of sandwiches that she took out of the sack. She slid the door closed and brought a large bag of barbecue chips with her to the front seat.

"Hungry? I got enough to last through the night. I don't like to stop too much. Who knows? They might put our mug shots on national television and someone would recognize us." She shut the door and pulled open the top of the bag.

"Oh, here's your card," she said, dropping the credit card on the console between them, then settled into her seat to munch on chips.

Ivy pulled away from the station with a smile on her face. She hadn't felt this peaceful in ages. The circumstances were still horrible and beyond her control, but the load she carried was lighter. Whatever came her way she knew God was in control.

{14}

"A flight to Omaha, please." Samson stood at the head of the American Airlines ticket line. The man behind him huffed and puffed as he moved up in line, pushing his suitcase and dress bag along the floor. Samson glanced back at the long line of customers waiting their turns and grinned at no one in particular. In fact, he hadn't stopped grinning since he talked to Ivy on the phone. He prayed that she would learn to trust again and yet when she told him it took him completely by surprise. Especially after her sudden departure.

"I can get you on a flight tomorrow. I'm sorry, but the last one out today is booked solid." The woman behind the counter looked down at the screen and tapped some keys.

"And it departs in three minutes. I doubt you could have made it." She smiled politely as she'd probably smiled at hundreds of passengers throughout the day. He wondered if her face ever felt frozen in place.

"Fine. Can I get a window seat, please?" He pulled out his wallet and handed her his credit card and drivers license.

"It's actually a good thing you weren't on the flight today, sir. It's been delayed," she said as she scrolled up the screen.

Samson frowned. Had Reynolds boarded the flight to arrest Ivy and Raven? When he spoke to Ivy on the phone, he got the impression they were well away. Maybe Reynolds had caught up to them after all. He wished he could be there and put a damper on Reynolds' nasty attitude toward Ivy.

"Does it say why?" he asked.

"No sir – just says delayed." She pushed his ticket toward him and gestured for the next person in line. "Have a nice flight, Sir."

"Could you tell me what gate that plane is leaving from?" he asked, a warm smile masked his impatience. He held out his FBI badge for good measure.

She eyed him as though perhaps he was a mad bomber before giving him the number.

"Thank you, ma'am."

He had his ticket, so he could go through security, but then he'd be stuck at the airport until his flight left in the morning. Not where he'd planned to spend the night. But what if Ivy was on that plane? He needed to see for himself and make certain that she was all right. He used his ID to bump to the front of the line, went through the security checkpoint and took off at a brisk trot. Following the green arrows, he began to run, dodging people and motorized carts. Maybe he'd get there before Reynolds did something stupid.

As he approached, he saw agents standing on either side of the boarding gate. He flipped his badge and entered the covered hallway that led out to the jumbo jet. Luckily, they didn't question his right to be there but just nodded him through.

On board the plane, a cluster of flight attendants whispered among themselves. They eyed him curiously as he passed.

In the midst of combing the plane for his fugitives, Reynolds looked up and spotted Samson immediately. He glared and stormed to the front like a bull seeing red. "What are you doing here? Didn't I tell you to stay away from my operation?"

The flight attendants scattered, apparently already familiar with Reynold's confrontational personality.

"As I recall you said to get my butt on a plane for Omaha. I believe *this* plane is going to Omaha," Samson said smoothly.

Reynolds turned dark red with frustration, turned on his heel and left the plane, signaling two other agents to follow.

The last agent stopped before disembarking, met Samson's gaze and shrugged. "We haven't turned up a trace of them on a flight out. Hope you have better luck in Omaha."

"Thanks," Samson said.

"Sir, do you have a boarding pass for this flight?"

A flight attendant stood expectantly at his side, her attitude back to business with the agents off the plane. It was past time to take off. The passengers were antsy.

Samson smiled apologetically and shook his head. "Sorry. Wrong plane."

He turned and made his way back down the ramp and into the airport. As he came out of the loading area, he saw Reynolds in a heated argument with an airport official. He went stomping off, leaving the other agents to trail along behind. Samson smiled. Reynolds had failed in his pursuit of Ivy. Now it was up to him to find her before she handed that disc over to the other side. There had to be some way to rescue Caleb and Riley without compromising the country's security. He prayed that God would lead him in the right direction. He couldn't get a direct flight back to Omaha until tomorrow. Would he be in time?

✝✝✝

Ivy purchased a map at the roadside rest area once they crossed into Arizona. The sun had set hours ago and yet the desert air was still hot and dry. She hurried toward the van parked in a nearly empty lot. Other than two semi trailer trucks, they had the rest stop to themselves.

Raven had fallen asleep in her seat a couple hours earlier, and Ivy had been glad for the quiet solitude to compose her thoughts and talk to God. It was strange at first – talking to the one whom she refused to acknowledge for so long – but soon her prayers winged their way upward with the earnestness of a child. She felt God's love melt the last remnants of her cold heart and turn her fear into peace.

Ivy stopped to put some coins into a machine and took the can of cranberry-apple juice that dropped down. It was ice-cold, and she rubbed it across her forehead before popping the top and taking a long, refreshing gulp.

She pulled open the door of the van. "Better hit the restroom before we take off. We've got to get going, and it's your turn to drive."

Raven yawned widely and stretched. She glanced heavy-lidded around the nearly deserted rest stop, then climbed out and walked toward the building without a word.

Ivy watched her go inside, then poked her head down by the front of the passenger seat and looked beneath. It was dark but not dark enough to conceal the pistol Raven had placed there earlier. She was loathe to touch it but knew she should. She didn't like guns or the idea of carrying a concealed weapon for protection. Raven had no such compunction and probably was quite adroit at using one, but it didn't make her feel any better about it being in the car. She reached under to slide it out and heard the crunch of gravel behind her. Before she could straighten up and turn around, a hand was on her backside and another clamped roughly over her mouth.

"Hey baby, what ever you're looking for, I got all you need."

Her hand tightened convulsively around the handle of the gun as the man groped and pulled her against him. She smelled liquor on him and felt him tremble with excitement when he took hold of her hair and yanked her head against his chest.

"This shouldn't take long at all, honey, and then you can be on your way," he said, his breath hot and foul on her cheek.

Ivy remembered the gun in her hand and some preservation instinct made her place her finger on the trigger as he tried to turn her to face him.

"I wouldn't do that if I were you," Raven said calmly from the shadows.

The man shoved Ivy back into the car and whirled to face the woman behind him. He made a show of looking her up and down, and chuckled low in his throat. He wore a cap with the bill turned to the back. It said *#1 STUD*. His saggy blue jeans and shrunken t-shirt allowed Ivy a three-inch view of his hairy backside.

"I'm sort of busy right now, honey, but if you'll wait a few minutes, I'll get to you too." His voice had a hint of the Deep South in it, and Ivy remembered seeing a picture of Georgia peaches on the side of one of the trucks as they pulled in earlier.

He'd tossed her carelessly aside and turned his back on her as though she were no threat. Ivy remembered another time when she'd felt completely helpless and unable to defend herself. This time she had no intention of passively sitting by and waiting for God to strike down evil with a bolt of lightning. She knew now that God didn't work that way. He *had* said that He would never leave her nor forsake her. That fact made her a bit fearless. She lifted the gun and brought it down with all of her might on the back of the man's head.

Raven grinned at her as the man crumpled to his knees between them. He groaned and fell face forward to the ground. A thin trickle of blood dripped from beneath his cap and around his left ear.

"Wow – I didn't know you had it in you," Raven said, wide-eyed. She shook her head and stepped carefully around his body. "I didn't even get to use my kung fu on him."

Ivy's laughter was a bit shaky. "I bet you don't even know kung fu, do you?"

Raven bent down and felt for a pulse on the man's neck. "He's still alive. Not that the world's a better place for it, but I suppose we should call an ambulance."

Ivy was momentarily stunned into silence, surprised that Raven would have any sympathy for such a man. She felt no sympathy for him herself, but she realized that she was condemning him to eternity without God if she just let him die. She reached for the cell phone and dialed 911.

Raven grabbed hold of the man's work boots and dragged him away from the van. She dusted her hands on the legs of her jeans and climbed into the driver's seat. "We better be a ways down the road before they show up."

Ivy made a wide circle around the man on the ground. Her gaze lingered for a moment, and then she jumped in the van and slammed the door. "Let's go. My kids are counting on me," she said through stiff lips, refusing to cry. She would cry later when Caleb and Riley were safe and sound. She would deal with everything later. Right now, was too full just surviving.

Fifteen miles down the road an ambulance flew by, lights flashing and siren wailing. Ivy didn't turn to watch. She stared straight ahead, her thoughts on her children.

"Are you all right?" Raven asked.

"Why wouldn't I be?"

Raven kept her eyes on the road and shook her head. "Heck if I know. Guess I'm just curious to see if a woman like you can stand up under the pressure. To be honest, I've never had a day quite like today myself. It would be understandable to fall apart – given the circumstances."

Ivy realized she was still clutching the gun in her hand. She slowly lifted it from her lap. The reflected light from a car's headlights glinted on the shiny metal. She felt a tremble begin somewhere in her chest and then her hands started shaking. She looked down at the gun as though it were a foreign object.

Raven glanced over, took the gun, and casually placed it back under the seat. "Good thing the safety is on," she said. "I'd hate to have to call that ambulance for you."

Ivy turned up the air conditioner and breathed deeply of the cool air coming through the vents. Her panic attack began to lessen and with nerves calm, she focused in on what Raven had said.

"The safety was on?" She shook her head. She couldn't have shot him if she tried. If Raven hadn't shown up, and if he hadn't turned his back on her, she wouldn't have even been able to hit him with it. That was a lot of *ifs*. Her heart sent up a prayer of thankfulness that God had been there, controlling a situation she had no control over. She relaxed her grip. Her fingers were stiff from clenching the gun for so long. "What do you mean by *a woman like me?*" she asked, curious.

Raven ran a hand through her short spikes and sighed. Taking her time answering, she pulled a stick of gum from her pocket and carefully opened it, steering with her knees. She folded it in half and stuck it in her mouth before putting her hands back on the steering wheel. "You know. The suburbanite housewife and mother who's never had anything more exciting happen to her than getting a letter from *Publisher's Clearing house* saying she may have won ten million dollars."

Ivy turned and stared out the window into the inky blackness of the desert. She leaned her forehead against cool glass. Until a short time ago her life had been fairly mundane, and she *had* received correspondence from the Clearing house, but it had never really excited her. She tried to remember the last time she was excited about something, but nothing specific came to mind. "I guess that description did apply to me a few days ago," she said, her voice thoughtful. "After all that's happened I'm not so sure that's a bad thing. You don't really live like this all the time, do you?"

"Truthfully? My life is a mess. I doubt I'd ever fit into the suburbs; I'm more of a nomad. But there are some things I'd like to change."

Ivy watched her through new eyes. Up to now she'd been blind to the vulnerability in this young woman. Raven put on a good show of toughness and savvy. Could her hard façade be cracking, giving a glimpse of the real woman inside?

"Does it have anything to do with a man?" she asked.

Raven kept her eyes on the road. She showed no sign of responding other than a tightening of her hands on the wheel. A few minutes later her voice broke the silence. "We'll be there in a couple of hours now. Not any later than 3:00 or 3:30."

Ivy opened her eyes and blinked owlishly. The hum of the engine and steady rhythm of tires on pavement had nearly put her to sleep. She rubbed her face and sat up straighter in the bucket seat. A glance at the clock indicated she not only was asleep but had been asleep for over an hour. She looked out onto the landscape shrouded by a blanket of darkness. She could make out a building of some kind in the distance and here and there a bush or tree, but overall it was flat and uninteresting.

"Where exactly is there?" she asked and yawned. There was no way they could reach Omaha by the deadline set by the kidnappers. So far, she had just assumed Raven had set up a meeting place elsewhere, and she had blindly followed. Now she was beginning to wonder.

Raven glanced over with a self-satisfied smile. "I wondered when you'd get around to asking. I have a friend who flies charters out of Arizona. Knowing our FBI buddies would be checking out flights leaving LAX, our only recourse was to find a private airport out of their range. We'll be in Omaha in plenty of time – don't worry."

"Actually, I wasn't worried until now. How big is this plane?" she asked, suddenly wide awake.

††††

Maggie kept her eye on the two men at the corner table even as she continued to run the register and wait on other customers. They calmly sat at a corner booth eating caramel and pecan covered sweet rolls and drinking coffee. One wore an expensive looking dark suit and silk tie, while the other was in jeans and a black polo shirt. But that wasn't what caught her interest. The reason for her concern was the two children with them. The same children who had come in with Samson and their mother just the other day.

She started to greet them by name when they came through the door but something in the young boy's eyes stopped her. While the fancy dressed gentleman took the children to the farthest table, the other paid for the coffee and rolls. Caleb and Riley sat quietly, not moving, which wasn't like them at all. She remembered them full of energy and curiosity. Something had to be wrong.

The man in the suit tried to talk to them a couple of times, but they just sat like zombies. Could he be their criminal father, the one that Samson was looking for? They didn't seem to like him much if that were the case.

During a slump in business, she went to their table on the pretext of serving more coffee. The men were both immersed in conversation, ignoring the children completely. Riley sat with her head leaned against her older brother while his arm encircled her protectively.

"Would you like more coffee?" she asked brightly although her heart ached at the sight of these children. They seemed to have no feelings for their father other than fear.

"Yes, please." The man she presumed to be their father raised his cup with a smile that could have chilled the heart of a crocodile. His mouth turned up but there was no light in his eyes, just gray steel.

She refilled their cups, then turned to the children with a warm smile. "Would you two like a free sample of my fresh batch of donut holes? They're still warm."

Riley smiled and looked hopeful, but Caleb shook his head. "No thank you," he said with quiet dignity.

The two men anxiously watched her interact with the children but seemed to visibly relax when she turned to leave.

Maggie returned to the counter and served two more customers, still watching the corner table. There was something wrong about that little get together. She absently scratched her head with a plastic fork and tried to remember exactly what Samson said about the man he was looking for. The FBI wanted him pretty bad; otherwise Samson wouldn't have been keeping an eye on his wife and children. She wondered if Samson knew he was in town.

She picked up the phone and dialed the number to his apartment. The answering machine came on after three rings and she sighed. This was too important to just leave a message. What if he didn't get it in time and the man got away?

She hung up and went to fetch her purse hanging on the hook in back. She found the little blue book she kept numbers in at the bottom of her over-sized bag and flipped to the S's, letting her finger slide down the page until it stopped below a number in red. Samson's cell phone number. She was only supposed to use it for emergencies, but this certainly qualified.

Resting her bulk on a tall stool next to the register, she dialed and waited impatiently, while keeping a watchful eye on her unsuspecting customers.

"Hello?" an unfamiliar female voice answered, surprising Maggie into silence for a moment. "Samson?" the voice asked cautiously.

"Hello," began Maggie, not quite knowing what to do. Why would a woman have Samson's phone? "I was calling for Samson Sinclair. This is his cell phone number, isn't it?"

"Yes, but he's not here right now."

There was something familiar about the voice. Then it hit her. This woman was the mother of the children sitting at the table in the corner. How much did she dare say? Would she give Samson the message or warn her husband of his imminent capture? "I need to get in touch with him. It's an emergency. Tell him Maggie called; he has my number."

"Maggie? This is Ivy. Remember me? I came into your shop with Samson the other day. My children were with me." Her voice cracked with emotion.

"Is something the matter?" asked Maggie with growing concern. Whether it was instinct or a higher power giving her insight, she suddenly realized that

Ivy's children were not here with her approval or even her knowledge.

"I can't talk right now, Maggie, but I'll do my best to get your message to Samson," she said, her voice soft.

"Wait, Ivy," Maggie called, afraid that she would disconnect before she could tell her. "The reason I need to talk to Samson is because there are two men here in the shop, and they have your children with them."

✝✝✝

Samson spent part of the night on the floor of the airport and the rest walking around. He didn't get much sleep, but he got a stiff back and a lot of thinking done. He was glad his flight was leaving early. He didn't think he could stand to wait any longer, unable to act. Anything could have happened by now. He ground his teeth together in frustration. It was an old boyhood habit. In stressful situations people nearly always reverted back to bad habits. He had watched people who hadn't smoked for a decade suddenly crave nicotine and light up. Human frailty.

He heard the call to board the plane just as Raven's cell phone started ringing in his jacket pocket. He pulled it out and flipped it open, eager for word from Ivy.

"Samson?" The voice was faint and surrounded by a crackling noise, but he could still hear the urgency in it.

"I can barely hear you, Ivy. Can you speak up?" he asked in a loud voice, assuming she was having the same problem.

"I got -- call -- -- phone -- -- Maggie." The line was cutting in and out, and he couldn't make out exactly what Ivy was telling him. Did she want him to call Maggie? He didn't give his cell number out to many people, but Maggie was at the top of his short list. She rarely used it, but he wanted her to have it in case of an emergency. Did something happen to Hank? He hoped that wasn't the case. His stomach tightened with dread. Hank had survived a heart attack a year ago. He didn't know if he could survive another.

"I can't hear you, Ivy," he said loudly, hoping she could at least hear him. "What about Maggie?"

The crackling grew worse, cutting out the words she was saying and then the phone went dead. He blew out a frustrated breath and flipped it closed.

The last call for boarding his flight to Omaha came over the loud speaker, and he moved into the line. The sooner he got in the air, the sooner he could use one of the phones on board the plane. He knew Ivy wouldn't call him about Maggie unless it was important. The last thing they needed right now were more problems. The flight attendant took his ticket stub, and he moved down the ramp to the plane.

{15}

The Cessna lifted into the air with a burst of speed from its jet engines that shook the small craft and its occupants as though it were made of paper rather than metal. Ivy gripped the arms of her chair. She was exhausted but flying in a plane this small sent her pulse racing in trepidation.

"Not afraid of flying, are you?" asked Raven, a small smirk of enjoyment on her lips. She had been chatting with their pilot before takeoff and seemed to know quite a lot about flying and planes.

"Not usually," Ivy said, "but in a plane the size of my son's toys, yes – a definite yes." She tightened her seatbelt.

Raven laughed and leaned her chair back into the reclining position. With a hand over her open mouth, she yawned and settled into the leather confines of her seat, getting as comfortable as possible. "Don't worry. Ben is the best pilot I've ever flown with – besides myself, of course." The early morning rays of the sun pierced their way through clouds floating like cotton candy and directly into their eyes. She reached out and closed the shade over the window. "You better get some sleep too," she said with eyes closed. "You look like you could use it."

Ivy stared through her own window as they rose and leveled off to cruising altitude before finally relaxing her death grip on the arms of the chair. The pilot, a mere twenty or so feet ahead of them, was busy charting his course or whatever pilots did in their little cubicle. She wasn't exactly sure. There was only one pilot and if something happened to him, who would fly the plane? She turned to watch her road-trip buddy sleeping peacefully. Raven could fly. At least she said she could. So, there was no real reason to fear, was there?

She released her seatbelt and reached for her purse on the table before her. The jet was small but not without its comforts. It boasted a wet bar and entertainment center, not to mention the most comfortable chairs she had ever encountered in a plane. They were pedestal mounted and could swivel as well as recline. There were four of them, with a table that flipped down in the middle, presumably to conduct business during the flight.

Ivy reached for a set of headphones and plugged them into her jack, then flipped on the CD player built into the wall to her left. The mellow, soothing tones of a saxophone solo came over the wire and calmed her nerves a bit. She leaned back in her seat and tried to relax, but a glance at her watch reminded her they only had a few hours until the deadline. Her mind churned with possibilities. When she called and tried to deliver Maggie's message to Samson earlier the phone had cut out and she realized the battery was completely depleted. There was no way to contact him now until they reached Omaha.

She hoped he'd understood enough to give Maggie a call.

She glanced across at Raven, asleep in her chair, and wondered how someone who led such a crazy life could sleep so peacefully and look so innocent while doing it. Ivy was exhausted through and through, but still unable to relax. She thought of Caleb and Riley and whether they slept last night or lay awake sobbing into a pillow out of fear and loneliness. Her eyes filled with tears at the thought of her babies alone with a madman.

Raven stirred beside her and Ivy closed her eyes and feigned sleep, not wishing to put her thoughts into words. Raven had turned out to be more empathetic then imagined, but she wasn't a mother and she couldn't possibly understand the bone-aching emptiness she felt without her children.

Finally, she fell into a restless sleep, but her mind continued to churn with fearful thoughts, like monsters, winding themselves around and around inside her dream world.

†††

Maggie was just about to go and offer the men at the corner table another warm-up when the telephone rang. She set the hot pot back down on the counter and picked up the phone on the second ring, already out of breath from her little dash across the small space. Pressing a hand against her chest, she puffed into the phone. "Maggie's Mocha Shack."

"Maggie? It's Samson. Is Hank all right?"

"Hank's fine. Why would you think otherwise?" She glanced around the counter and into the back kitchen area where Hank bent over the open door of the oven pulling a long pan of fresh, cinnamon rolls out, oblivious to anything else. When he was baking, he was in his own world. She hadn't let Hank in on the current predicament playing out in their store, for his own good. His heart didn't need to be excited any more than necessary. She could be wrong about those men and getting Hank all agitated about nothing was silly.

Samson breathed a sigh of relief into the phone. "Thank God! When Ivy told me you'd called, I assumed the worst. You never use my cell phone except for emergencies. Hank was the first thing that came to mind," he admitted.

Maggie lowered her voice and spoke into the phone with her hand cupped around the receiver, afraid the sound would carry, and those men would overhear her conversation.

"Samson, didn't Ivy tell you about the children?" she asked, a puzzled frown creasing her plump face.

"We had a bad connection and her phone went dead. What children?"

"Ivy's children. They're here right now at the shop. They're with two men whom I've never seen before, but I assume that one of them is their father."

"Maggie, their father is dead. As far as I know, those men are responsible."

She let out a small gasp. With that announcement ringing in her head she twisted her bulk around to keep an eye on the table and found the man with the black polo shirt staring right back at her. She tried to look less guilty, but she wasn't sure if he was buying it. He rose from his seat and walked toward her. Her heart skipped a beat when he pointedly stopped at the counter and waited for her to end her conversation. His glum expression now seemed much more sinister.

"Hold on a moment, please. I have a customer," she spoke as brightly as she could into the phone and set it down. Pasting a smile on her face she approached the counter. "Can I help you, sir?"

"Do you have a restroom I could use?" he asked. His gravelly voice sent shivers down Maggie's spine.

She pointed down a short hallway to the left, hidden by the half wall dividing the kitchen from the dining area. "Right through there," she said.

He walked around the divider and down the hall without a thank you or another glance in her direction. Keeping her eye on the bathroom door, she picked up the receiver.

"Samson, that was one of the men with the children. He's in the bathroom. They've been here almost an hour, so they're probably about ready to leave. What shall I do? I don't think my coffee is going to keep them here much longer."

"Offer them free sweet rolls, I don't know, but be careful. If they try to leave don't do anything. They're dangerous men. Don't let them know you recognize the children. Maybe they're staking out the place to use for the swap."

Samson's voice was tense with worry and love for the children and their mother, and Maggie felt it as surely as though he was her own flesh and blood. "You care about those kids don't you, Sammy?" The childhood name came back so easily to her lips. She remembered when he was as young as Caleb and just as brave when his mother died. She had tried to be a mother to him as best she could, but soon realized that no one could ever replace the real thing.

"Yeah, Maggie. I care. And I don't want anything to happen to them, but I'm still on a flight from Los Angeles and I won't be getting in to Omaha for a couple of hours yet. I'll call my partner and see if he can get over there before they leave. Pray, Maggie. Pray hard." He hung up without saying goodbye, and Maggie held the phone to her ear for a few extra seconds, not willing for the link to be broken.

The man came out of the bathroom and walked around the counter without a word. He returned to the table and sat back down, glanced out the windows, then turned and spoke to the other man in a low voice. The children were growing antsy. Riley had wandered to the next table and was busy beating on the top like a drum.

The bell over the front door jangled and six young women came in for morning bagels and coffee. They were busy talking and laughing at the counter looking at the display of fresh rolls and other sweets.

"Can I help you ladies?" Maggie asked, hoping her face didn't show the worry in her heart.

The tallest, a beautiful woman with short red hair and full, pouty lips, stepped forward and waved her hand to encompass the entire group. "Whatever they want, just ring it all together. I'm buying," she announced. Ignoring half-hearted arguments, she ordered coffee and a Danish for herself, then stood back.

Each of the women ordered and took their items to a double table in the middle of the room, where they continued their conversations. The redhead was paying for the order just as Maggie noticed the two men stand and take the children by the hand. They were leaving.

She handed the woman her change rather clumsily and half of it slipped past her outstretched palm and onto the floor, rolling right into the path of the well-dressed criminal.

"I'm so sorry," Maggie apologized breathlessly.

The man bent down to retrieve the coins. He sent a dismissive glance in her direction but when his eyes rested on the young redhead his lips curved up in a smile so smooth it must have been oiled. Maggie watched him reach for her hand and slowly drop the coins into her palm, closing her fingers around them. The girl appeared too stunned by his charm to pull away.

"Better keep a tight grip on them this time," he murmured softly before releasing her hand with practiced reluctance and opened the door. The children and their bodyguard followed.

The redhead stared after them, frozen in place. But Maggie quickly snatched up a pencil and piece of paper and followed.

A black limousine waited outside the strip mall. The driver waited for his passengers to get seated then shut the door and climbed into the front. Maggie didn't want to look too conspicuous in case they looked her way, so she walked to the mailbox and pretended to mail a letter.

The limo pulled away and Maggie scribbled furiously on her scrap of paper. She was glad she could still see distance without glasses even though she required a pair for reading at night. It was a weakness she wasn't fond of. Growing old and flabby was one thing, but losing her sight and hearing was quite another.

A dark blue jeep pulled up just as she turned to go inside. She recognized the man behind the wheel. Samson had brought his partner into the shop on more than one occasion. Special Agent Andrew Timmons was always welcome at Maggie's Mocha Shack, but at this moment he was a Godsend.

She didn't wait for him to step out of the open Jeep but hurried over and spoke, her voice urgent with worry. "Andy – thank God you're here. They just left in that black limo." She handed him the piece of paper. "This is the license number. The children are in the backseat with two men. Hurry and catch them!"

Andy didn't hesitate but began backing his vehicle out of the space. He turned and gave her a grim smile and quick wave before tearing out of the parking lot and back onto the street in the direction the limo had just taken.

Maggie watched until the Jeep was out of sight. She returned to the shop with a heavy heart, praying that God would intervene and save those two precious children from the wicked men who held them.

†††

Ivy jerked awake as the plane hit a patch of turbulence. She sat up and looked around, her eyes heavy-lidded from sleep. Leaning forward, she looked out the small cabin window and realized they had begun their descent. Farms like patchwork quilts sewn together stretched as far as the eye could see. Soon they were low enough to see cars and trucks speeding down the interstate as they made their final approach and prepared to land. She was back in Omaha. It seemed like she'd been gone for a month when in reality it had only been twenty-four hours.

Raven's chair was empty. She was leaning over the pilot, chatting, a glass of something in one hand, the other placed intimately on his shoulder. Ivy saw him smile, and then he waved her back to her seat as he continued talking to the tower on his headset.

Ivy readjusted her seatbelt, making sure it was secured and took hold of the arms of her chair once more for the final part of their flight. She looked up and found Raven watching her with a speculative expression on her young face. Raven buckled her own belt in a nonchalant fashion, as though she was doing it only because the lighted sign said so and not because she thought it necessary.

"Did you get enough sleep?" she asked. She emptied her glass with one last swallow and set it on the table, where it slid across the smooth surface as the plane's wing dipped for a turn.

Ivy didn't like to talk when she was concentrating on survival, but she forced her eyes open and looked at Raven. "I'm fine, if that's what you mean." The grip she maintained on the arms of her chair belied that fact and she tried to ignore the sound of the landing gear being lowered. This was the part she hated most. In a large jet you hardly felt the landing, but in one of these it was a major amusement ride and she wasn't keen on amusement rides.

The plane's wheels touched ground so lightly that Ivy didn't realize they'd landed until the roar of the engines made her eyes fly open and she looked out the window. They were already slowing on the runway. She expelled a breath of relief when she saw the familiar buildings of the airport.

"I told you he was the best," said Raven smugly. She didn't wait for the plane to come to a full and complete stop but unbuckled and stood up to stretch.

"Hey, Bree!" the pilot called over the intercom as he coasted down the runway. "If I stick around, are you free for dinner tonight?"

Raven laughed and moved to the front of the plane. Ivy saw her shake her head as she apparently gave him some excuse and kiss him on the cheek before turning to scoop up their few belongings.

"Raven, why did Ben just call you Bree?" Ivy asked. She turned in the swivel chair to reach for her purse on the table.

Raven hesitated and then shrugged. "I guess it's time I tell you my real name." She stuck out her hand. "Hello, I'm Brenna Blackman. It's been nice flying with you."

Ivy ignored the proffered hand and stood up, her gaze hard. Her purse was sitting on the table where she'd left it, but it had been opened and the disc was missing. Anger filled her. She had traveled with this woman under the mistaken assumption that she wanted to help rescue her children when in reality she only wanted to get her hands on the disc like everyone else. It wasn't enough to run off with her husband, and talk him into stealing government secrets, now she was putting Caleb and Riley's lives in jeopardy for a measly few thousand dollars.

"How dare you take the one thing I have to bargain for my children with! Where is the disc?" she demanded.

Raven pulled back as though stung. Her smile turned into a mask of indifference. She took the disc from her back pocket and held it out on the palm of her hand.

Ivy snatched it up. How in the world could she have been so naïve as to trust this woman? She put it back into her purse again and turned her back to pick up her overnight bag, when it suddenly hit her – Raven didn't have to give it back at all. What could she do about it? Go to the FBI? She was running from the law as well.

"Why did you take the disc?" she asked, fumbling with her bag, afraid to meet the other woman's eyes.

The plane came to a rolling stop, and they heard the engines shutting down. Outside Ivy could see two men driving by on a train of luggage, their ears covered for protection against the loud roars of the jet engines. The sun was shining brightly, glinting off the top of the control tower in the distance, and she could tell it was going to be a hot day in Nebraska.

"I was planning on having it back in your bag before you woke up. I'm sorry but I got sidetracked," she said, slanting her eyes toward Ben.

"If you weren't stealing it, then what were you doing with it?" This time Ivy's tone was soft. Had she been wrong again? Raven tried to hide it, but Ivy thought she might have hurt her feelings by her accusation.

The pilot stepped out of the cockpit and opened the door. A man below secured a set of stairs to the plane for their departure. Raven slung her bag over her shoulder and stepped to the door. She stopped long enough to thank Ben and blew him a kiss at the bottom of the steps.

Ivy had no recourse but to follow, her bag and purse in tow. She also thanked the pilot and hurried to catch up with Raven.

The air hit like wet wool after the cool, dry climate-controlled cabin of the plane. Nebraska was known for high humidity in the summer months and today was no exception. She imagined her hair going straighter by the second.

They walked briskly across the tarmac, climbed a set of stairs to the door and went inside the terminal. She had to jog a few steps to catch up with Raven's long stride. She refused to slow down until they stepped on the escalator. They rode down, not speaking. Ivy followed Raven in silence through the parking area until they stopped before a sleek, black, convertible, sports car. It was beautiful, and no doubt expensive, but it fit Raven to a tee.

"Nice car," Ivy said, and threw her bag in the back.

"I like it." Raven pulled the door closed and turned the ignition. The air-conditioning started to cool things off after a couple minutes, but apparently not Raven. She turned to Ivy, her eyes sparks of anger. "Let's get something straight. I don't have to help you. I could walk away right now, and you'd be on your own."

Ivy opened her mouth to speak but Raven cut her off.

"If I wanted to steal that disc, I would have had it a long time ago and you would have never been the wiser. I took it, so I could make a copy. The copy is the one we are going to give to them. The original we give back to your boyfriend."

With that announcement she put the car into gear and backed up with a squeal of tires. She paid the parking fee at the booth as they exited and pulled out onto the road. Her jaw was firmly set as though she had nothing more to say.

Ivy turned away and stared out the window at the familiar landscape rushing by. She wondered what was ahead and prayed that she hadn't messed everything up beyond repair with the only person who was willing to help her. She needed to set things right with Raven before it was too late.

"I'm sorry I jumped to conclusions about your motives, Rav– I mean Brenna, but I'm still not clear about why you made a copy. A *copy* of the disc in the wrong hands isn't going to fly with the FBI any better than the original in the wrong hands." The new name felt strange on her tongue. The name Raven seemed to fit this girl as well as her black sports car.

"You might as well call me Raven. I'm used to it now. Besides, no one calls me Brenna except my father," her hands tightened on the wheel as she sped smoothly in and out of lanes and between cars, definitely making record time to whatever destination she had in mind. "The copy I made is only good until they try to download it or copy it or access it for longer than a minute. Then it starts to disintegrate. Get the picture?" She accelerated through a yellow light, her eyes on the rearview mirror.

Ivy reached into her purse. She opened the small square case and looked at the tiny disc that was worth so much to so many people. A shudder ran through her at the thought that she was, in a very strange way, holding her children's lives in her hands.

"So, this disc has a special virus included?" she asked. She held it up and looked at it as though she would be able to see it eating into the plastic laser grooves like a human virus eating into the immune system.

"Let's just hope they don't realize we've tricked them until we have the kids and get out of there. Otherwise we'll have to go with Plan B."

"What's Plan B?"

"I don't know yet. I'm hoping we won't have to find out."

She turned at the next corner and pulled into a 24-hour grocery store. The sales of the week were plastered in the windows with red letters and prices at least two feet tall. Shopping carts had not yet been gathered and corralled for the day but were here and there throughout the parking area, some turned on their sides, others pushed into parked cars.

"Are you hungry again?" asked Ivy in disbelief. This girl ate more calories in a day than she was allowed in a week and was still willow thin. Another injustice in the world she lived in.

"I could use an omelet about now but that's not why we're here." Raven pointed at the public telephone at the front of the store.

Ivy was shocked to see a working pay phone. She couldn't remember the last time she'd used one. Cell phones had made them nearly obsolete.

"Our phone's dead, remember? I have to call to set the time and place for the exchange. I'll be right back."

Raven climbed out of the car and stepped up to the phone with a purposeful stride. In jeans, t-shirt, and leather boots, she looked like a teenager, except for the confidence she exuded. Her short hair was no longer sticking out in severe spikes but had relaxed into a softer style that framed pale skin and accentuated her blue eyes, making her appear more vulnerable than Ivy had any reason to believe was possible.

She watched Raven dial a number on the phone, her back to the car. She leaned casually against the side of the building with one shoulder as though she were calling a friend rather than the man who had already sanctioned murder and kidnapping.

It didn't take long. Raven got back in the car, her face unreadable in the morning light.

"Are the kids all right? He hasn't hurt them, has he?"

Her gaze softened. "Don't worry, he won't hurt them. They're his life insurance on the off chance that the FBI catches up with him, and his business insurance policy that entitles him to one free disc of government secrets."

She pulled out a stick of gum, folded it in thirds and chewed on it for a minute in silence. She seemed to be a million miles away, deep in thought, but her gaze was on an old guy leaning against a lamppost. He looked homeless, with two or three layers of old clothes on his back and a cart of junk parked beside him. Smoking a cigarette, he stared defiantly back as though they were in a junior-high stare-down contest.

Raven broke contact first. She turned to Ivy and grinned. Apparently, the gum had been brain food because she had the look of someone with a plan.

"Do you know where Peony Park is?" she asked, excitement glowing in her eyes.

"The old amusement park? Sure, I've been there. Why?" she asked. Amusement parks were right up there with small planes in her book and even the *thought* made her feel a bit queasy.

Raven combed her hands through her hair and leaned back in the bucket seat, a look of purpose on her face. She put the car into gear and backed up.

"That's where we're meeting them. Anderson wanted to make the exchange in some warehouse, but I'm not crazy. I don't trust him. What we need is lots of people around. So, I suggested the amusement park and he agreed. It doesn't open until 11:00. That gives us time to get over there and get in before Anderson and his thug show up."

So close to actually making a deal made Ivy's stomach knot. Her kids meant everything to her but what if she were wrong going in without the FBI? What if they screwed it up badly and irrevocably? If she were responsible for something happening to Caleb or Riley, she would never forgive herself.

"Maybe we should call Samson and let him know. We could use the backup."

Raven shot her a look of commiseration but shook her head. "No. I know you trust him, but he's a straight arrow and those kind always go by the book. He'd have to call it in and there'd be a couple dozen cops swarming all over that place. Mr. Anderson isn't stupid. He'd be long gone before they ever made him."

Ivy leaned her head back and closed her eyes, not wanting Raven to see her fear slipping out in the form of tears. She drew a deep fortifying breath and slowly released it, coming to terms with what they had to do.

"I hope you're praying because that's our best bet right now." She gave her a sidelong look, stepped on the gas and slipped into the passing lane.

{16}

Samson pulled up at the Mocha Shack at 10:39. Traffic was a bear getting across town from the airport, but he'd made it in record time. With his adrenaline pumping the way it was he was amazed that he made it without a serious accident. He shut off the ignition and sat for a moment to pull himself together. Maggie would be worried enough without seeing him hopelessly out of control.

Control. That's what he lost along the way. Or maybe he never had it. He thought if he did his job well and followed the rules, he'd be rewarded with everything turning out the way he planned. But God had other plans.

When Ivy dropped into his life as a job assignment, he thought he could handle it the same as he handled everything in his life. In a purposeful, well thought out, planned manner that would end up with the job being done to the satisfaction of his captain and perhaps another rung added to his ladder of success. But Ivy turned out to be the woman he was falling in love with.

His plans for love and marriage weren't written in his personal planner yet, but God's planner was a whole new ballgame. This woman came with a ready-made family; two small kids he already loved and cared for. How could he plan for that?

He sighed and lowered his head to the steering wheel. He didn't know how much time he had left to find Ivy, but God did. In the scheme of things his planning had left a lot to be desired. He had been floundering around, worrying about what to do, when all the time he should have been praying and asking for help.

"Samson, what are you doing out here? I saw the car and ran right out."

Maggie stood at the car door peering in at him, a worried expression on her face. She wore her favorite apron that stated, "*Don't Worry, Be Happy. God's taking care of everything!*" Her hairnet covered about half her hair as usual and she had a smudge of raspberry jelly on one cheek.

"Maggie, I don't know what to do. Ivy hasn't called, and I haven't heard from Timmons. The children could be anywhere." He shook his head.

"They *could* be anywhere, but I happen to know exactly where," Maggie said with a lift of her penciled brows.

"What are you talking about?"

Maggie smiled and patted his hand where it gripped the top of the door. "One of the men came back in a while ago. He had dropped his wallet under the table. As he was leaving, I heard him talking on his cell phone. He said something about Peony Park at 11:30."

Samson grasped her hand and pulled her down to his level, so he could kiss her on the cheek. "Get going then," she said and stepped away from the car, folding her arms across her ample chest.

"It's 10:45. God sure keeps a tight schedule. Pray, Maggie," he called out as he drove away.

Peony Park was a good twenty-five-minute drive. He waited at a red light wishing he had a strobe light in his car to get through traffic. Twenty-five minutes didn't give him a lot of time to get in the gate and look for them in the crowd. He had no idea if they were meeting at the entrance or inside at a certain ride.

He pulled the cell phone from his pocket and dialed Timmons number as he sat at the light. The phone rang but instead of Timmons grumbly voice, the automated answering service came on. He left a message to meet him at Peony Park and flipped the phone closed.

His car darted in and out of traffic closing the distance to his destination. But it seemed as though the faster he drove, the more red lights he had to stop for. He began to worry that he wouldn't get there in time, then traffic slowed to a crawl and suddenly came to a complete stop. Traffic was backed up too far ahead to see what was causing the congestion. He waited, fingers tapping a staccato beat on the steering wheel.

He lifted his eyes to the rearview mirror as a police cruiser went past on the shoulder of the road, the siren wailing a warning of alarm. With an accident up ahead blocking access he might never get there in time.

"God, why did you bring me this far just to stop me now?" he asked aloud. With the words barely out of his mouth, he felt remorse for calling God into question. God just answered his prayer to find where the children would be, and he was on his way to find them. If there was an accident up ahead, surely God knew about that too. God didn't react to circumstances; He already knew what was going to happen.

Samson remembered a bit of a verse in Isaiah when God told Israel, *"in quietness and trust is your strength."* He needed that strength more than anything. The strength to trust.

A horn sounded behind him and he looked up to see the line of traffic slowly moving forward again. He took his foot off the brake and moved along with the flow, still anxious but calmer of spirit.

†††

"Are you sure this is the best idea you could come up with?" asked Ivy. She looked down at her new wardrobe, her nose wrinkled in disgust.

On the way to Peony Park Raven had made a detour, stopping at a thrift shop that bore the name of *Used but Usable*. The window displayed a mannequin wearing fairly attractive but out of date clothing.

They went inside and were immediately hit by the unmistakable odor of mildew and mothballs, which set off Ivy's allergies. She began sneezing and coughing while her eyes watered, and her throat itched.

It didn't take Raven long to find what she was looking for. She pulled old clothes off the racks as fast as a construction worker clearing off an all-you-can-eat buffet. Soon her arms were full. She paid the lady at the front of the store and asked if they could use the dressing room, which consisted of a cubicle with a curtain, to change into the *jewels* they'd found.

Now they stood beside the car, across from the park. Raven popped the clip out of the gun and back in and wrapped it in a newspaper. She looked Ivy up and down, scrutinizing her handiwork.

"Personally, I think you look swell," she said. "You saw the guy at the supermarket. Nobody ever looks twice at someone like that, and if they do," she lifted her shoulders dismissively, "they don't really see them."

"That's sad, you know?" Ivy said. "To be invisible to the world around you – has got to hurt."

"Yeah, well be glad because today you need to be invisible." Raven held out the newspaper. "Keep this close. You may need it." Ivy hesitated, and Raven grasped her hand and placed it around the concealed weapon. "I know you can do this. I saw how brave you were at the rest stop, Ivy. Your children are counting on you."

Ivy took the paper and tucked it into the pocket of the oversized coat she wore over an old baggy, brown plaid dress. The dress reached nearly to her ankles and was trimmed with dingy lace. On her feet she wore black socks and a pair of red canvas tennis shoes that looked as though moths had gotten the best of them. A yellow straw hat, a bunch of plastic fruit perched precariously along its brim, covered her head. She felt anything but brave at the moment. Besides being terrified for her children, she felt inadequate to do what was required. She nodded grimly and with shaking hands picked up the paper sack filled with extra clothes Raven had purchased. Apparently, a smart bag lady never went anywhere without her possessions. She'd left her purse under the seat of the car since it didn't go with her new outfit and Raven had the disc to exchange for Caleb and Riley.

"Good luck," Raven called softly as she watched Ivy move toward the gate. She would wait a couple of minutes and then follow.

The carnival rides filled up fast. Mothers stood on the sidelines and watched their offspring being latched into swinging seats. It was stiflingly hot, and Ivy could feel sweat trickle down beneath her layers of clothing. The sights and sounds of the park mingled with traffic from the busy street outside the gates. She sauntered slowly along, her eyes peeled for any sign of the children or their abductors.

She moved past the Octopus, mechanical tentacles filled with screaming kids being thrust forward and back and around and around until she had to look away to keep her breakfast down. Throwing up on the sidewalk might draw a bit of attention whether she was dressed as a homeless woman or not. She swallowed down the sour taste in her mouth.

The smell of freshly popped corn and the sugary sweet scent of cotton candy hung in the air when she neared the concession stands, nearly overpowering the heavier oil and smoke perfume that wafted around the motorized rides. Two young men behind the counter spun giant pink and blue cotton fluff onto paper handles and stuffed them into plastic bags as a teenage girl waited on the group of short customers who wanted ice-cream bars. Ivy's glance swept over the children hoping to see two familiar, sweet faces. But they weren't among them. The kids paid for their treats and ran past her heading in the direction of the roller coaster.

She turned in a slow circle to get her bearings, trying to remember where the Carousel was located. Raven would meet Mr. Anderson there to make the swap. It was public enough for safety but busy enough and loud enough to be private for the exchange. Ivy looked around at all the mothers with small children and worried that more innocent people might be put in danger. There was no time to reconsider though. She had to get to the meeting place and blend into the background.

She headed toward the sound of music blaring from the speakers of the old merry-go-round. The tune was familiar; a waltz she'd heard on numerous occasions when she came to Peony Park as a teenager. It had been a great place for her and her friends to hang out and get away from the rest of the world.

She followed a curve in the path and came upon a line of parents with children now waiting for a turn on one of the brightly painted horses. Manes flew in the wind as they continued their unending course around and around the carousel, the music blaring forth. It was a call to step up and have an adventure, if only in your imagination.

A group of teenage boys rushed past her as she paused on the path watching the happy faces of the children as they pointed out the horse they wanted to ride when it came their turn. One of the boys shoved against her in his hurry and she fell back into the bushes, scratching her hands and arms. He paused and looked unsure what to do. One of the other boys laughed and yelled for him to hurry up.

"It's just an old bag lady, come on!"

The boy hesitated for a second before running after his friends, leaving Ivy still floundering in the shrubbery, her eyes wide in shock.

If she had any doubts that someone would spot her and becoming suspicious, she didn't anymore. But she'd never felt as angry and alone. The boys treated her as though she didn't matter. She pulled herself awkwardly from the bushes, brushed herself off and looked around to see if anyone had noticed. As far as she could tell she was quite invisible. The few who dared look at her at all gave her a glance of disgust, as though she were some worthless drunk tottering on the path rather than a woman who had been pushed uncaringly into the Rhododendrons. Others ignored her completely. Out of sight, out of mind.

The carousel had stopped, and passengers were disembarking. Children and parents streamed from the exit gate, their eyes lit up with excitement as they pressed on for the next ride. The music started up again with another happy waltz, loud enough for hearing loss.

She drew her hat down over her eyes as she approached the line of people forming at the gate. She glanced over the area, her shoulders rigid with nerves at the thought of what would transpire in a matter of minutes. Raven was nowhere in sight, but she had a feeling she wasn't far away.

She walked toward an empty bench positioned near the exit gate, hoping to be in a prime position to move fast when the time came. People automatically edged away from her as she passed, as though she might carry lice or bedbugs. People looked anywhere but at her.

She plopped her bag down on the bench and sat beside it in the shade of the overhanging canopy. Overhead, clouds were gathering to the west. The wind had picked up as well, whipping loose scraps of trash across the path and along the fence line, and she had to take hold of her hat with one hand as a strong gust nearly tore it from her head. With humidity as high as it was today, it wouldn't be long before a nice thunderstorm broke out. Possibly even tornado weather. She turned her gaze from the skies to scan the faces of the newest arrivals, hoping for a glimpse of Caleb and Riley in the crowd.

"Mind if I sit here?" asked a familiar voice.

Ivy didn't look up but kept her face concealed from Samson by the brim of her hat. She scooted her bag closer to her side and he seemed to take that as assent. He sat down on the other end of the bench. His hands pressed into tight fists as he leaned forward, elbows on his knees. When he sighed heavily, she dared take a peak at his face. He looked exhausted and tense at the same time. The small lines in his forehead were more pronounced, his face drawn into a frown. She felt guilty for what she'd put him through but elated that he'd actually found her. Of course, he didn't know he found her yet and that was the rub. Should she say something? She wanted to throw herself into his arms and put this whole mess into his capable hands, but Raven said they couldn't trust him to do what had to be done. She didn't want to believe that. Wouldn't it be better to have someone with experience in charge rather than a con and a mother of two who had absolutely no idea what she was doing here besides sheer desperation to get her children back?

Samson's cell rang, and he flipped it open. The noise and music were so loud he had to ask the caller to speak up. He covered his other ear with the palm of his hand. "Yes, I'm here. No – just wait there. I'll meet you at the gate. I have no idea where to look," he said with a shake of his head. "We'll have to spread out and cover as much area as we can. Ok. See you in a minute." He flipped the phone closed and stuffed it in his back jeans pocket, stood and headed for the entrance gate.

Ivy didn't know what to do. Samson had brought someone with him. It was probably his partner, Timmons, but it could be more agents as well. It was one thing to want Samson here for backup but quite another to have men running all over with loaded weapons who considered retrieval of the disc their top priority rather than her children's lives. She shuddered at what would transpire if Mr. Anderson thought they'd set a trap.

A pair of long shapely legs encased in tight jeans stood in front of her. She looked up and recognized the set of Raven's shoulders. Her head was tilted to the side as though listening but with all the noise around her Ivy doubted she could pick any one thing out of the jumble.

"That was smart not to let him get a look at you. He'll only bring trouble, mark my words. Agents are like ants; where there's one, there are dozens. Let's hope he doesn't bring his whole colony down on us," she said before sauntering over to the row of people already lining up for the next ride. She fell into line and ran her fingers casually through her hair, her gaze meeting Ivy's with reassurance.

"I don't want to ride on the Merry-go-round. That's for babies!" At the sound of Caleb's voice so close to the bench, she nearly spun around in excitement but instead willed herself to remain calm and stay put, not moving a muscle.

"You're going to ride on it with your sister and me whether you like it or not, so shut up," a gravelly voice threatened.

Ivy's jaw clenched. That man wouldn't get away with taking her children and speaking to them like that. She pushed her hand deep into the pocket of her coat and felt the reassuring bulge of the gun.

She didn't turn to watch them when they passed but waited until they were in line a few feet behind Raven before she let her gaze rest on her two

children. They were both sober and quiet, which
wasn't like them at all, but they seemed whole and
unharmed, at least physically. She ached for them
when the man placed a hand on each of their frail
shoulders and pushed them ahead of him in the line.

The man was on the short side with dark hair
combed straight back from his forehead, revealing a
thin white scar. He wore dark glasses, so she couldn't
see his eyes, but she imagined they were cold and
hard. She couldn't tell if he carried a weapon but no
doubt he was quite capable of harming her children
without one. Dressed in black pants and a dark green
t-shirt, he didn't fit in with the summertime crowd. He
also didn't fit the description of Mr. Anderson that
Raven had given her. The man had to be Lionel, the
lackey. Raven had mentioned him. She didn't like
him one bit. His boss was apparently not going to
show. Anderson wouldn't want to chance being
arrested for the crimes he committed. Better to send
in a fall guy in case the whole thing went sour.

The carousel ground to a stop, and small
children slid from the horses' backs and jumped to the
ground running. Their parents followed at a slower
rate, calling out for them to wait up. Once it was
empty, the ticket taker let the new crowd through the
gate and onto the ride. Ivy watched Raven step
carefully up onto the platform and walk slowly
through the circle of wild horses, taking her time
deciding which one to ride, as though the decision
was of optimum importance. Finally, she swung her
leg over a white stallion. Frozen in time with its mane
flying and its eyes wide, it strained against the leather
bridle. The saddle was painted red and gold, the color
chipped in places from many years of service.

Caleb climbed up on the platform and turned to
help his sister who stopped and balked now that she

realized they were going to ride on horses. Riley had a fear of animals larger than herself, but Ivy hadn't realized it included mechanical ones as well. She tensed when the man bodily lifted Riley and carried her to a horse directly behind the one Raven sat on. Riley's lip quivered, and two fat tears rolled silently down her cheeks. Caleb climbed on behind her and placed his arms around her with big brotherly concern. Ivy felt moisture well in her eyes. The man stood with his hand on the mane of the horse, his head turning this way and that, ever vigilant. Ivy saw him glance her way briefly and then turn back to the other passengers boarding around him. The horses and buggies filled quickly, and the gate was shut. The carousel started up again, its horses galloping up and down to the tempo of a Johann Strauss waltz.

She felt the first drops of rain from the storm clouds darkening the sky. The air was heavier than before. Ivy looked up at the sky, now a sickly green, reminding her of storms when she was a child and her parents shepherded her and Holly down to the dank underground regions of their cellar.

What should she do? The wind kicked up gravel dust and blew it into her face. She blinked it away and wiped at her eyes with the sleeve of her coat, not wanting to miss a second of the exchange. Lionel had sidled up closer to Raven's horse, who quickly slid to the other side, leaving the wooden beast between them. Ivy watched Raven slip her hand into her back pocket and pull out the disc. She passed it across the empty saddle to the man on the other side. He took it, handed her an envelope in return, and climbed into the vacated saddle while Raven walked back toward Caleb and Riley.

"You seem quite interested in those children." A tall man in a navy-blue suit stood beside her, his hand thrust casually in his jacket pocket. His hair and mustache were perfectly groomed, the color of steel. His eyes were a flintier color, hard to describe, but they appeared full of shadows. "You wouldn't be their mother, would you?" he asked, with a flash of teeth.

Anderson slipped onto the bench close beside her and she could feel the blunt end of the gun he held in his pocket pushed painfully into her side.

"I knew Bree would try something, but I didn't know what," he explained smoothly. "That's why Lionel is here. I wasn't about to go into the thick of things without an advantage. Looks like you've given me that." He chuckled as though he'd told a joke.

"What do you want? We brought you the disc. I just want my children back," she pleaded, turning toward him. She felt the jab of the gun harder this time and flinched. Her fingers found the handle of the gun in her own coat pocket and she flicked the safety off.

"I don't want much. Just assurance that we'll leave this park without any undercover agents popping out of the bushes. I have no intention of going to prison." He smoothed his mustache with his free hand and she noticed the diamond and onyx ring he wore. It was engraved on the side with his initials AA. Her hand tightened convulsively on the gun and she remembered what Raven told her. *"Don't put your finger on the trigger unless you intend to use it."* She quickly relaxed her grip.

"We didn't bring any agents with us," she said with more bravado than she felt. "You asked us to come alone and we did." She prayed Samson stayed out of sight. She didn't think Mr. Anderson would believe the FBI just showed up on their own.

He lifted his shoulders in a shrug. "Just call me cautious. Don't hold it against me if I don't trust you.

I'm sure that you'd say anything to get your kids back, wouldn't you, Mrs. Winter?" He leaned closer, and brushed his fingers across her cheek, sending a shiver of alarm through her entire body. His eyes slanted narrowly. "I will kill you and your children if you don't do exactly as I say."

The carousel slowly came to a stop. Ivy caught a glimpse of Raven talking to the children before pulling them down from the horse, ready to exit the platform. Her eyes widened in alarm when she saw Mr. Anderson beside Ivy. She glanced back at Lionel, unsure what to do.

"Ladies and Gentlemen, may we have your attention please. There is a severe thunderstorm coming our way any minute, so we will have to close the rides down for now. They will reopen once the storm passes. Thank you." The announcement over the park speaker system put a smile on Mr. Anderson's face. He stood and pulled Ivy up by her baggy coat sleeve.

"This is turning out perfectly. With all the people exiting the park, no one will notice us, now will they?" His grip on her arm tightened as he guided her toward the main gates.

Ivy saw Raven and the children jump from the platform and put some distance between themselves and Lionel. Mr. Anderson pulled her around a bend in the path and she lost sight of them. He walked briskly, his iron grip tightening even more when she slowed. A few people stared at the sight of a well-dressed man escorting a bag lady, but most were too busy exiting the park to notice.

"Just mind your manners and everything will be fine. Lionel is keeping an eye on your children until I'm safely in the limo. Then you may have them back. I certainly don't want to keep them." He maneuvered around a tipped over trashcan, his lip curled in disgust. "I can't promise to let your friend off so easily though. She did fail me after all."

The smug satisfaction in his voice gave Ivy the impression that Raven was now expendable. Anderson was a cruel man who apparently enjoyed making people suffer. After all he had murdered Todd and tried to have Samson killed as well.

"She didn't fail you. She brought the disc. She didn't have to come here today. She could have let me do this on my own or stole it from me and sold it to another buyer, but she didn't." Ivy realized she was wasting her time. He wasn't even listening. He scanned the faces of everyone they passed, looking for cops or FBI.

The weight of the gun in her pocket was reassuring, a last resort, like a buoy in the ocean when you're drowning. But as long as Lionel dogged her children's steps she feared for their safety. That changed things a bit. She couldn't do anything until she knew they were out of danger. She pushed the gun safety back on with her finger.

The wind blew wildly, sending trash and leaves flying through the air. A flash of lightning rent the blackened sky, followed closely by a crack of thunder. She jumped at the sound although she had been expecting it. The first clap during a storm always set her nerves on edge. Huge drops of rain began to fall, soaking Mr. Anderson's expensive suit. He swore and started to run, pulling her along with him. Her baggy clothes whipped in the wind and tangled around her legs, slowing her stride. He glared at her as though she were the cause of the storm.

"Can't you go any faster?" he yelled into the wind. "My suit is going to be ruined!"

"So is mine," she yelled back, unable to keep a smile from her lips.

They were a dozen feet from the open gates when the wind whipped her hat from her head and sent it flying. She watched it skitter down the path until it stopped at the feet of a man in jeans and a white t-shirt. He bent down and picked up the fruit-laden hat by the tattered brim and looked around for its owner. Anderson yanked her arm harder, and she stumbled along beside him, hoping Samson recognized her under all the layers of clothing and grime.

{17}

Samson watched the tall man in the dark suit lead the bag lady forcefully from the park. Something didn't sit right here. He looked down at the battered straw hat in his hand and frowned. Something nagged at the back of his mind. Of course! When he sat beside the woman earlier, she had a paper sack with her. Why would she leave it behind? Homeless people never willingly abandoned their belongings. But there was something else bothering him. He replayed the short scene in his mind, trying to recall each small detail before he was called away to the gate. She had pulled her bag to the end of the bench but never spoke or looked up...as if she were hiding behind her hat. That wasn't unusual for people living on the streets, they seldom made eye contact, fearing those around them, but...

He shook his head. What was it that bothered him so much? He watched her being helped, or rather forced, through the open gates and into the street. She glanced back, her face streaked with dirt and grime. That was it! Her face was filthy but when she'd pulled the sack to her side of the bench earlier, her noticed her fingernails were clean, carefully manicured, and polished.

He strode toward the entrance, covering the distance in seconds. Pausing out front, he looked up and down the street, hoping to spot them before they drove off. With each passing moment the sky became darker, and the wind blew with such force he felt as though he were swimming against the tide. He spotted them getting into a long, black limousine half a block down.

With the battered hat in hand he pushed forward against the wind and caught up to them just as the driver was about to close the door. He grasped the top of the door to keep it from being shut and gallantly held out the hat. "I believe the lady dropped this," he said with a southern drawl. The driver stepped back, and Samson slid smoothly around the door to lean inside. "I wouldn't want you to have to buy a new bonnet just because of a silly ol' storm."

His southern gentleman act didn't hold much water with the gray-haired man, but Ivy's eyes lit right up. Even in the dim interior of the car he could see she was frightened. Hesitantly, she reached out and took the hat.

"Well, were you expecting a reward, or did you want to ask her out on a date?" The man stared at Samson with obvious impatience. He gave a curt nod to the driver, who quickly moved Samson away from the door and shut it.

Samson couldn't see Ivy through the limo's tinted windows, but he knew she was watching him. He smiled and started down the sidewalk. Behind him, the limo pulled away from the curb.

He flipped open his phone and called Timmons.

Before it rang, he heard his partner's voice on the sidewalk directly behind him, "You rang?"

Samson spun around, automatically reaching for the gun in his shoulder holster, which he remembered too late, he wasn't wearing.

His partner laughed and shook his head. "So, what's up?"

"They have Ivy in the limo that just pulled away.

"My Jeep's right here." Timmons pointed across the street to his blue CJ7.

"Let's see if we can catch up."

The seats were slick with rain since Timmons had left the top off. He found a baseball cap under the seat and pulled it on over his wet crew cut.

They pulled out and made a u-turn. Samson pointed at an old, brown Buick parked a few car lengths up the street. Their headlights caught the driver full in the face, and Samson saw him clearly. It was the same man who stood outside Ivy's apartment watching. The same man who shot him in the park. The car pulled away from the curb, and Samson nodded at Timmons to follow.

"He'll get us there a lot faster. Just don't lose him, whatever you do."

Timmons turned the jeep in a half circle and followed the Buick at a discreet distance. The suspect didn't seem to be in a hurry. He drove the speed limit like a real law-abiding citizen.

"Were the kids in the limo too?" Timmons asked, stopped at a red light. There were two cars between them and the Buick.

Samson shook his head and wiped his face with the sleeve of his t-shirt. "I didn't see them. Maybe they want to check out the disc before they release them."

"*If* they plan to release them," Timmons said and swore. He took off from the light, tires slipping and finding purchase on wet pavement.

Samson knew Timmons well enough to know he had taken the blame for the kids' abduction squarely on his own shoulders. But there was no use casting blame. There was plenty to go around. His gaze swung back to the brown Buick.

"We'll get them, Timmons," he said, clenching and unclenching his fists. He imagined what it would feel like to get his hands around the neck of the man who took Ivy's children from her.

The Buick took a quick left and they followed, staying three cars behind. Rain fell steadily, but they'd left behind the worst of the storm. The sky ahead was clearing, sunlight trying desperately to peak through rain-heavy clouds. He glanced back and saw streaks of lightning rent the sky three or four miles away.

He removed the gun from his ankle holster and stared intently down at it as though it were a living thing. He hoped he didn't have to shoot anyone, but if he did he prayed his aim was true. With Ivy and the children involved...

"I think he's getting ready to stop. He put his blinker on and pulled into the right-hand lane. There's a snazzy hotel on that side of the street," Timmons said, slowing.

The Buick pulled into the hotel's underground parking ramp. Timmons put his blinker on and pulled over to turn in after him. The automated gatekeeper announced, "Please take a ticket", and he pulled off the stub. The bar went up, and they slowly moved forward.

"This could be some sort of trap, so be careful," warned Samson. He took the safety off his weapon and released his seatbelt. The man had already shot him once, he doubted he would have any compunction about doing it again. It was possible they'd been spotted and were being led on a wild goose chase, but he doubted it. The storm and heavy traffic were perfect covers for tailing.

They wound slowly down until they spotted the taillights of the car ahead searching for a space. It turned in between a little sports car and an SUV. They drove around to the next aisle, so he wouldn't get a glimpse of them passing and quickly pulled into an empty space.

"Ready?" Timmons pulled off the wet cap and climbed out of the jeep.

Samson tucked the pistol into the back of his jeans and followed Timmons toward the elevator. They heard the doors open, and saw the man they were following get in. Staying out of sight until the doors closed, they waited behind a cement pillar. Then they ran to the doors, watching to see what floor it stopped on. The arrow landed on six. Timmons pushed the button to bring it back down and they both stood tensely waiting for all of five seconds before Samson couldn't wait anymore.

"I'll take the stairs, you take the elevator," he said. He ran for the stairwell.

He took the steps three at a time, up one flight and then another. At the sixth-floor door he paused, breathing hard. He opened the door a crack and looked out into the hall. It was empty. He stepped out, glanced up and down the hall before advancing. The whirr of the elevator heralded Timmons ascent. He knew he should wait for backup, but it might be too late. He heard a quiet knock on a door. He moved as quietly as possible down the thickly carpeted hallway until it branched off to the right, then with his back to the wall, cautiously peeked around the corner.

Still wearing dark glasses, his hair slicked straight back, all the man needed was a black pinstripe suit and he could pass for a short Italian mobster. When the door opened, he leaned forward and held out a small plastic case. The disc. Samson would bet on it. But how did he get the disc if the other man had Ivy? Was Raven still mixed up in this and if so, where was she? And where were the children?

The door shut, and the man turned to leave, heading back toward Samson. Samson pulled back around the corner before he was spotted and quickly knocked at the nearest room, hoping against hope that no one was there. When the man rounded the corner, Samson leaned in toward the door, keeping his face turned away.

"Honey, le'me in. I forgot my key," he mumbled against the door.

In unwelcome surprise he heard the rattle of the chain and then the deadbolt shot back. The elevator doors opened behind him. He glanced over his shoulder as Timmons stepped right into the path of their quarry. Suddenly the door he leaned on was pulled open and he went sprawling headfirst into the room, knocking a woman in a pink terrycloth robe and slippers down with him. She screamed and made a mad scramble for the phone. Samson rolled to his feet, pulling out the gun from the back of his waistband. It only caused her to scream louder. Before he could get back out into the hall, his partner had already pushed the little mobster into the elevator, up against the wall. Timmons had one large, beefy hand wrapped around the little guy's neck, holding him in place, while the other twisted his arm behind his back to cuff him.

Samson turned to show the frightened woman his badge and apologize but she had run into the bathroom, locking herself in. He tapped on the door and tried to explain briefly through the barrier, but she didn't respond.

"You really shouldn't open your door to strangers, lady. It can be dangerous," he called out helpfully and let himself out of her room.

Heads appeared down the hall as people peeked out the doors of their rooms to see what the commotion was all about. He ducked into the elevator and pushed the garage level.

"Thanks, Timmons. That was quick thinking."

Timmons shrugged and tightened his grip on their prisoner. "No problem. Looked like you had your hands full with something pink." His shoulders shook with amusement.

"I guess I had that coming," Samson said and grinned.

Their prisoner had remained silent so far, except for heavy breathing. Timmons had the side of his face pressed up against the wall of the elevator, condensation from his breath clouding the mirrored surface of the metal. Now he sputtered in a gravelly voice, "Who are you and what do you want with me?"

"Shut up!" growled Timmons. "You don't get to ask the questions here, we do. If I want you to speak, I'll let you know."

Samson pulled the man's wallet from his hip pocket and opened it. "It says here your name is Lionel Templeton. Is that right?"

The elevator ground to a halt on the garage level, and the doors opened. Raven stood there with her hands on her hips, a defiant glare in her blue eyes.

"Well, it's about time!" she said. Then she recognized Timmons's prisoner and blanched. Her eyes darted left and right as though considering escape.

Timmons pulled Lionel out of the elevator and pushed him to his knees on the cement floor of the underground garage. Raven stared down at the man, a sultry smile turning up the corners of her mouth. She bent and patted his cheek in a condescending manner. "Hello, Lionel. It's good to see you, sweetie. I hope they give you a nice room in the state penitentiary."

Lionel gazed up at Raven with a look of absolute hatred on his ruddy face. He bared his teeth. "You better hold your tongue, woman, if you want to live to see another day."

"Take him to the jeep, Timmons. Raven and I are going up to get Ivy." Samson grasped the dark-headed woman by the arm and led her into the elevator.

"Are you sure?" Timmons stood over Lionel, his feet braced apart and looked back over his shoulder at the two of them as the doors closed.

"We'll be fine."

The elevator started up again.

Raven leaned against the reflective wall with one shoulder, eyeing Samson speculatively. "Are you going to marry her?"

"I don't think this is the time to discuss my personal life. I need to know where the children are and whether or not the man that has Ivy can get to them."

Raven pushed away from the wall. "Don't worry about Caleb and Riley. I took them somewhere safe. It's Ivy you need to worry about. Anderson is a very dangerous man."

She ran fingers through her hair, her eyes narrowed in thought. "Why don't I knock on the door and draw him out? Then you can come and save the day – and the girl."

"You've got a deal."

"One more thing," she said with just a touch of worry reflected in her eyes. "Ivy has a loaded gun and she doesn't really know how to use it."

†††

Ivy sat in a red upholstered chair in Mr. Anderson's room and looked around. The suite consisted of three rooms; the front room where she sat, a large and separate bedroom, and a bathroom.

He emerged from the bedroom now, wearing a robe and slippers, courtesy of the hotel. She'd heard the shower running minutes ago and his damp hair was parted on the side and neatly combed.

The chauffer had been her watchdog while she waited. He stood with his back to the door, hat in hand, unmoving and incommunicable. God knew she'd tried to talk him into letting her leave. Now Mr. Anderson waved him away. He turned and went out the door without a backward glance.

She glanced nervously at the closed door and felt the hairs on the back of her neck stand up. She didn't want to be alone with this man.

"You seem tense, Mrs. Winter," he said. He moved toward her, and she cringed, wishing she could disappear between the cushions.

"What do you want with me, Mr. Anderson?" she asked with more bravado than she felt. "You have the disc. Lionel brought it to you before you took a shower. I want to see my children now." She stood up, but he pushed her back into the chair.

"Ivy. May I call you Ivy? It's so much friendlier than Mrs. Winter. You may call me Ace," he said with a strange light in his eyes.

Ivy rose again and faced him, her tone pleading. "I don't care what you call me, but could you please let me see my children? Just tell me where they are."

He sighed and turned toward the table by the bed where a bottle of champagne chilled in a bucket of ice. Ivy assumed Mr. Anderson and his cohorts were planning to celebrate after finally getting a hold of the disc. Now she sucked in a breath as he pulled it from the ice, letting the bottle drip onto the floor. He smiled, and she couldn't help but shiver under his gaze.

"Would you have a glass of champagne with me, Ivy? I don't like to drink alone. Though sometimes I do." He poured two fluted glasses full without waiting for a reply and crossed the room with one in each hand. He held one toward her.

"I don't want champagne. I want my children," she insisted.

At the repeated mention of her children he frowned. "I'm sure that Bree is taking perfectly good care of your two little brats," he said, his voice hard. He withdrew the glass at her refusal and drank it down as well as his own, then tossed them both onto the sofa nearby. With one quick stride he took hold of her shoulders and pushed her up against the wall. Ivy gasped and struggled to free herself.

"I think it's about time that you and I got to know each other," he whispered harshly. He tried to kiss her, but she turned her face away in disgust and his lips grazed her cheek.

She tried to scream but he put his hands around her neck and squeezed so tightly that she could barely breath. She choked and gagged against the pressure and his mouth came down on hers blocking her oxygen supply completely.

There was a ding from his laptop computer and he pulled back, breathing heavily. "Saved by the bell," he said and patted her cheek before turning his back on her and walking to the desk. He sat down and read the instant message, then typed his response.

"My buyer is online and ready for his package. Isn't technology wonderful!" He turned in the chair and met her frightened gaze. "I'll just be a moment, beautiful, and then we'll continue what we started."

Ivy watched him take the disc from the pocket of his robe and insert it into the computer. She held her breath. He pressed *send* and sat back with a satisfied sigh.

"That's that then. They get the information, and I get forty million dollars in my Swiss account. Everyone goes home happy. Except for Todd of course." He shrugged as though killing someone was all in a day's work.

Ivy cringed as he stood and advanced toward her again. What would happen if he looked back and realized the disc contained a virus and it was eating away at not only the weapon plans but also everything on his laptop? But he didn't look back; he just kept coming, his long thin hands on the belt of his robe.

He reached out and grasped the front of the baggy, old coat she wore and pulled her hard against his chest. She shivered with revulsion when he ran a finger along her cheek in a gentle caress. Suddenly he drew back and looked down at her in disgust, as though just realizing he was seducing a bag lady. She sucked in a breath of relief at the reprieve.

"Take those ridiculous clothes off, Ivy!" he commanded in a voice that brooked no argument.

Before she could react, he grabbed the old hat off her head and tossed it across the room. She hadn't even realized she was still wearing it. She must have put it back on after Samson retrieved it for her. He reached for her coat next, and she pushed him away. Her hand slid into the pocket, and she felt the cold metal of the gun. She grasped the handle tightly but hoped she wouldn't have to use it.

"I'll do it myself," she said backing away, her fingers flying to the buttons of the coat.

He stood back and folded his arms, clearly amused. "Don't keep me waiting."

Ivy froze. Her stomach churned, and she felt physically ill at the thought of this man touching her. "Oh God," she whispered.

"God isn't here, Ivy. I am," he said, anger creeping into his voice.

She moved back until she hit the wall. His eyes turned steel gray with determination. He gave up waiting for her to take off the clothes and moved to help. She pulled the gun from the depths of her pocket and aiming it directly at his chest.

"Stop right there, or I'll shoot," she said.

He stopped and stared at the gun in her hands with a mixture of disbelief and fear. Her hands shook as she held it and she saw his confidence return.

"You won't shoot me, Ivy. You *can't* shoot me," he said, still advancing.

"I will. I swear!"

He shook his head and a smile of pure evil spread from his lips to his eyes. "You have the safety on."

The next thing she knew they were struggling for possession of the gun. He yanked on it and it flew across the floor, spinning like a top. It came to rest against the leg of the small table in the corner. He pulled back his hand to hit her when there was a knock at the door. He stood motionless, his hand still upraised, apparently waiting for whoever was there to go away, but the knock sounded again, insistent.

He pushed her into the chair and picked up the gun. Stuffing it into the pocket of his robe, he went to the door and looked through the peephole.

"Well, well, well," he drawled. "Looks like your friend has shown up to rescue you."

Ivy pushed the hair out of her eyes, confused. Why would Anderson look so self-assured if Samson were out there? Didn't he even fear the FBI? Was he that insane that he thought he was above the law? She looked on in surprise as he released the chain and thrust open the door, waving in his newest guest with a cold, calculating, smile.

"Nice to see you again, Bree. Won't you join us?"

Raven entered the room but stayed just inside the door, her glance taking in Anderson's robe and slippers then resting on Ivy's pale face. She stopped before he could shut the door.

"What's going on in here, Ace? You're not holding Ivy against her will, are you?" she asked with a lift of her dark brows.

"I don't see how that's any of your business."

He started to shut the door and suddenly it flew back against his shoulder, making him wince and cry out.

Samson charged in and tackled Anderson to the ground. They wrestled there on the floor, struggling to get the upper hand. Anderson tried to shove Samson off but when that didn't work he grasped him around the throat and choked him. Samson landed a blow to his abdomen. Anderson yelped and released his grip long enough for Samson to roll him over to his stomach and jerked one arm behind his back. He reached for his cuffs and didn't see Anderson easing his free hand into the pocket of the robe.

"Samson, he has a gun!" yelled Ivy, jumping from her chair.

Raven already spotted it and brought her heel down on his hand while it was still in the pocket. He cursed and jerked out his hand, minus the gun, examining it minutely for injury.

Samson yanked the injured hand back with the other one and cuffed him, then reached into the pocket of Anderson's robe and carefully withdrew the gun.

"Is this yours?" he asked Ivy, frowning.

She shook her head.

He glanced at Raven, but she gave him an innocent, wide-eyed look and threw her arms around Ivy. "Thank God you're all right!" she burst out melodramatically, which was so unlike her.

Ivy hugged her back and whispered, "Thanks." Then she pulled away and demanded, "Where are Caleb and Riley?"

Raven smiled. "I got them a babysitter."

"You left them with strangers after all they've been through?" she asked, incredulous. What was Raven thinking? Her children had just been through something no one should have to endure, and she callously deserts them into the hands of strangers? She shook her head. "How could you do that?"

"They're safe, and they're being taken care of. In fact, I wouldn't be surprised if they're already back with your sister." She folded her arms across her chest and shrugged. "As I was leaving the park I left them with a policeman in a cruiser. He promised to get them home. Don't worry. They looked anything but scared. Last I saw them they were being shown all the cool gadgets in the patrol car," she assured her.

"I'd like to know how you accomplished that," Samson remarked dryly. He lifted Ace Anderson to his feet and shoved him toward the door. "I don't really have time for explanations right now, but I'd like to talk to you both later and get the full story, so don't disappear." He stared pointedly at Raven before moving Anderson out the door and down the hall. The last they heard of Ace Anderson he was threatening Samson with a lawsuit for not allowing him to change into proper clothes.

Ivy felt a bit shaky, so she sat back down. She took long, deep breaths and a look around the room that had been her prison only minutes ago. She was free, and her children were safe. She breathed a quiet prayer of thanks and finally looked up, feeling much stronger.

"Let's go. I need to see my children."

Raven took her arm, and they walked out together, letting the door swing closed behind them.

{18}

When Ivy and Raven finally pulled up outside across the street from Holly's house, a patrol car was parked at the curb. The officer who had brought the children home was standing on the porch saying his goodbyes. They watched when he finally got into his cruiser and pulled away.

Ivy reached for the door handle, but Raven didn't move to get out. She just sat there staring straight ahead. "You aren't coming in?" she asked.

It had started to rain again, big fat drops that thumped like olives falling on the hood of the car. She stared out at the street. The wet blacktop gave off a sheen of oil in the path of the car's headlights.

Ivy wanted to rush into the house and pull her children into her arms and never let them go, but she couldn't leave without saying goodbye to Raven. Raven had stuck by her and was the main reason she had survived, and Caleb and Riley were now safe. She reached out and touched her arm, giving it a soft squeeze.

"Thank you, Raven. I couldn't have done any of this without you."

She shrugged and gave her a playful grin. "Of course not. You don't even know Kung Fu."

"No, I don't. You'll have to teach me sometime."

Raven looked past her at the house alight with welcome, and Ivy followed her gaze. The curtains on the front window were open and she could see Caleb and Riley getting hugs from Holly. Tears of joy filled Ivy's eyes, and she turned back to see that Raven was crying. But Raven quickly dashed a hand across her cheeks and turned back toward the steering wheel, gripping the leather cover.

"What will you do now?" asked Ivy. "You can't continue in your line of work, or you could turn up like Todd. I wouldn't want to see that happen," she said, her voice soft with worry. She cared about this young woman in spite of past misgivings.

Raven glanced her way, a frown between her black brows. "You really care what happens to me, after my involvement with your husband?"

Ivy accepted the challenge. She nodded. "I care about you, Raven. No matter what you did before. I haven't exactly been a saint myself, but ever since I let go of the past and let God control my future, I've learned to trust again. In Him – and in people," she said.

Raven's face filled with a child's yearning, something just out of reach. She swallowed hard and drew a deep breath. "That would be great, to be able to erase the past," she said, "but I've done some things that can't be erased. I can't forgive myself. I don't expect God would either."

"Raven, you're wrong. He can, and He will. You just have to ask." Ivy reached out and covered

Raven's hand with her own. She knew only God could change her mind. "I'll never forget you, Raven – or should I say, Brenna Blackman."

"I'll never forget you either." Brenna Blackman, alias Raven Black, waved a hand as Ivy opened the door and climbed out. "Wait!" she called before Ivy could shut the door.

She reached across the stick shift, opened the glove box, and pulled something out. She held it out to Ivy in the palm of her hand. Ivy looked down at the mini disc in surprise and then back at Raven. She had actually forgotten about the original disc. Raven could have taken it at any time, but here it was, a shining example that sometimes you *can* trust people to do what's right.

"Please return that to your boyfriend. I'm afraid I won't have time to meet with him after all."

Ivy smiled and tucked it into her pocket. She shut the door and stepped back from the car. Raven revved the motor and sped off down the street, her tires squealing as she took the corner too fast.

Ivy watched the car out of sight, then turned and ran to the house, her arms aching to hold her children once again.

†††

Ivy had fallen asleep sitting on Holly's couch, an arm around each of her children, all three of them exhausted from the emotional stress of the last few days. Holly and Bill asked questions until she was drained. They finally let her and the children alone and went into the kitchen to rehash the extraordinary set of circumstances that had occurred in the short time Ivy had been back in Omaha.

Ivy heard voices in the other room and stirred. She opened her eyes and watched Caleb and Riley sleep, their heads in her lap, their small faces peaceful, softly snoring. She brushed the hair back from Riley's forehead and smiled as her daughter turned her face and tried to burrow closer into her side.

Holly stepped hesitantly into the living room. "I didn't want to wake you," she began, "but your FBI agent is here to see you."

Her FBI agent? Ivy smiled, and her heart beat faster in anticipation. There were questions in her sister's eyes, but Ivy decided they would have to wait because Samson was here. Now that she had her children safe and sound, she needed to see him to confirm her own feelings. Had she imagined the attraction between them? Was it real, or just a temporary feeling brought on by a stressful situation? She needed to know.

She gently repositioned the kids on the couch and stood up, smoothing the tan slacks and pink t-shirt she had changed into after a shower. They were already a little wrinkled from the children sleeping on her lap, but they were a world better than the outfit Samson had seen her in earlier. A grin spread across her face. Maybe he liked the bag lady look. She glanced in the hall mirror as she passed and fluffed her hair with her fingers. She couldn't remember the last time she had worried so much about what she looked like. It felt like a first date.

She followed Holly to the kitchen where Bill stood leaning against the refrigerator in shorts and a t-shirt, a can of cola in his hand. Samson sat at the table, a polite look on his face. He fiddled with the placemat before him. He still wore the same clothes she'd seen him in at the hotel. His white t-shirt was streaked with dirt from wrestling with Anderson on the floor, but it stretched tautly across his muscular chest and looked really good. She felt a blush rise in her cheeks at the thought.

Samson pushed back from his chair and stood up to face them, his eyes searching hers eagerly. It felt strange for him to be in her sister's kitchen, with Holly and Bill looking on as though they were protective parents. His face was lined from exhaustion, but his eyes lit up at the sight of her.

"How are you, Ivy?" he asked, breaking the silence that seemed to stretch forever.

"Fine – now that the kids are safe." She stepped forward and grasped Samson's hand. "Take a walk with me," she said brightly. Without hesitation Samson let her lead him out of the kitchen and toward the front door.

"But Ivy, it's dark outside!" her sister called after them.

Ivy paused on the front steps, Samson's hand still snug in hers. "It's all right, Holly. I've got my own personal FBI agent."

"Make that–Special agent," he teased.

He matched his long stride to her shorter one as they walked down the rain slick sidewalk. The rain had stopped earlier, and most of the clouds had blown away. A sliver of moon glowed in an inky black sky. The boulevard was quiet. Ivy paused at the corner under the streetlamp, not sure which way to turn.

Samson pulled her to face him, his hands resting lightly on her forearms. The light shone down at his back, leaving his features shadowed. Ivy wished she could see him more clearly and know what he was thinking. He pulled her against his chest and held her there, wrapped in his warm embrace. She sighed and leaned against him, more content than she had ever been.

"Thank God you're safe," he mumbled against her hair.

Ivy closed her eyes and relaxed. Something she hadn't done for a very long time. Here in Samson's arms she felt safe and complete. It had been a long road getting here, but God knew what she needed before she did.

She tilted her head back and looked into his brown eyes, completely sure of her feelings. She loved Samson Sinclair.

His lips covered hers, and they stood there locked together for a heart pounding moment before Holly's voice rang out down the street.

"Ivy! Ivy!"

Samson pulled away and squinted into the dark. "Do you think she's coming after us?" he asked.

Ivy laughed and slipped her arm in his. "We better go find out what she wants. Maybe the kids woke up."

Holly ran toward them. "Ivy! There's a phone call for you," she panted.

"Really? Is it the president?" Ivy teased.

Holly sent her a scathing look but shook her head. "No, it's not the president," she said, "It's someone from NBC News and they want your story."

Ivy frowned. "Tell them, no comment."

Holly fell into step with them. "What do you mean? Don't you want to do the interview? You're a hero! You stopped secret information from getting out of the country, and you saved your children from kidnappers. They'll probably want to put your story on 60 Minutes!"

"Holly, when you have children of your own, you'll understand. We don't need any more

excitement. We've had quite enough for a lifetime."
She squeezed her sister's arm. "Go – tell them we're
not interested – please?"

Her sister looked dubious. "All right. If that's
what you want." She ran lightly up the steps and back
inside.

Samson stopped on the sidewalk and frowned.
"I hate to ask you this, but I have to. Do you know
where I can find Raven? She made a copy of our disc
and got away with the original. Did you know she
planted a virus on the one you gave to Anderson?"

Ivy reached into her back pocket and pulled out
the case. She had kept it with her even after changing
clothes, afraid something would happen to it before
she could return it to Samson.

"Honestly, I don't know where Raven is, but
she left this for you. Her exact words were – *you can
give this to your boyfriend.* Are you my boyfriend?"
she asked, a hint of eagerness in her eyes.

"She did have a way with words." He scratched
his chin thoughtfully as though he didn't know quite
how to answer her question.

"Don't answer all at once!" she said, perturbed.

"I'm thinking," he teased. Then he pulled her
close and kissed the top of her head. "Ivy, I'm thirty-
four years old, and I'm in love for the first time. I
don't want to be your boyfriend. I want to be your
husband."

She couldn't speak through the lump forming in
her throat. He drew back and looked into her eyes
now damp with tears of happiness. She nodded her
answer. He sealed it with a kiss and the porch light
came on, illuminating their love for the whole
neighborhood to see. Ivy looked up at the door and
saw her brother-in-law's face peering out at them

from the glass. They laughed, and still holding hands, went in to talk about their future together.

†††

"I don't care whether she gave back the disc and helped rescue the children, she's still a known fugitive and I want her found!" Captain Herndon said. His desk was cluttered as usual with stacks of folders, little notes to himself on scraps of paper, and used Styrofoam coffee cups. Dry, brown rings decorated the folders and desktop where coffee sloshed out over the rims. Some cups were still half full, others lay empty on their sides. He picked up his latest cup and downed the last dregs, frowned at the bitter taste, then tossed it toward the trashcan in the corner. It missed and fell to the floor amid crumpled papers and trash.

Samson refrained from arguing. He knew it would do him no good. The captain was adamant that Raven be found and arrested. He tried to explain that without her help they never would have gotten the disc back and the information would have been downloaded to Iran, but captain Herndon reminded him she had been working for Anderson from the start and had committed crimes that needed to be answered for. Samson knew it was true, but he had a soft spot for her in his heart since she rescued Caleb and Riley.

The captain leaned forward across the desk, glanced out the open door and lowered his voice so just the two of them could hear. "I said I wanted her found, I didn't say *you* had to find her," he said softly. Then he leaned back in his chair, placed his arms behind his head, and yelled loud enough for every agent in the offices to hear. "Now get out there and get to work!"

Samson and Timmons didn't dare look at each other until the door closed behind them, then they grinned like two Cheshire cats. Timmons slapped his partner on the back, nearly sending Samson careening into the desk beside him. He caught himself just in time and straightened, still grinning.

"This should make your woman happy," Timmons said, strutting toward the coat rack to retrieve his suit jacket. He struggled into it, making Samson grin even wider.

Samson pulled on his own jacket. He had worn a navy-blue suit today, intending to take Ivy out for lunch. He adjusted his tie and buttoned his double-breasted suit coat.

"How do I look?" he asked Timmons, who looked ridiculous in his own tight suit, his arms bulging at the seams.

"You look tall," he said gruffly, "and business like." He ran fat fingers over his black crew cut and sighed dramatically. "How do I look?" he asked with a lift of his brows.

"Short!" Samson replied. He pushed open the door. "Catch you later, Timmons."

{19}

A week after Caleb and Riley returned safely home they all stood in the White Funeral Home. Ivy planned a memorial service for the children's sake, even though Todd had already been cremated upon arrival in the United States. The children needed a chance to say goodbye.

Todd's only living relative was the aunt who had raised him. Other than Wilma, Ivy, and the children, Todd didn't have any relatives or close friends. He had not been the *best-friend* type; he was always too busy stabbing them in the back. The chairs were empty except for the front row where the family sat as the organist played a solemn tune.

Samson sat next to Ivy squeezing her hand gently and she held Riley on her lap. Caleb sat on her other side, his face much too grave for a boy his age.

Todd's Aunt Wilma sat two seats away from Caleb, dabbing at her eyes. She wore a black skirt with a gray blouse. Ivy had only met Wilma once, the day Todd and she married. She seemed like a cold fish at the time, and Ivy often thought it was no wonder that Todd turned out the way he did. But now she actually seemed broken up. Ivy returned her attention to the podium where Pastor Nichols, the preacher from Samson's church, was speaking.

At the front of the room was a large picture of Todd. She'd put it in a gold colored frame and set it on a small table for them to view. She thought the children might need something to connect to during this service. It was hard to think of someone as gone when you hadn't watched them go. When someone died suddenly and unexpectedly, it was unreal and for the children it was doubly hard, having their father go away for a trip and never return. They knew Todd had done something wrong and that he'd been killed, but she didn't go into details, and thankfully they didn't ask.

Pastor Nichols spoke for a few minutes and then stepped down and came forward to give them each his condolences. He was a quiet spoken man with a kind heart. Ivy shook his hand and thanked him for leading the service. As he went to speak to Todd's aunt, Ivy caught the movement of someone leaving through the back door.

"Excuse me, Samson will you watch the children for a minute?" she asked. She stepped around the seats and out of the room, closing the door carefully behind her.

"Raven!"

Raven paused, not turning, her hand on the handle of the door. She wore a pair of black slacks and a dark blue shirt. Her hair was once again spiked, and she wore dangly gold earrings in each ear. "I just wanted to pay my respects," she said.

Ivy stood beside her and placed a hand on her arm. "I'm glad you did." Raven's eyes were covered with a pair of black Ray Ban sunglasses, so Ivy

couldn't see what she was thinking but she thought
she knew. "It wasn't your fault, Raven. Ace Anderson
was an evil man. He probably would have killed you
as well as Todd if he'd had the chance."

"Well, it was nice seeing you again," Raven
said, pushing the handle of the door.

"Wait. There is someone I think you should talk
to."

Raven shook her head. "I'm not going to turn
myself in to your special agent."

Ivy tightened her grip. "I don't expect you to. I
was talking about Pastor Nichols. Samson told me he
knows a lot about forgiveness, and I think he can help
you."

Raven remembered the sermon she'd heard
from him not that long ago. He might be an expert on
forgiveness, but she doubted *anyone* could help her.
She shook her head. The door to the viewing room
opened and Pastor Nichols slipped out into the hall,
eyeing them both with interest.

"Pastor Nichols, I'd like you to meet a friend of
mine. Raven Black," Ivy said smoothly.

He stepped forward, his smile warm and open.
"Very glad to meet you at last, Miss Black. I believe
you were in one of our services not long ago. I'm
sorry I failed to introduce myself."

Raven lifted her brows. "That's one way of
saying I skipped out," she said with a laugh. "I'm
sorry now that I did," she said.

"Would you walk with me?" He glanced back at
the door he'd just come through, and Ivy realized he
knew who Raven was and was trying to protect her
from Samson. "I need to clear my head after a sad
service like that."

Raven glanced at Ivy, hesitant, but then she shrugged. "Sure – why not? There are a few things I'd like to ask you while we're out."

"Thank you," Ivy whispered as Pastor Nichols held the door for Raven and then followed her out.

†††

Ivy stood at the sliding glass doors with Samson's arms around her waist, and leaned against him, feeling his solid strength behind her. The past year had flown by with the children in school and she in her teller job at the bank. Samson and she had taken things slow, dated like regular people, and built a relationship that grew stronger with each passing day. Danger and excitement may have pushed them together, but mutual faith, trust, and love bound them for life.

"I see the kids have made some new friends," he said against her ear.

She looked down by the pond and spotted Caleb talking to another little boy about his age who was trying to fish in the murky water. Farther up the hill Riley played with two little girls; their three heads bent low over a doll stroller. Ivy wondered if it contained a baby doll or something more Rileyish, like a couple of plump toads. She smiled and turned in Samson's arms, giving him a playful poke in the ribs.

"When are you going to marry me, so we can get a puppy and a fish tank and be a real family?"

Samson lifted one brow. "Is that what it takes to be a real family? I didn't know." He pressed his lips together and looked up at the ceiling as though deep in thought. "Will next week be too soon? Pastor Nichols said he had an open afternoon on his calendar. Afterwards we could go house hunting. Once all of that is accomplished, I certainly wouldn't be averse to a puppy and a fish tank."

Ivy laughed at his smug expression. She stood on tiptoe and pressed her lips to his. His arms came around her and pulled her close once again and she sighed with contentment, trusting God for their future together.

ABOUT THE AUTHOR

Barbara Ellen Brink lives in the great state of Minnesota with her husband, their two dogs, Rugby and Willow, and their two adult children living nearby. She spends much time writing, reading, motorcycling, running, and enjoying life with the family and friends that God has given her.

Made in the USA
Las Vegas, NV
22 October 2022